James and the

CW00516291

A ghost mystery set in Lincolnshire,
England, United Kingdom.

The fourth of the
James Hansone Ghost Mysteries

By Paul Money

*Dedicated to the Men and Women of Bomber
Command whose sacrifice can never be forgotten.*

Copyright Notice

Acknowledgements

The author would like to acknowledge the support and help of his wife, Lorraine, in listening to the idea of the third sequel, how it developed and giving both invaluable advice, encouragement and editing ideas as the story progressed.

He would also like to thank the following for their advice, informed wisdom, patience and encouragement as this book progressed from a few pages to a full-blown novel:

Gill Hart
Patricia Money (Mum)
Keith 'Ackers' Money (Dad)
Margaret Slater (Mum 2 aka Mum in Law)
Rev Charles Thody

And finally acknowledge the wonderful help and support of Simon Ross/Paper Planes Gallery for his work on the cover for the e-pub/POD editions.

Preface

A ghostly WW II airman
The old RAF Grasceby airbase
A chair that won't behave itself
A terrible wartime injustice
The trip of a lifetime…
A new mystery at Wolds View Cottage

James and Sally finish renovating Wolds View Cottage only to discover there was more to the cottage than at first met the eye.

They embark on uncovering the truth about the ghostly airman and why Jenny's ghost won't return to the cottage.

Along the way they take on a new member of the family and James faces his most difficult challenge yet…

… looking after Scruff!

Prologue

1944

The war looked to be finally turning in their favour and there was no doubt in Bomber County, as Lincolnshire was known, that the RAF and Bomber Command had played a crucial role.

All across the county were airfields buzzing with the sound of Merlin engines as Lancaster's took off on their sorties heading out deep into the heart of Europe. The last few years had been rough on everyone but they had persevered. There was even talk that with luck the war would soon be over and that fascism would be defeated, never to return to blight the world again.

RAF Grasceby was a small subsidiary airfield supporting the effort in conjunction with RAF Bardney and the men and women who served on the base knew that despite their high losses they were getting the job done.

Edward smiled as he approached the base on foot from his home a mile down the road from Grasceby itself. He was lucky, for most of the early war years he had been stationed in Kent but when an opportunity had presented itself to be stationed back on his home territory he had jumped at the chance knowing he could return to the small family home at Wolds View Cottage.

The path through the woods was well known to him since childhood when he had played under the two old oaks that he'd found all those years ago.

Sometimes he made the slight diversion to go and see them, bringing back fond memories of swinging and climbing the branches.

As the path opened out onto the base he could see in the distance the hangers with their doors open and the ground crews busy working on the Lancasters that had been damaged in the most recent raids over enemy territory. It was a non stop affair and he admired the ground crews just as a much as he did his colleagues who flew those magnificent machines.

He knew he was lucky. He'd now survived over twenty sorties, not many got past a handful before being shot down, ending up either dead or captured becoming a POW. Plus he was close to home now and so could be with his son and daughter-in-law along with their adorable daughter, Jennifer. She'd only been born the previous year and he ferverently hoped she would not grow up with a war still going on around her.

Little did he know or suspect that his life was about to be turned upside down and cut short through no fault of his own…

\#

Just a few months later and it was the day of reckoning.

No matter what he had said, all the words he had mustered had not counted for anything. He knew his fate was sealed and regardless of the truth, without actual proof, his version of events sounded absurd even to his own ears.

A ground crew member failing in his job, the ill-fated flight, the last-minute stand-in airman vanishing without a trace, all had been brushed away as a flight of fancy.

Despite his impeccable record he was now pretty sure that he would be court martialled. He was only grateful he had been allowed a last evening with his son and daughter-in-law along with their one year old baby Jennifer. It was a quirk of fate that he'd been assigned to RAF Grasceby this last couple of years which had brought him back to the family home. It saddened him that his family struggled to accept his version of events and indeed Barbara was particularly distant. He had brought shame on them all according to her and the accusation struck painfully deep.

If he could have got the ground crew to dish the dirt on their dishonourable, so called colleague, then he might have been able to exonerate himself. Without the missing part for proof, he was lost. His fellow crew members were all dead from the crash and one mysteriously missing, indeed he apparently did not exist at all. A mystery, yet he had been on that fateful flight when the crash itself had destroyed any further evidence.

He was in a hopeless situation.

Getting up from his favourite chair, pushing it slightly ajar as he always tended to do, he looked around the kitchen.

They would discover the paperwork of his will and last testament signing over his half of the semi-detached cottage to Jack and Barbara when they awoke later that morning.

Now it was time for him to leave. His solicitor, two days earlier, had confirmed all was in order but did not realise it would be needed sooner rather than later.

Picking up his holdall, Edward carefully unlatched the back door and, walking around to the front of the cottage, he looked up at it smiling briefly, reliving a few happy childhood memories. For a fleeting moment he thought he saw a strange woman looking down on him but then she was gone. He brushed the sighting off as a mirage then thought about the cottage. 'Wolds View' had always struck him as a bit odd as you couldn't actually see the Lincolnshire Wolds from the ground floor so why it had been called that, he guessed he would never know. The connection to his family tree however, was strong and he hoped it would continue well into the future.

He checked his uniform was clean and tidy then made his way carefully out the front gate and turned right for the airfield. There was the usual shortcut through the woods and he walked towards it, climbed over the freshly made gate with its warning sign that he was entering MOD property.

As he followed the faint animal path, a path he had run along as a child when he played in the woods, he reached a spot he knew well from those seemingly distant days.

Instead of carrying on towards the base, he turned off the track and headed deeper into the wood until he reached a small clearing where two familiar oak trees stood proudly defiant.

He reached into the holdall he had slung over his arm and brought out the rope. He needed it as the old tyre swing he had used as a child had been taken down several years earlier when the airbase had been hastily built due to the war. He knew it was a weak and foolish thing to do but he was not prepared to be humiliated any more. He certainly was not going to be shot for something he had no control over, and was not responsible for.

He knew it was time to depart and allow his son and family a fresh start without him...

James and the Air of Tragedy

Part I

Wolds View Cottage

The present day

1: Wolds View Cottage

It had taken some time but James and Sally Hansone had nearly completed the renovations of Wolds View Cottage. It was still an odd feeling being in the cottage, James thought, as he sat in the lounge pondering how it had come about. Who would have thought that a simple unplanned road diversion would have changed his life completely.

It didn't seem like five minutes, yet just four years earlier, that diversion had taken him past a rundown cottage that triggered several ghostly encounters over the following months. Incredible to think that it led to his discovery of a missing person for over fifty years due to seeing her spirit wandering at the cottage. Jenny Portisham had, in a shocking twist, turned out to be the deceased elder sister he had never known. In the process he'd discovered an earlier life of his mother that he had been unaware of. It had dramatically affected his marriage to the point of separation when his wife, Helen, took up with a, now former, work colleague. James had also discovered a new love interest, the local detective superintendent, Sally Fieldman. She had closed the case of Jenny's disappearance and arrested the culprit, Jenny's boyfriend of all those years ago, Richard Dreyer. He was now behind bars awaiting news of his appeal against his sentence.

Along the way James had accidentally discovered the remains of the long lost first manor of the village of Grasceby and inadvertently, found himself unofficially known locally as a ghost hunter. That had led the following year to Lord Grasceby approaching him for help when workmen began to experience paranormal activity at Grasceby Manor as it was undergoing renovations. That eventually lead to the solving of the mystery of the ghostly apparitions, much to his Lord and Ladyships appreciation, especially as it had helped boost their tourism plans for Grasceby Manor and the estate.

James sighed as he recollected the shock of seeing the ghost of his ex-wife, Helen, whilst he and Sally were on a brief trip to Scotland, staying at Jenny McClackens' B&B. With help from Sally, he'd eventually found out what had happened to Helen and her fiancé in Snowdonia. Then they'd returned to Lincolnshire only for him to become roped into the ghostly affairs of the original De Grasceby Manor. It had been a long-held belief that Charles De Grasceby and his family, originally from France in the 1700's, had perished at sea whilst being hounded back to their former country. However, excavations at the site had uncovered the grisly truth, that they had been murdered by a rival, Earl Chichester. Tragically buried alive in their cellar before the first original manor was demolished and lost for three hundred years.

Still, something good came out of it all when Sally proposed to James on February 29th and he accepted. Not long after that she surprised him again by admitting she had managed to buy Wolds View Cottage and handed him the keys to what was technically his ancestral family home long before he had been born. So, life had turned full circle and here they were in the final stages of renovating the property with just a few finishing touches needed.

James looked over and down at the love of his life and smiled.

Sally sat cross-legged on the living room floor with sheaves of paper scattered around her. She was mulling over several new guidelines that were being considered concerning the rise of illegal hare coursing that was taking place in the rural county. That was one of the problems urban regions didn't have to deal with, he mused, knowing that in some cases the people responsible had turned violent to anyone trying to arrest or report them.

She looked up at him, almost as if she knew he was watching her.

"Just a thought, what did you do with that tin we found in the corner of the garden the other day?"

"Oh, the one with the medals and teddy bear in? I've put it in the garage for now and will get them cleaned up. Must be a time capsule sort of thing, wonder what the medals were? The teddy looked a bit worse for wear, but they could be worth something to a collector."

"Ahh that's an idea. A project for another time then."

Her phone pinged, catching her attention and she saw she'd received a text. James looked on bemused at how engrossed she had been in her paperwork.

"Ahh, Jenny McClacken asks if we are OK and have any idea if we might be able to reschedule the week away. Shall I suggest we'll re-book for a few months' time and we'll go on her web site to see what dates are free?" asked Sally as she looked up whilst still listening to Jenny McClacken on the phone.

"Yes, that'd be a good idea. Once we've got all this decorating behind us, I reckon we'll need a holiday."

Sally put Jenny in the picture and hung up. "She's a good 'un is Jenny, wonder if Marcus will try again to win her over?"

"We can always put in a good word for him when we see her. Anyhow, I'm getting hungry, shall we eat out? Pop down to the Star and Crescent Moon and see what Marcus has got on special this evening?" James asked hopefully.

"Good plan, don't fancy cooking anything tonight." Sally replied.

"Me neither, let's get someone else to do the work!" James picked up his phone and tapped speed-dial to call the inn.

#

She still hadn't told him about seeing the blue uniformed man in the front garden again, albeit briefly. It was beginning to prey on Sally's mind as she couldn't understand why she was seeing a ghost at the cottage that didn't seem to have anything to do with James deceased sister, Jennifer Portisham. Sally was also puzzled, why her? She had never been prone to see ghosts even after becoming involved with James.

She'd tried to work a conversation around to whether James had seen anything else at the cottage, she didn't want to cause undue worry if it was nothing. Yet, since moving into the cottage around three quarters of the way during the renovation, she'd begun to see the ghost. It was as if something during the renovations had triggered it and for most parts it always seemed to be in the front garden that she had seen him. Always heading away from the cottage, stopping, turning around, and looking at the cottage before heading off across the road and fading from view. She shuddered and again wondered if she should come clean with James. But why had Jenny not appeared instead? That would have been more logical, that's if you could say anything logical about ghostly sightings!

Sally decided to keep quiet for the time being and make a note of every time and where she saw the apparition. At least her police training and detective skills would be of help.

#

Just a couple of weeks later, Sally was leaning against the new work surface next to the sink sipping her Earl Grey tea and looking thoughtful as she gazed around the room.

"You know, I reckon now we've got the main work in the kitchen diner finished we could do with a decent table and a few wooden chairs just to give it that finishing touch. Something in keeping with the cottage I reckon, instead of this cheap tat we have."

James popped his head round the door.

"Say what? Something about the kitchen?"

She looked at him and shook her head.

"Typical! What I was saying was that I should sell my body to the highest bidder and see what we can get…"

James stared open mouthed at her not knowing what to say but she saw the look on his face and burst into a grin.

"I said, now we've got this room sorted with new units and cooker, it's large enough to have a modest table and I think some good old-fashioned wooden chairs just to set the scene. Better than this cheap excuse for a table. We could put cushions on the chairs so they won't be too hard on your delicate bum, so to speak…"

"Cheeky. Anyhow that was my first table, mine and Helen's first table when we moved up here. Anyhow, what's wrong with my rear?"

"Exactly my point, best look after them cheeks you know, they're not getting any younger!" she quipped.

"Very funny indeed!" he replied and stuck his tongue out at her, somewhat childishly.

"Charming, I'm sure." she fired back flippantly.

"Well, we could pop down into town and have a mosey around some of the antique dealers there. Since Dreyer is effectively out of business some of them are pretty pleased with us and may offer a bit of a discount if we're lucky. I know he's been forced to sell the main business as a going concern and it's now re-opened under new management, although to be honest his old place is the last one I'd like to visit, so what about the others?"

"Worth a try I suppose. Let's go after lunch then?" she smiled sweetly at him and James knew it wasn't a choice but effectively an already decided issue.

#

Four hours later and what seemed like a hundred miles of walking they still had not found '*the*' chairs or for that matter a suitable table. Sally was becoming bored and wishing she hadn't suggested the idea. However, despite aching legs from trudging up and down stairs in what seemed like every single shop, she knew James was now set on the idea as a task they just had to complete that day. One way or the other they would be going home with something and she just hoped it wasn't going to be tacky!

Still, it was only another half hour before the shops would be shutting up for the day. Secretly she began to hope that they would run out of time.

They popped into the newsagents on the corner of the marketplace, picked up their pre ordered magazines and just as they headed for the door saw Fred ambling towards them.

"Aye up, how are you both doing?" he asked as they realised they were not going to be able to elude him.

"Well, not too bad, especially as I've now taken early retirement and have a lot more time on my hands." replied James. Sally smirked at him.

"More time on your hands? You seem to be busier than ever, especially now you are giving talks about the old De Grasceby Manor. Fred, he's hardly at home now in the evenings, starting to think he ought to wear a badge so I know who he is when he does finally come home!"

James shrugged but said nothing, then had a thought.

"To be fair Fred, I wasn't sure if you'd be speaking to us after, well, you know, the Dreyer circumstances." suggested James.

"Oh good grief no! Dick, ah, Richard I mean, deserved what he got. For heaven's sake he was let off lightly regarding your sister and I can honestly say that he damned well got what he deserved. So what're you two doing then, spot of shopping?"

"Sort of, we've almost finished renovating 'Wolds View' and wanted something like a nice antique table and chair set for the kitchen/dining room but so far we've drawn a blank. Not found anything that really takes our fancy." Sally replied and sighed. Fred looked at them slightly mischievously as if he was hatching something.

"Have you been into Dreyer's old premises? Been taken over since he was incarcerated and he had some of the best stuff on the top floor. Doesn't normally let most people up there but now there's new owners you might find something to suit you? I believe they kept all of the original stock as part of the going concern."

Fred stepped to one side as if to leave then changed his mind and nodded to them before heading into the newsagent, leaving them to their thoughts.

James looked at Sally trying to gauge her potential reaction as they had both been deliberately ignoring Dreyer's old antique and second-hand shop just down the road from where they stood. Sally looked at him with that knowing look, nodded and turned to head off in its direction.

"You sure about this?" James enquired but she just waved her hand at him and he dutifully followed on behind. On seeing them arrive and noting time was running out before closing, the woman sitting just inside the front door did not seem so happy on seeing them enter.

"I'll be closing shortly so I hope you know what it is you are looking for." she said brusquely.

Sally thought to herself that clearly the woman did not have a head for business nor politeness to potential customers. She almost turned around to walk out but James was already twisting the woman around his little finger with tales of how he was the local man who discovered the De Grasceby Manor ruins and the woman quickly changed her tune.

"So, tell me Christine, is it true that Dreyer had some good stuff up on the top floor? We're after a decent wooden table and a set of four chairs to match and at the rate we are going we'll be taking our custom to Lincoln after today."

Christine eyed him up then glanced over towards Sally smiling at her as she changed tack sensing a possible good sale.

"Ahh, now I know who you are. If it wasn't for him being incarcerated then I wouldn't have been able to acquire the business. I've only just got to the top floor as there is so much here that, to be honest, is pretty much junk and tacky rubbish. But I did see something that might be of interest. Come with me."

They followed her up three flights of stairs until Sally began to think the top floor had to be a figment of Christine's imagination. They finally emerged through a wide opening onto the top floor, the last few steps creaking spookily. The top floor was the smallest and one side appeared partitioned off. Apart from a few bedroom dressing tables and a couple of tall wardrobe units, there was little else of interest, much to James' dismay. There was plenty of dust too, so it was clear very few had ventured as far as this floor, which didn't surprise him. He wondered idly if anyone suffered from altitude sickness if they ventured this far up the building.

He was about to say as much when Christine beckoned to him and Sally from a curtained off opening in the partition. They stepped through. Christine pulled on a light switch cord hanging to one side and the harsh glare of the bare light bulb dazzled them briefly. Again, at first glance, the room did not hold much promise. Sally stepped over to one wooden table but shook her head on spying the decay on one side. James too was beginning to feel despondent, but he felt drawn to the right-hand side where a large tarpaulin covered something.

"What's under here then?" He asked and Christine came over scratching her head.

"Well as I said, I haven't done a full inventory and from the dust I'd say Dreyer can't have been up here much at all. Probably forgot he had stuff up here if you ask me. But I did spot a table and chairs here so they might be of interest."

As Sally wandered over, James and Christine rummaged around to find the edges of the tarpaulin and began to pull at it as dust motes lifted to fill the air causing them all to cough briefly.

A set of four neatly engraved wooden chairs were arranged upside down on a similarly ornate polished but slightly tarnished, wooden table. James smiled and then managed to catch one of the chairs as the tarpaulin caught and toppled it off the table.

Sally coughed and waved to clear some of the dust but could see why James appeared to be enamoured with their find.

She and Christine stood back as James pulled the table away from the wall and then set the four chairs around it before standing back to admire the arrangement.

"Well, apart from a layer of dust, looks like a lick of polish or a quick buff up with a soft cloth would soon put this right" offered Sally and James nodded as he felt a warm glow come over him. He could just imagine the furniture in the kitchen diner and knew instantly they'd found what they had been looking for. He glanced at Sally to see if she too felt the same.

He didn't need to ask.

2: A mind of its own

"Told ya!" Sally said triumphantly as James stepped back from setting out the chairs.

"Ok so you were right, it does look better turned that way round after all. I bow to your superior judgement" he replied and together they admired the, now polished, table and chairs arranged in the dining part of the large room they'd converted from the original kitchen and separate dining room.

"Works well I reckon. When I get back from the station tomorrow night, we ought to have a proper sit-down meal to christen them don't you think?" she replied thoughtfully and James nodded in agreement.

"You in at the HQ then tomorrow? James queried and she sighed.

"Yeah, sad day though as Harriet texted me to say she'd received confirmation. The powers that be have decided to go ahead and amalgamate the crime lab with the Nottinghamshire one so ours is being closed down. Harriet is taking redundancy instead of the offered move to Notts and is talking about setting up on her own as a freelance forensic expert. Hope she gets enough work is all I can say. Bloody cuts!"

"Huh, typical, well I hope you two stay in touch as she's quite a force to be reckoned with – much like you if I dare say it…" he ducked but there was no retaliation, Sally just shook her head as her mind was wandering off at a tangent.

"You know, funny how Fred seemed to guide us to finding these. Wonder what his game was?"

James walked round then adjusted the nearest chair a centimetre as Sally smirked at his action.

"Don't think there was a motive, perhaps he just knew that Dreyer had kept these to one side for himself but never got round to doing anything with them. Pure coincidence that's all."

"Yeah, guess you're right. Anyhow, small glass of white before retiring to bed eh?"

"Why not, mustn't break a habit of a lifetime!" he replied and they both headed out, James fetching the wine glasses from the cabinet.

#

Sally had left early, around six am, managing not to wake him. At seven thirty James' alarm went off on his smart phone and he turned it off, rolling over, only to realise Sally had already gone. He rolled onto his back and gazed up at the ceiling as he shook off the sleepiness of the night.

Heading downstairs he heard the front door letterbox rattle slightly and wandered through only to find an electricity bill lying on the floor. He couldn't help thinking that he'd cancelled paper bills just the other month and in theory they were now on paperless billing, but somehow the message had not registered with the company. He opened and scanned it quickly, satisfied it was a reasonable amount and promised himself to make sure he paid it online later that day.

Wandering through to the kitchen he popped a couple of slices of bread into the toaster, tidied the chair that was at an angle to the rest of the table and headed into the lounge. Activating the wall screen, he began to scan through the world news as he sat down on the sofa.

He couldn't help thinking they'd got a bargain with the TV watching the long running ad campaign on the screen for wall mounted large flat screen TV's.

"Bugger, meant to put the coffee pot on!" he scowled at himself, got up and walked back into the kitchen, sorted the the coffee maker with a new filter and set it to work as he headed back catching the side of a dining chair.

"Huh, I'll have to remember we've got these now. I will end up with a bruise and Sally will wonder what I do all day now I'm retired" he chuckled to himself. Setting the chair straight, he sorted his drink as the coffee maker was almost done, collected his toast, added butter and marmalade for good measure and wandered back into the lounge.

Despite their good-humoured banter about James now being retired, the next few days were going to be quite busy and followed a similar routine. Along the way he was to prepare and deliver a lecture to the Nottingham Historical Society on the Wednesday, then write an article for the 'Lincs Speaks' newspaper courtesy of Annouska, on the possibilities of further discoveries being made in the county using modern technology.

She had been quite helpful when she had learned of the ghostly goings on at the archaeological site of the original De Grasceby manor the previous year, being gracious enough to hold off so that they'd give her the full story. Since then she'd become a useful contact at the paper.

On the Thursday he was booked to pop into the local radio station in Lincoln to chat about the De Grasceby discovery of the previous year and finally on the Friday he had a luncheon appointment with a book publisher keen for him to write it all down.

Yes, early retirement certainly did not mean he was lounging around the house all day tidying chairs whilst Sally was busier than ever with her work, especially with the various cutbacks Lincolnshire Police had been forced to endure.

He grabbed his coat and set off out the front door not noticing a chair was once again slightly ajar from the table …

#

It was quite funny really, mused James as they walked along on the grass verge. They'd lived now at Wolds View for over a year and had done the mile or so walk into Grasceby village but never gone in the other direction.

Well, they were making up for it today. He and Sally walked along the verge, occasionally stepping onto the road as they chatted about everyday life and swapping stories about the week that had gone by.

A car whizzed past them interrupting the conversation as James looked up, at first glance seeing a metallic blue that caused his heart to skip a beat. For a split second he thought Dreyer was back out and on the road. However he relaxed as he saw the car was a Ford, not a Mercedes. Sally noticed his expression and chuckled.

"I know, I thought the same thing as I saw the colour. Dreyer won't be out for a while yet, but I must admit it still catches me by surprise when a metallic blue car overtakes me when I'm driving."

James nodded and looked ahead towards a poorly kept sign but as he turned to say something Sally suddenly dashed ahead of them catching him by surprise. He enjoyed seeing her rush off and admired her figure from the distance.

Ahh, a butterfly, he realised, as he walked up to her whilst she used her smart phone to try to get a picture of it. The white butterfly, with flashes of orange, was having none of it however, lifting off then settling down before lifting off again just as Sally was poised to take the picture.

She followed it a little way further along the verge then stood up and looked back at him in triumph, brandishing her phone as much to say 'I got it!'.

As James caught up with her again, he passed a rough, dirty and grassy entrance that was gated with a semi broken down wooden gate with PRIVATE handwritten across a small board. The entrance led into a dense wood to which the butterfly had seemingly decided to escape preventing further harassment by Sally.

"Well, what was it then clever clogs?" he asked as she sidled up to him and showed the picture.

"Orange Tip. Male."

"OK then, how do you know that's a male, can't exactly turn it upside down and have a look can you!" he replied a little more sarcastically than he'd intended.

Sally looked at him sternly.

"My dear sir, are you forgetting my powers of deduction, observation and sheer knowledge of lepidoptery?"

James knew he was about to get a lecture and shrugged as innocently as he could but that didn't stop her launching into one of her favourite subjects.

"My dear ignorant hubby, for your future reference, only the males actually have the orange tips, oddly enough the females don't have them. Actually, it's often the case that the females can be confused with either the Green Veined or Small White butterflies. So now you know!"

'Yep I sure do..' he thought but kept that to himself. She shook her head at him and pocketed the smart phone continuing on the grass verge a little further. It finally petered out giving way to a rough surfaced entranceway with just a few small potholes beginning to make their presence known. A faded and dilapidated sign stood at a slight angle and Sally wandered over to it putting her hands on her shapely hips.

"Ahh, yes, this is the former site of RAF Grasceby. It's an industrial estate now, well that was the plan I gather.

There's only one company on it and they've expanded to take over pretty much the whole site."

James caught up to her, briefly looked up at the main arch that had the company name on it but didn't take much notice of it as Sally was bent over looking at yet another butterfly that had landed on the ground next to her.

"And how do you know all about that then my love?"

She stood up and looked at him with an air of superiority, then smiled.

"There was a spate of burglaries here a few years back that I had to investigate so naturally I did a bit of research. The company is a storage and haulage distribution centre for a regional food retailer, Smith-Lincs. Arthur and Son is the company. Mind you with the competition so strong there are rumours they may not last more than a few more years, if indeed that long."

"Oh, guess that would be a shame but commerce is commerce and it is a cutthroat world out there. Stop just where you are and I'll take a picture of you set against the edge of the wood."

Sally stepped back a little as James fished out his own smart phone and began to frame the view. She immediately began to pose in silly ways until James let out a loud 'hurrumph' and she settled down as he took several pictures of her. He looked up and shook his head as he glanced past her then moved a little to one side and began to take more pictures.

"Hurry up then old man, I can't keep posing all day you know."

"Shush! Less of the 'old man' as well! I just needed to avoid the chap in the distance, didn't want him in the view."

Sally looked round, much to James annoyance then back at him.

"What chap?" she asked innocently.

James looked up again and peered past her but there was no one there.

"Oh, he must have been crossing into the wood from the industrial estate. Gone now, so no worries." He finished up and stood next to her as they scrolled through the pics.

"Well where is he then?" Sally tried not to sound sceptical. James frowned, puzzled.

"Well I could have sworn there was someone well off in the distance. Oh, look, there's some form of bluish gatepost. Ahh, must have been part of the airfield I guess."

"You thought there was a ghost didn't you!" Sally lightly punched him in the ribs and James mockingly fell back in shock at her attack on his integrity.

"Of course not, now what makes you think I'd jump to that conclusion, Mrs Detective dearest?"

"Old habits and all that. Never mind let's get back as I'm getting hungry!" she retorted.

He put his phone away and they turned to head back but on the other side of the road verge.

Roughly halfway back another butterfly fluttered by and Sally once again became excited and tried to follow it as James shook his head.

He delved into his pocket fishing out the phone again and started to film her antics as she attempted to catch up with and photograph the brownish butterfly. Suddenly she tripped on a tuft of grass and fell over onto the verge with a loud curse. James hurriedly put the phone away and naturally went over to help.

"Stupid man over there put me off" she said as she brushed off grass and a little dirt from a molehill she'd manage to catch on landing.
James looked ahead but shook his head.

"What man?"

"Him, over there…" she stopped and looked perplexed then looked back at James.

"Seriously, he was over there - in some sort of uniform. Oh hell, now *I'm* seeing things. Honest I did see someone; he was walking back in the direction of Grasceby."

"Perhaps it was the chap I saw earlier and he knows a short cut - we've not really explored this way since moving into Wolds View. I bet there are plenty of public footpaths dotted around here, especially with this old airfield nearby. There would have been paths to the village I expect and maybe someone from the estate lives in Grasceby?" offered James and Sally shrugged then looked round.

"Oh, well it's gone now but I think it was a Speckled Wood butterfly, but I didn't get it on the camera. Let's get home so I can clean up - and no laughing, OK?"

James just nodded, knowing his life would be hell if he joked about her little trip and together they set off again on the grass verge for home.

#

"You know, it's getting a bit old and boring now." Sally said as she walked into the kitchen/dining room and put her hands on her hips.

"What is, love?" asked James as he finished taking his shoes off and putting his slippers on. He joined her and looked around the room but was none the wiser.

"I'm sure I left everything neat and tidy. Blooming chair is out of place again. You don't think we have another unwelcome guest here do you?" she asked folding her arms across her chest. James just looked at her perplexed for a moment.

"Ghost, ghost! James, of all people I'd have thought that would be the first thing you'd think of!" she looked at him and shook her head.

"Well, not always, and anyway, I'd have thought we'd have seen Jennifer if we were going to see something like that." He turned and headed out of the room just as Sally almost began to tell him of the strange blue suited figure, but she stopped short. Instead she ventured upstairs to clean herself up after her little trip earlier and put thoughts of the mysterious figure to the back of her mind.

James sat in the front room and wondered if he should've said anything. For he too had seen the same ghostly figure on a couple of occasions, mainly outside in the front garden, but had decided not to say a word in case it was just his imagination.

But then, Jenny had not been a figment of his imagination just a few years earlier …

3: Things that move in the night…

Sally looked at James with her mouth wide open in disbelief.

"What do you mean '*tidy up before I go to work*'? Look who's talking! Pretty much every morning when I come downstairs there's at least one chair always out of place. It doesn't take a genius to put it straight before they come to bed now, does it?"

It had been a long day and she was in no mood for jokes or accusations. James knew he'd bitten off more than he could chew and tried to put on his apologetic look, but something she had said struck a chord with him.

He looked slowly down at the table then back up at her with a perplexed look about his face. He looked down again and pointed to the chair nearest the wall.

"Always that one by any chance?"

Sally shook her head and pointed to the one opposite it across the table.

"Good, as I wanted to see if you pointed to the right one." he looked serious as he said it then looked upwards at the ceiling.

"JENNY! Stop messing around with the kitchen chairs!" he bellowed and Sally suddenly looked bemused at him, forgetting her anger and frustration with him.

"Really? You think it's your ghostly sister after all the time we've been in 'Wolds View' without a sighting of her?"

He looked at her and shrugged.

"Well it's one explanation! Anyhow it's more likely that the floor is slightly sloping and it slowly drifts a little."

"Ahh, so now perhaps you've realised that it is better to call upon science than accuse the wife. Hmm?" she looked at him with as serious face as she could muster knowing she'd got him squirming now.

"OK, I apologise. It was out of order. But still, quite odd it's always *that* chair."

"Anyway, I thought you hadn't seen Jenny here since we moved in? Doesn't feel right that she would do this, not her style" offered Sally and James raised an eyebrow.

"Now look who's talking about ghosts! True I haven't seen her for a long time and I didn't really expect her to appear, but it was worth a shot. Odd though, that it's always that particular chair?" he again pointed to the offending item.

Sally nodded and walked over to examine the floor but stood up and shook her head.

"There really doesn't seem to be any sign of a slope under it. When Jack and his team did the work they did a darn good job. There's got to be a simple explanation." she added.

"Well love, it's late so why don't we both check the room now then both go up at the same time, agreed?" James looked at her and she smiled.

"OK, one more thing. You get up with me in the morning and no monkey business popping downstairs to mess with my head during the night. I have enough on with work at the moment without you playing silly buggers."

"Deal!"

34

#

"So, there you are, nothing out of place, so what have you got to say for yourself Mr Hansone?"

Sally stood defiantly in the kitchen just moments after they had come down the next morning only to find nothing amiss. James scowled and shook his head.

"Doesn't mean a thing…"

…"if it aint got..." she quipped, anticipating the lyrics.

"Ha, ha, very funny. OK, perhaps we're overreacting to this and it's just one of those things that we'll just have to shake our heads over and let it be."

Sally grimaced then set about sorting her breakfast and lunch. Twenty minutes later she kissed him on the forehead as he sat finishing his toast, then headed out to leave James home alone.

He had a fairly lazy day lined up except for setting up a wireless router upstairs on the landing to provide better Internet and connectivity throughout the old cottage. He couldn't help musing that Wolds View would have seen many changes since it was first built. In his research he'd discovered the cottage was almost two hundred and eighty years old. Built before anyone could even dream of regularly flying around the globe, keeping in touch with just a press of a button or accessing tons of information via a handheld device.

He chuckled as he finished off the connections and powered everything up, going through each of the rooms upstairs and downstairs checking signal strength. He wandered into the kitchen diner so engrossed in his tablet and the app that was testing the wireless signal strength that he didn't see the chair. Not until he found himself plunging forward, only just managing to grab the table to stop his head crashing into its edge.

James looked round and once again the same chair was out of place, moved round slightly but just enough to get in his way. A ripple of cold passed through him.

He didn't have time to think things about further as the tablet chirped to say he had a call. He didn't recognise the number.

"Hello?"

The voice on the other end explained who it was and he slowly pulled the annoying chair round and sat down on it as he took in the news.

"Thank you, I appreciate you calling. I'll let you know and get back to you, OK. Thanks, bye."

James sat there in deep reflection as he forgot about the chair and reflected on the bad news he'd just received.

#

"That's sad" Sally said. "How old was she?" she enquired as they sat together at the dining table that evening.

"I think in her early seventies, perhaps seventy three or four. Sarah, Bridget's neighbour became suspicious when she heard Scruff constantly barking late in the morning. She went round and could just see Bridget lying on the floor in the living room from the window. She has a key so quickly let herself in but it was clear Bridget must have collapsed early on as she was still in her dressing gown. Scruff was going frantic and barking at her body, poor thing must have known something was wrong.

Real shame, Helen gone, now her. I wonder if she ever got over losing Helen and seeing us break up?" James mused quietly as he thought about both his ex-wife and ex mother-in-law, both now deceased.

Sally lightly held his hand and he looked into her eyes and smiled. She shuffled a little closer then looked a little perplexed.

"What'll happen to Scruff now? Is the neighbour looking after him. Bet he's in shock as well."

"I don't know, must admit I didn't give him a thought, but he is a dog after all. Can't feel or understand like we can." He pulled his hand away sharply as Sally rapped his knuckles.

"*Don't* ever tell me dogs and for that matter cats, that are pets don't feel for their owners. I only met Scruff the once but the affection that dog had for Bridget and come think of it for you too, was overwhelming. He loved you and you can't tell me you didn't have any affection for him either. I saw the way you two acted together. Even Bridget said he pined for you when you left the house."

"Wow! Didn't know you felt so much about pets. OK, OK, yes, I do feel for him then and he is funny with his antics." James went quiet and Sally looked thoughtfully at him until he looked up at her again.

"Let's give him a home here" she said.

James didn't need to give it a second thought and picked up his phone.

#

The car drive had been a little traumatic and the journey had seemed to take forever so he was glad to jump out of the vehicle but was very patient as the leash was reattached. Scruff sat on the grass sniffing the air then spotted that his new owners were pointing at a cottage and a garden gate. He wagged his tail, stood up and obediently followed them through the gate and along the path as it wound round to the back of the property. Oddly they didn't use the front door. A porch awaited with a closed door and again he sat down on a paving slab as his new master seemed to fumble at the door with a key.

He still felt sorrow. His mistress had gone to sleep on the floor for some reason and despite his best efforts he had not managed to wake her. After what felt like an eternity, someone had come to the house and found him so his barks for help had worked. Strangely his mistress had appeared to him and stood next to the body lying on the floor but she had helped calm him down. After a while, staying with the next door person who had that horrid cat, he had been relieved to see a familiar face with his favourite rubber toy and his tail must have let the person he knew as James, know how happy he was to see him. Even the new lady with him seemed pleased to see Scruff and he remembered she had visited with the master once before.

The door opened and it was clear he was allowed to enter. The door shut behind him and for a moment Scruff was unsure, then the leash was taken off and he was shown to a newly made up bed - it was his from the old home!

He jumped into it turning round several times but couldn't sit down as he rushed out and barked at his new humans wagging his tail to show how happy he was. Master James picked him up and the new mistress tickled him under his right ear then they put him back on the floor and he looked up at them wondering what to do. His master gave a smile and they both left him to go into another room, his mistress looking back at him and waving for him to follow and he assumed it was OK to explore this new place.

He gladly rushed around each of the ground floor rooms missing the one his new owners had gone into, wanting to leave that till last. He found the stairs and rushed up them to explore further. Turning right he trotted into the bedroom and cocked his head. She looked at him and smiled and he felt a wave of happiness spread over him even though she seemed ill at ease before fading from view. He wagged his tail and wandered back out and across the landing into the next room.

He looked in through the slightly open door, it seemed peaceful and he turned and saw a smaller room and popped his head round the door to investigate. Hmn, not a room for him and he wasn't keen on baths so he headed downstairs and trotted into the room he had not ventured into yet. They were standing by the sink embracing and pushing their faces together.

Scruff trotted round and looked at the person sitting on one of the chairs. The man looked at him then scowled, but in a friendly sort of way and Scruff took the hint heading out into the other room where his bed seemed to be calling to him.

But he was puzzled.

Odd that, he thought in a way only a dog can, they didn't seem notice or be bothered by the person sitting on the chair by the table ...

4: A surprising trip

James arrived home late in the afternoon, parked up and let Scruff out whilst trying to put his lead back on. Scruff was a little confused and it was no surprise really as he and James had just come back from Grantham Crematorium after the funeral of Bridget, Scruff's original owner and James' ex mother in law.

Sally let them in and gave James a hug then picked up Scruff and gave him some attention too.

"So, always a sad event, but how did it go?" she asked as she put Scruff down who promptly went over to his basket and lay down. He really did look sad, Sally thought.

"It was the usual. Sad that first Helen dies in a freak accident, then Bridget passes away. Apparently the coroner suggested natural causes associated with her old age. I suppose it was no surprise but when we were outside for the burial of the ashes, I saw them both standing there hugging, then they seemed to see not just me but Scruff too. He also seemed quite subdued and was looking in their direction intently so it must have been a bit strange for him. He seemed to be straining at his leash as if he wanted to go over and be fussed by them. Everyone else just thought he was cute and then that was it. Ceremony over and they faded from view so I guess that's the last I'll see of them.

Sally embraced him and he fell quiet, contemplating his past life with Helen and how well he had always got on with Bridget.

#

It was most unexpected, but for a few months the saga of the moving chair subsided. Sally commented that perhaps having Scruff with them had driven wherever spirit or force it was away and they at last could get some sleep. James had to smile at the change in her in the last few years compared with when they had first met, he as a reluctant ghost hunter and she the sceptical real-life detective.

Well at least they were happy and Scruff had settled in, although he did occasionally bark for no reason in the kitchen next to the table.

Sally again surprised James by handing over an envelope one day with a card until he realised it was only a few days from his birthday. His *real* birthday as he'd discovered once the full facts about his mother and his families past had come to light. He did try to get two birthday cards a year but Sally insisted he should start to celebrate the proper date and he reluctantly agreed. It was still quite a change to him after all those years of thinking his birthday was in August when instead it was actually in May.

He opened up the envelope before Sally had chance to stop him and she tut-tutted at him as he realised he was supposed to have waited for the right day - it was going to take him a long time to get used to it. It was a gift certificate for two people to attend a 'Ghost walk' in Lincoln for two hours, *'exploring the hidden and mysterious ghostly happenings'* near to the Castle, so the certificate stated.

James chuckled and Sally frowned at him.

"You don't like it!" she stated rather than asked and he quickly looked into her eyes.

"Yes, yes, of course I do. I didn't really ever give it a thought to go on one of these, so, yes, thank you love."

She eyed him up then gave him a hug.

"Good, we don't have to use the voucher up yet but when we decide on a date we can book online and use the voucher then. They only run them apparently when the moon is bright, so I guess it takes place close to full moon, they'd use that to help people see in dark places - oh, so *mysterious places*." She waved her hands spookily above her head and he shook his head at her.

"So, you're coming too then?"

"What? Let you have all the fun? Of course I am. Anyway - it will be funny to see what they plan and if there are any tricks or if it's just walking around in the dark telling porkies about what happened at such and such a site."

"Methinks you be a bit sceptical my dearest!" he retorted, and she laughed.

"Yep, but I'm game if you are. What's the worst that could happen - we see a real ghost - we've already been there and done that and you've done it by the spade full! You'll probably be able to tell them a thing or two."

"Yeah, I suspect it will all be staged anyway but worth seeing what they get up to. Thank you love, it will be good to see something different than my own family eh?"

Sally shrugged and picked up her folder.

"Anyhow, gotta dash, we have a health and safety inspection at HQ and you know how I *really* love those things!"

James gave her a kiss and she headed out the door but stopped as Scruff ran up to her looking expectant as he cocked his head from one side to the other.

"No Scruff, - Daddy over there will take you for a walk, I've got to go to work." She tickled him under his right ear and he barked happily but looked back at James as she closed the door behind her.

James knew he had little choice and reached for his coat and for Scruff's leash.

#

They reached the gate, Scruff obediently waiting for it to be opened before they both walked through together. James turned left towards the village where Scruff had become a bit of a celebrity with the locals, especially with his antics at the village pond. However, as James started to walk towards Grasceby the lead pulled taut and he realised Scruff was not eagerly following. He looked round and realised Scruff was looking the other way up the road.

"Come on Scruff, this way boy!" James called out, but Scruff stood still and alert, still looking up the road.

"Now come on Scruff, you know you like to see the ducks on the pond."

Scruff was having none of it however today and pulled at the leash with a low growl which surprised James. He'd never heard Scruff growl like that before. Like a warning or as if something was annoying the dog.

James looked down the road then stood stock still. A figure in a slate grey-bluish uniform stood on the verge in the distance looking towards them then turned, headed into the woods and disappeared.

Scruff growled then barked and pulled at the leash and James reluctantly began to walk in that direction unsure of what to think. For now, Scruff seemed to be in control rather than James.

They walked or rather James was 'towed' as Scruff continued to strain at his leash and it took them just over a couple of minutes to reach the spot where the person had been. Before James had a chance to explore the area, Scruff turned left sniffing around on the verge. James saw there was a little used and quite faint impression of a path or animal track leading off into the woods and he realised it was the place that Sally had chased the brown butterfly just a few weeks earlier. He allowed Scruff to explore a little along the path and as the undergrowth became taller they came across a dilapidated wooden fence with what looked like old rusty barbed wire running along it's top.

A small gate with a rusted padlock barred their way further, although Scruff was determined to push his way under the gate. James pulled lightly but firmly on the leash and Scruff trotted back to him standing next to his right leg looking for all the world as if he was annoyed at being stopped.

"Hold back there Scruff, we might get into trouble if we venture in there." James noticed a wooden sign had fallen into the undergrowth below the gate and he carefully picked it up wiping it as clean as he could. The wording was badly faded but it's intention and meaning was clear regardless.

James stepped back a little to get better lighting on it.

RAF GRASCEBY
MOD PROPERTY
UNAUTHORISED ACCESS IS STRICTLY
FORBIDDEN.

"Well Scruff, me old bean, looks like we can't go in there".

James was about to turn and leave when Scruff let out a spine-tingling whine that James had never heard him utter before and he looked up…

… straight at the uniformed person standing looking at them through the trees several tens of metres away. Not for the first time in his recent past, James felt a creepy sensation and a tingle trickle down his spine as he looked down at Scruff then back up - only to see the person had disappeared.

"Oh heck, now what am I getting into?" James muttered as Scruff gave out a little growl then pushed forward to the gate, managing to get under before James could stop him.

James shook his head, hooked the leash onto the gate post and taking extreme care, managed to climb up over the gate just missing the barbed wire. He took hold of the leash keeping it short so Scruff could not try that trick again and together they headed slowly along the barely visible path.

A pheasant suddenly took flight startling both James and Scruff but they pressed on deeper into the wood. After just a few more minutes Scruff stopped and sniffed around then tried to bolt to the left through the undergrowth as James held on. For a few moments James could only wonder at how Bridget had managed to keep hold of her dog on their walks. But just as he thought this, they stumbled out into a sparser patch of the wood with a couple of ancient trees holding sway just off centre. Both were large and quite grizzled old oak trees.

Walking over, Scruff once again straining at his leash, James looked round but there was no sign of the uniformed man. He looked back to where they had disturbed the grasses and ferns and looked down at Scruff shaking his head. Scruff in turn looked up at him but had his tail lowered and James realised something.

Scruff wasn't looking up at him, but up and off slightly to one side.

He followed Scruff's gaze and startled, stepped back as he looked up at the uniformed person hanging by the neck with a rope from the thickest branch before the apparition faded before their very eyes.

#

Back home, several hours later, after spending time pouring over what online newspaper records he could find, James had to admit he couldn't find any reference to anyone reported being found hanging in the woods.

He sat back, picked up his coffee then scowled as it had gone cold. He headed over to the microwave and placed the cup inside to heat it up.

He looked down at Scruff who was asleep in his basket.

"You know something don't you boy, eh? You can sense something and maybe even see whoever it is. If only you could talk."

Scruff seemed to stir but remained asleep as he turned over onto his side then his little feet began to jiggle as if he was running, perhaps he was dreaming…

"That's it Scruff, you chase whoever it is and find out for me!"

He wandered back through into the living room and settled on the couch examining and searching the web on his tablet.

#

A noise at the door and Sally entered as James stirred, realising he had dropped off to sleep. Scruff too came awake and rushed off to greet her happily. She came in and looked at James putting her hands on her hips.

"So, this is what you get up to when I go out to work, slaving away whilst you just lounge about at home!" Scruff barked happily wagging his tail expectantly as James yawned and stretched his arms.

"It's alright for you, you've not been off in the woods finding a ghostly body hanging from a tree!"

Sally stared at him for a second not knowing what to say, then walked into the kitchen over to the kettle, filled it up and put it on.

She came back into the living room.

"OK, spill, and I mean all of it!"

"Yes, miss detective miss, yes indeed ma'am as long as you don't arrest me for trespassing!"

"Well, I'll be the judge of that m'lordy."

With that, James told her of that morning's excitement.

5: A walk in the wood - take 2!

"You know there was something I remember Helen saying when we were at the Lincoln archives a few years back whilst looking for information on Jenny." James said to Sally over the lounge coffee table that evening whilst Scruff slept at her feet.

"What's that then love?"

"There was a reference to my family having had more than one tragedy but when we were looking for any more records I seem to remember the assistant at the desk saying that there had been a fire some years earlier and some of the early records had been destroyed. Perhaps something else happened here, or nearby, that involved someone related to me in the past before Jenny was accidentally killed?"

"You'd have thought Jenny would have mentioned it to you on the few times you have seen her, wouldn't you?"

"I'm not sure. I don't know, but I haven't seen her here since we resolved what happened to her. I might just be off on the wrong track."

"Well why not go to your family's graves tomorrow and see if she will appear to you?"

James nodded thoughtfully.

"Yes, might try that. Might be a bit of a long shot but hey ho, worth trying. Don't know about you but I'm for bed as it's gone eleven thirty now."

"Good point. You taking Scruff outside, or am I?"

Scruff had awoken, immediately headed to the door and looked over at James.

"I think he's already decided. I'll see you up there in a few minutes when I've sorted his lordship out down here!"

Sally just grinned and picked up the coffee mugs as James duly led Scruff out to do what he needed to do.

#

At first it seemed quite distant, but as he came awake James realised that Sally was now awake too and prodding him in the ribs. He leant over and managed to focus on the alarm clock noting it was about an hour or so before Sally's own smart alarm would be going off. The sky was already light and he realised what the noise was.

Scruff was barking like a mad dog!

Grabbing his dressing gown, Sally also jumping quickly out of bed, they both rushed downstairs flicking the lights on and making enough noise to ensure that if it were burglars they would be in for a fright.

But there was nothing and no sign of entry as they quickly scoured the downstairs rooms until they were left with the kitchen/dining room. They looked quizzically at Scruff who sat bolt upright on his bed looking at them expectantly.

"So, what's the panic then Scruff?" asked Sally as she went over to him. He jumped out of his bed and rushed over to her wagging his tail. She tickled him under his ear and he seemed to settle down. Despite an extensive search, when James came back, he just shrugged and shook his head.

Then noticed something.

The chair was again moved out of place.

"Err, Sally, the chair…"

"Oh, sorry, that was me. I was going to sit down and let Scruff jump up onto my lap but I didn't get a chance to sit down."

James sighed with relief then ruffled Scruff's head.

"Now what's up with you boy eh?"

Scruff just looked at him nonchalantly, turned, went over to his bed and settled back into it. Sally looked at James then looked at the kitchen clock.

"Well, I'm not going back to bed as I'll not get any more sleep. I'll do a little paperwork then slip off to work, so if you want to go back for a couple more hours kip that's fine by me."

James smiled at her, sidled over and kissed her on the forehead before nodding, turning and giving Scruff a little wag of his finger before heading back upstairs. Sally put some toast on and filled the kettle and shook her head as she thought about what to do first before heading out herself.

#

James heard the noise as he came awake from a deep state of sleep and for a moment felt disorientated, then realised he had rolled over and was on Sally's side of the bed lying diagonally across it.

It was Scruff barking again, quite furiously. He stumbled out of bed and shouted down to Scruff before throwing on his clothes and rushing downstairs.

He entered the kitchen diner with an annoyed look at Scruff who'd stopped barking as James entered.

"Come on Scruff, give me a break mate!" James said as he bent over and ruffled the hair on the back of Scruff's head. Scruff enjoyed the attention but kept moving his gaze past James, who didn't notice.

At first that is.

He looked up, caught a reflection of the room in the microwave door and was about to stand up when a thought struck him about the view.

Sally had left the chair out to one side again.

Slightly annoyed he turned round.

Only to look straight at the man dressed in the RAF uniform he'd seen the previous day. James quickly glanced back at the reflection in the microwave door but there was nothing there.

As James turned back, the man was still present but appeared oblivious to him seeming to look towards the door with a decidedly sad expression on his face. Indeed, to James he looked a worn and beaten man. He stood up, straightened his uniform and headed for the back door.

James paused for a few moments then looked at Scruff who had stood up and trotted to the kitchen door into the hallway, looking out towards the back door. Realising the ghost wouldn't use the front door as it was a modern feature, he grabbed Scruff's leash, quickly attached it, then hurried out only remembering to lock the door just in time. Together they ran round to the front of the cottage in time to see the man appear to open an invisible gate, step through then begin to walk down the road off towards the right.

Déjà vu crept over James as he remembered following another ghost from the cottage just a few years previous and a shudder went down his spine. But if there was a second ghost at Wolds View then why hadn't Jenny warned him about it?

They began to follow at a discreet distance and James noted that the RAF man turned into the woods along the same path he and Scruff had found only the other day whilst following him at a distance.

Following, this time James made sure Scruff waited until he had climbed over the gate and cleared the barbed wire before setting off down the small and almost indistinct path. Just ahead James could still see the ghostly figure and he realised they were close to where he and Scruff and turned off the path before but as he watched the man carried on past the turning and James hurried to keep up.

Maintaining a discreet distance, James realised that the ghost wasn't aware of him and they passed through a low hollow in the ground then up a slight rise as the trees began to thin out.

James could see buildings ahead.

The Grasceby industrial estate.

Without stopping the ghost carried on out of the wood, seemingly opening another gate that didn't exist in the modern age, but now he appeared to be following a different path, as if he was skirting around a building. There was nothing there until James and Scruff reached the same place and he could see the faint outlines of foundations where a building had once been. Long and rectangular he thought by the looks of the faint remains.

James looked up. He couldn't see the ghost anymore but approaching him was a man who looked solid and serious in his demeanour. He appeared to have come from what looked to be the control tower building a little further on near to several old converted hangers. Perhaps a throwback to the old airfield, James mused as the man approached.

"Excuse me sir, can I help you with anything?" the newcomer asked rather brusquely.

"Oh, sorry, Scruff here got a little carried away. Hi, I'm James, James Hansone." He held out his hand as the man eyed him then held his out in turn and they shook.

"Greg Sanders. Scottish?"

James looked at him perplexed. Then Greg pointed down at Scruff.

"Oh, sorry, thought you meant, well never mind. Yes, Scottish Terrier. My apologies, I thought it was a public path and didn't realise it ended up here."

"Well, let's put it like this, I haven't seen anyone using this path since I came here and that's at least eight years now."

Greg looked at James oddly.

"Seen anything odd on your walk?"

This caught James by surprise and for some reason he just shook his head.

"No, why, should I?"

"Nah, just curious why someone would be on a path that's not been used for who knows how many years."

James thought quickly.

"Well actually I own the cottage just beyond this wood on the road to Grasceby and we've been exploring the neighbourhood recently with the better weather. Haven't we Scruff?"

Scruff looked up at the mention of his name but quickly looked away as he'd spotted a rabbit in the rough grass not far from the outline of the building they'd just found. He pulled eagerly at his leash, to no avail.

"Oh, so you're the person who's done it up? Looks a good job. Nice to see it no longer deserted, although I have to say it always looked a bit spooky for my liking."

James kept quiet, knowing what he knew about the history of the cottage.

"Well I'd best be off and sorry to have intruded."

"That's OK but bear in mind that this is now private property. Looks like I need to get a sign done for the old path next to the road then doesn't it!"

James nodded and they shook hands as he turned around and Scruff realised he wasn't going to be able to chase the rabbit after all.

They started to head back the way they came when James heard Greg behind him.

"Best take the main entrance off to your left, leads you back to the road without having to go through the woods and over the old gate."

James turned and waved as he did as he was told.

#

Greg started to walk back to the main building but was a little troubled. He couldn't shake the feeling that he'd either met or read about James but just couldn't place where or when.

And there was one other thing.

For he too had seen the airman on several occasions recently and had noted that Mr Hansone had not mentioned it although he'd watched the ghost and then James appearing to follow with his dog. It was clear to him that James too had seen the ghost and was following it.

It unnerved him as he stepped into the converted control tower, a throwback to the days of the site being an airfield and now the company headquarters with a small museum at the back commemorating the old airfield.

#

He used to like the walk, through the woods and to his airfield. Yes, it wasn't an easy life but war was never easy and he just counted his lucky stars that he kept returning after each mission. He had completed twenty three sorties with the same crew as their flight engineer. Pilot Mark 'Chappers' Chapman, wireless Basil 'Hairy' Harris, bomb aimer and front gunner Neville 'Trumpy' Trumper, mid-upper gunner Kevin 'Bondy' Bonderson and navigator Anthony 'Ackers' Anders. Sadly, flak during their last but one mission had claimed the life of their rear gunner, Oliver 'Olly' Martens.

Olly was missed but that was the nature of being in a Lancaster bomber in 1944, especially for rear gunners. His replacement had big shoes to fill, Jack 'Jackers' Jackson, but he seemed a decent enough chap. Shame it had been their last mission and his first and last. As for the imposter…

Yes, he used to like the walk, but now it was different, things had not been the same since.

6: A reverential meeting

"I tell you, go and see if you can raise her or whatever it is you do to contact Jenny. If there is another ghost here, I want to know so we can try and do something about it as it's no longer funny finding the chair moved almost every morning."

Although difficult to say out loud, Sally just felt that something had to be done once she'd heard James' story.

He just nodded feeling a sense of unease at the turn of events but knew Sally was right. It couldn't carry on as it was and it was clear Scruff could see the airman and now of course so could James.

Well at least on those occasional times as, for a few days, everything had gone quiet.

He nodded, she pecked him on his cheek and made sure she was looking respectable.

"You think I look OK?" she asked. James inwardly chuckled as there was only one answer he was supposed to give.

"Yes, you look lovely dear. I'm sure Harriet will not be bothered as long as you both have a good time."

"It'll be good to have a day out with her as I haven't seen her since she left. Now don't do anything daft like trespassing on an abandoned airfield again - I might not have a phone signal so there'll be no one to get you out of jail - again!"

James smiled as he remembered how she'd swept into the North Wales Police HQ and taken the local detective to task for detaining James the previous year. He nodded as Scruff followed her to the front door and realising as she left that she wasn't going to take him for a walk. Head lowered, he wandered back into the front lounge, found his rubber hammer toy and began to chew squeakily.

James had a few notes to make for the presentation he was giving to the local WI at Grasceby village hall the next month, so he headed upstairs to Jenny's old room.

He stood just inside the doorway and for a brief moment memories came back of a damp afternoon when he and his former friend, Craig, had explored the abandoned cottage looking for clues to discover who the young girl was that James had been seeing as he drove by.

So much had happened since then, he mused, then a resolve took over him.

"Jenny? JENNY? Are you here?"

Nothing.

The room remained silent with not a hint of anything unusual.

"JENNIFER?"

He stood listening as he heard Scruff barking and he rushed downstairs only to realise Scruff was only barking because he'd heard James upstairs shouting for Jenny.

He quickly took Scruff outside for his ablutions then made sure there was plenty of water and food in his bowl, patted him on the head as Scruff gave him a look as much to say 'you leaving me then?' before heading out to his car and setting off for Grasceby church.

He didn't see the airman looking out wistfully from the living room window as he left Wolds View cottage…

#

He stood looking down at the gravestones and for a moment smiled at the good job that had been made of the headstone.

It still seemed so far-fetched, yet all those years he had not really known his mother as he had thought. It must have been incredibly hard keeping her secret from him all that time. All just so that he could have a normal life.

Normal!

Well that had certainly gone out the window since he and his first wife, Helen, had moved up into the area.

"Jenny?, Jenny, are you there?" he called out again but she didn't appear to him. Not surprising once he'd discovered the truth about her disappearance all those years ago. Her spirit was probably now at peace and had passed over to wherever it was they went to once they were settled.

He remembered the brief view of the three of them, his mother who had managed to restart her life and raise him, his father who he'd never even met but only knew when he saw him as a ghost. And of course, Jenny, the sister he had never had the chance to get to know, again only as a ghost.

"Can I help you Mr Hansone?" The voice seemed to come out of nowhere and he involuntarily jumped in his skin. He turned to look up the path and saw the Reverend Sarah Cossant smiling at him from a few feet away.

"Oh, sorry to startle you. You did seem to be deep in thought and I wasn't sure if I should say anything." she added.

"No problem Reverend. Just paying my respects and wondering what it would have been like if I'd known my father and sister if they'd lived."

"That's understandable, it must have taken much courage for your mother to move away and try to make a new life for you both. I'm glad you managed to find some closure, and of course the loss of your first wife must also have taken some toll. Would you care to come into the rectory and have a chat about it? It's often the case that all people need is someone to listen to them and not say a word in judgement."

"You know what Reverend, I will. I'm sure you know I'm not particularly religious but events and circumstances over the last few years have made me question much about the way I look at the world, indeed the universe."

Sarah smiled. "Come along then, cup of tea always helps sooth the path regardless of where we are heading. I'm sure I can find a biscuit or two as well."

#

The artificial gas fire glowed warmly and James felt settled as Sarah poured the tea.

"If I may say, you have seemed somewhat distracted of late. I have passed you a few times in Horncastle and you've hardly said a word, as if something deep is on your mind. Do you want to talk about it?" she asked.

"Well, let's put it like this. I'm sure you are aware of my family connections with Grasceby and with Wolds View Cottage and that I saw my long dead sister who I'd never even knew existed."

"Yes, quite a convoluted situation wasn't it?"

"You can say that again. Well, Sally and I thought it was all done and dusted since we solved Jennifer's missing persons case, but now I'm not so sure." He paused wondering how much to tell the reverend.

"Yet clearly it isn't or you wouldn't be at your family's graveside calling out for your deceased sister ..."

"Oh, you did hear me then. Sorry."

"Why?"

"Why what?" asked a puzzled James.

"Why are you sorry that I heard you. There is nothing wrong with talking to the graves of loved ones lost. I hear it all the time. It brings great comfort to many, even non-believers such as yourself, knowing there may be a chance they can still hear us. But it shows that deep down we still have a connection with our ancestors, and it is a way of maintaining that connection."

"To be fair, I was actually trying to ask for Jenny's help." he replied as he thought about what he should say.

"Why?" she gently pressed for him to open up more.

"Well, since Sally and I renovated the cottage, we seem to have disturbed or awakened something. And it's not Jenny."

"Interesting, this can happen when a property has been reclaimed for the living. I have heard of cases where a past spirit, long dormant, has taken umbrage at the new owners and makes sure they know it."

"You sound as if you know something about our cottage?"

"Not at all, well, not quite. But this sort of happening does come with the collar you know." Sarah smiled as she tugged gently on her collar and a little grin appeared as James too smiled.

"Yes, I guess it does. Sally and I have seen what looks like an airman, perhaps RAF walking away from the cottage, down the road and into the woods in the direction of the old airfield. Even Scruff can see and sense him and has even led me after him, on his lead of course."

"Scruff? On his lead? I've heard Charles, the estate manager called a few things in my time but never a scruff despite appearances! And as far as I am aware he is not into 'that sort of thing'." She shook her head a little mystified then realised James was looking at her and chuckling a little to himself.

"Oh no, nothing like that." he said.

For a moment James tried to push away the odd thought of Charles into something rather exotic then brushed it aside. He chuckled again. "We have taken on my ex mother-in-laws dog after she sadly passed away a few weeks back. He seems to be able to see the airman."

Sarah laughed out loud, startling James.

"Oh, I am so sorry, that was in poor taste considering her passing, but it was the mental image of Charles being more scruffy than normal. I hadn't realised you meant your dog. You have to admit Charles is not really the tidiest of people, but I guess that goes with his job, doesn't it!"

"Yes, your reverandship…" James mockingly bowed to her and they both smiled. It seemed they both had a similar sense of humour after all.

"Touche'. Is there anything else on your mind?"

James sat and wondered about what to say.

"Well there's another aspect to it. I think he may have committed suicide." he said quietly.

"Good Lord, that is a little extreme. And of course, a sin in the eyes of the Lord. What makes you say such a thing?"

"Well, on one of the times Scruff led me into following the airman, he diverted off into the woods near to the cottage and not far from the old disused RAF base. There was a clearing and.." he paused.

Sarah looked at him then gently motioned for him to continue.

"I realised that Scruff wasn't looking at me but up at the nearer of two oak trees and for a moment I could have sworn I saw the same airman hanging from a rope tied to one of the thicker higher branches. He then faded away."

"You have intrigued me, RAF you say? Perhaps from the second world war?"

"Yes, possibly, yes, I think that is the case. Why?"

"I'm not sure but I will have a look in the rectories library as I know there are quite a few old diaries of the many clergy who have been here before me. Who knows if they have recorded anything that may help. I'm sure something like that would have been recorded somewhere. Have you tried the archives in Lincoln for newspaper reports and the like?"

"Yes, but quite a lot was destroyed in a fire many years ago, so some records are lost probably forever."

"Oh dear, I've only been here about nine years so didn't know about the fire. It must have been a while ago. But I will have a look for you in my library and see what I can find. It is a most interesting story and I think one that is worth investigating, don't you think?"

"Oh yes, it seems Sally and I have started something that neither of us could ever have expected."

"Talking of starting something, did you hear that we have been successful in our lottery application for funding?"

"No, funding for what?" James was intrigued.

"Well the rectory and church are around three hundred years old and in our modern world access for those with walking issues is a real problem. So, we've worked with the council planning department and despite the hurdles, we have found a way to provide disabled access and a special pathway around to the church. The church can't have much done to it as it's listed, but we've now secured a lottery grant so we can have what amounts to a conservatory built at the back of the rectory, with a level path coming round from the front. Anyone with mobility issues, scooters or wheelchairs and such like can come in to see me. The second path then winds its way to the church and again will give easier access into it from here. I'm pretty pleased I can tell you. Work may start in a few months' time so I'm sure when it's all finished we will have a special opening day and you and Sally can come over if you'd like?"

"That sounds really good and quite appropriate. I'll let Sally know to expect the invitation."

"Very well. Sorry to do this but we'll have to finish now as I am supposed to meet a young couple to talk to them about their upcoming wedding vows. Although to be fair, one thinks it could be a shotgun situation if you get my drift!" Sarah gently tapped her midriff and winked at him and he couldn't help think how well they had got on.

He knew she was highly respected, but he had seem a more humorous side to the reverend than he had thought possible. Shaking her hand he noted the time and knew a certain dog would be pining away at the front door waiting for him to come home, so he bade farewell and left the rectory just as the young couple walked up the gravel driveway.

He could see what Sarah meant…

\#

"So, Jenny was a no show then?" asked Sally as she buttered a slice of toast. She waved it at James who nodded eagerly, whilst Scruff too watched her just in case it should fall miraculously from her hand and he could pounce on it.

She didn't drop it but put it on a small plain orange and yellow plate and handed it to James who quickly scoffed it, much to Scruff's dismay.

"No, but I did end up spending the afternoon with Sarah. You know, the reverend."

Sally turned slowly and eyed him up with a stern look on her face. "Oh yes?" she asked in a police style of interrogation.

"Not like that you daft thing! She heard me calling out to Jenny and invited me back to talk about my family and things in general. I was quite surprised how well we got on. I know she was a great choice for the wedding and she did seem a good egg and all that. Especially letting her hair down at the reception, but I'd never really had such a conversation before with her in the rectory.

"So anything interesting to report?" Sally asked smiling, looking into his eyes but making sure he knew he was now under interrogation.

"Well, Sarah is going to check the rectory library for any possible records relating to an airman who may have committed suicide. It's a long shot but as many of the archives records were destroyed all those years ago it might be the only way of knowing the truth."

James licked his lips.

"Any more toast? *Pleeease?*"

Sally rolled her eyes and proceeded to look after the poor male human being who was unable to make his own supper.

7: Tripping back the time fantastic

"Whose a good boy then, yes you are, you are."

James looked round the door from the kitchen into the hallway and shook his head as Sally played with Scruff. He knew it wasn't him she was talking about!

"Best not mention the 'V' word to him. He thinks he's going for walkies!" James called out to Sally.

"Thanks a bundle, he's just heard the 'W' word and now is even more excitable" Sally retorted.

In one deft move she managed to pick Scruff up, swing round and quickly put him in the dog carrier before Scruff knew what had happened. However, as he began to whine, Sally put a doggie biscuit in and Scruff soon settled down as he chewed on it. It was a tough one, meant to keep his teeth and gums strong and healthy but also worked to help Sally settle Scruff, so win, win, she concluded.

"Good job it's my day off and I'm the one taking him in as I don't think you'd cope hearing him whine when he gets to the vet."

Scruffs ears pricked up, he knew that word and it was never a good thing. He gruffed his annoyance but settled down now that he'd been captured and had a biscuit to try to crunch through.

Sally put her coat on and popped her head around the door.

"OK, we're off now, should just have enough time to get there so whatever you do, don't go wandering off after ghostly airmen trying to top themselves eh?"

"Yes dear, I won't."

Sally grabbed her car keys, reached down and carefully lifted up the dog carrier as Scruff looked forlornly out from the wire front.

"Byee." she said, opening the front door and trying to gently close it whilst being careful with Scruff.

The door instead slammed shut and James realised there was a window open upstairs that must have created a draft. He shook his head and didn't think any more about it.

He used his tablet to flip through various channels on the wall screen but soon became bored with what was on offer. Getting up he decided to make a coffee but as he did so, James glanced out to admire the view out of the kitchen window and immediately caught the side of one of the kitchen chairs, just managing to stop himself falling over.

He looked down at the chair with a dawning realisation.

It was the same chair that used to be out of place when they came down in the morning. It had been quiet for a few weeks now so had caught him by surprise. He looked slowly around the room but there was no sign or hint of the airman so James set the chair back into place tucked under the kitchen table and waited.

Nothing.

No change or movement at all.

Ten minutes that seemed like an eternity but again no change as he fetched his coffee then decided to go upstairs and check their broadband router as it had been playing up intermittently for a few days now. A job right up his street considering his past work with computers, software and data processing. He fondly remembered the days of working with his friend, and technically his boss, Mark. Then he remembered the new chap, Craig who he'd got on well with at first, until of course Craig and his now dead ex-wife Helen had begun an affair.

Still, at least he had met Sally and the two had fallen for each other. Shortly after that, Helen and Craig decided to live together once Helen and James became separated, then divorced. He couldn't help think about how fast things had happened.

He wandered into the master bedroom and over to the window to look out over the front garden and stopped in his tracks.

The airman was just leaving, heading off towards the right as usual, crossing the road and walking away on the grass verge in a purposeful manner.

James raced downstairs and out the front door, just remembering to lock it first, Sally wouldn't forgive him if they got burgled whilst he was out chasing a ghost. He briefly remembered she'd hinted he shouldn't be doing it again, but he shook it off. For a moment he thought he had lost the airman, but then realised he would have reached the turn off into the woods. James ran along the road, listening out in case of a car or for that matter one of the occasional lorries that came from the industrial estate surprised him.

No sign of the airman as he reached the turnoff and he quickly clambered over the run-down gate, avoiding the barbed wire along the top.

Then he saw him.

A chill ran down James's spine as the airman appeared to be looking directly at him, almost as if he was waiting for him to catch up. He then turned, satisfied, and carried on walking, this time not turning to the left towards the clearing, but once again heading in the direction of the old airfield. James followed but kept a wary distance back.

His curiosity was piqued and he just had to find out where the airman went to on the disused airfield. Even if it meant running into Greg again. He followed as he brushed away some of the overgrown foliage and he wondered if he should have put on some sturdier shoes. James involuntarily shuddered as the grass path became neater and almost well-trodden and a shock awaited him as he looked up.

The path was indeed far neater than he'd remembered it and up ahead was a small gate and beyond…

He stopped suddenly and let out a gasp of shock as he took in the unfolding scene before him.

The gate led out onto a fully functional RAF airbase and in the distance he saw a Lancaster Bomber had just landed and was swinging round to taxi up the side runway. He reached the gate and could see various buildings, hangars, a control tower and a dozen or more Lancasters parked up with ground crew milling about them, working on some and several affixing wooden chocks under the wheels to stop them rolling away of their own accord.

There was no sign of the airman but a military vehicle with emergency markings raced away towards the recently landed Lancaster and he realised as the latter turned, it was badly shot up.

The sound of the Merlin engines was almost overwhelming as two of the parked Lancasters struck up their engines and moved away into the distance, readying for take off. Six more joined them and lined up for take off.

James carefully opened and passed through the gate, mesmerised by the sights and sounds, and now smells of aviation fuel. It felt surreal. A fuel truck parked up near a large, indeed huge, tank and the driver jumped out to attach hoses to the tank to fill up. No one had noticed him yet, so James followed the well beaten track down the side towards a series of out buildings that he figured looked like maintenance hangers. He recognised the lower brick part of the structures as matching the outlines of foundations he had noticed when he'd last come onto the airfield. That time it was the industrial estate but now James felt a chill run through and down his spine.

It appeared to be sometime in the 1940s. How? He had no idea but thoughts raced back a couple of years to when he was exploring the Grasceby Manor and had found a toy room which didn't exist in the present. He'd scoffed at the idea of any form of time travel, always dismissing it as fantasy and scientifically impossible.

Yet.

One, it had happened.

Two, he had not believed in ghosts but that had dramatically changed since encountering Jenny, the dead sister he didn't know he had, and *three*, he was now somewhere back in the 1940s!

Whilst he had been musing on all this an officer had approached then drawn a gun, pointing it at him.

"Drop to your knees and put your hands on your head and explain who you are quickly or I'll shoot." the officer barked.

James stood, flustered but his wits raced back.

"Sorry sir but I was dropped off at the wrong entrance and came through the woods so I'm a bit lost."

"Flight, ground or officer?"

James wasn't quite sure on the answer so took a gamble. "Err, ground, Sir."

The officer looked him up and down then shook his head. "Send us all sorts now. Let's hope you're up to the task. You look a tad familiar, are you local? Have you relations on the base or in Grasceby, perhaps Bardney?"

"Erm, sort of local you could say" James answered carefully. He kept pondering what Einstein had said about going back in time and changing the timeline. He had to come up with something and quick."

"You look like Teddy, but he's never mentioned anyone like you, you're nowhere near like his son, Jack. Although come to think of it…no, not really!"

James heart pounded. "No, I'm originally from Essex, don't think any of my lot got up here but you never know what with the war. Name's err, Mike…" He looked frantically past the officer searching for a name then blurted out… "Mike Barracks."

"Hah! Hope there's no army in you, can't have one of those in the Royal Air Force, just wouldn't be right! Ground eh? We need you chaps more than ever. Jerry seems to be getting desperate and keeps having a go at the airfields trying to get our planes, so get going, main office is over there to the left and report in for duty. Someone will assign you a bunk and a decent uniform. Don't know how you lot dress down in Essex but up here that will not do. Dismiss!"

The officer waved James away and strode off towards the Lancaster that had just landed. James breathed a sigh of relief, but it was short lived as sirens began to blare out across the base and suddenly people were running frantically around. The officer raced back to the main control tower whilst others quickly disappeared down into what James assumed must be bunkers and for a moment he froze on the spot not knowing where to go.

High pitched engine noises from above, then loud explosions rocked the ground as concrete and dirt flew up into the air over in the distance. Suddenly several dark shapes raced across the airbase strafing the ground. In shock he saw several people in the distance cut down and then heard a shout and he looked in that direction.

A man in overalls covered in dark stains and grease was frantically beckoning to him and James ran for his life towards him.

Several more explosions getting closer rocked the ground making him stumble, but he kept running. The overalls man was near to one of the gun emplacements with sandbags surrounding it, the gun was pointing off to one side and firing into the air as another larger aircraft was passing overhead. From the films James had seen he thought it was a Junkers or Heinkel, but he couldn't be sure in such a fast moving situation. A bunker appeared ahead as he caught up with the man and they headed towards it just in time as a bomb struck the gun emplacement and blew it to kingdom come, killing the two men operating it. Bombs were now falling nearby and getting closer but James realised it wasn't a bunker but a storage hut that had previously been hit.

Overalls man, grabbed James by the arm and they were almost there when they were thrown to the ground by a, much too close for comfort, explosion. James sat up groggily and realised the man was knocked out so he grabbed him and hoisted him up, shaking him groggily awake. James realised they had to be close to a Lancaster due to its shadow, then saw in horror a large bomb was lodged in the cockpit area but had not detonated. He turned as the man spotted it and James hauled both of them away diving behind the thick wall of the hut just as the bomb finally slid further into the cockpit and detonated, blowing the front of the Lancaster off in one go.

He could hear the outside walls being struck by shards of metal and for once in his life, James prayed.

Several other shadows quickly crossed the airfield and James braced but then heard the cheers. He looked gingerly out from the side of the wall and just spotted three Hawker Hurricanes and a couple of Spitfires streak over and head up to take on the enemy.

He could have cried with sheer joy at the sight. It was a strange feeling watching them, knowing that all he had ever seen were such planes in flying displays and in the movies. This time it was for real and it was a sobering sight.

Overalls man sat up, grabbed his right hand and shook it repeatedly.

"Thank you. Thank the heavens you were there. I might not have made it. Name's Arthurson, Eric Arthurson, ground crew. You are?"

James had to think then remembered what he'd said to the officer. "Mike Barracks. That was pretty frightening I can tell you. Nothing like in the movies, a lot louder and quite terrifying."

Eric looked a little baffled but just shook his head.

"Bet we've lost a few planes today. And good people too. They must be getting desperate. We'll get them, you'll see."

"Oh indeed we do, we do. Er well, at least we'd hope for that wouldn't we…" James realised he was babbling and also remembered he couldn't say too much.

"Well, if ever you need anything then just ask for me. Best get over and see what's left. With luck only a few will have been hit as I noticed several were scrambled. They must have been warned to get as many in the air as possible. On the ground they are sitting ducks, as are we."

"Oh, yes, right ho and all that." replied James but Eric just looked at him, shook his head.

"Here, you're clearly new here, look I need to get over there to help check out the damage to the remaining Lancs, so take this over to the garage hanger over there and leave it with George. He'll know what to do with it.

Eric handed over a small, but complex, mechanism then turned and hurriedly left in the direction of the remaining Lancasters, some of which looked somewhat worse for wear after the attack.

The all clear sirens blared out as more people emerged from several nearby bunkers and hurriedly went about their duties. James looked about, wondering what to do and where to go.

He pocketed the mechanism in his inside jacket pocket and, remembering the control tower was still standing in the present, well, his future, he started in its direction. Without warning he felt a little lightheaded, shook his head to try to clear it then looked about, stunned.

He was back in the present on the industrial estate and someone was coming towards him with a look of astonishment on his face …

8: Roped in again...

"Excuse me, I did tell you that this is private property, so not to come back unless you had an appointment."

The voice was oddly familiar, James looked at him only to recognise the same person he'd run into just a few days earlier when he'd been told not to come back.

"Err, I can explain, well to be honest, I'm not sure if I can as I don't believe it myself."

"You're Mr Hansone, aren't you? Hmm, you are as white as a sheet, but I'll have to ask you to come to the office with me and I'm afraid I can't let you off this time. I'll have to call the police."

James groaned inwardly knowing that Sally would probably be alerted and he knew she'd enjoy telling him off in no uncertain terms. Her voice echoed through his head... *'Don't go wandering off after ghostly airmen...'* the words came back to haunt him, although at the moment he'd had enough of ghostly goings on.

James began to follow the man as he tried to remember his name, then it came to him, Greg Sanders.

"I'm really sorry Greg, it's a bit hard to explain that's all."

"Not got your dog with you then this time so you can't blame him now can you?" Greg replied and James had to admit he had a point.

"No, he's been taken to the vets. Sally, my wife took the day off to take him as I seem to be hopeless when it comes to taking Scruff to the vets. I seem to have too much sympathy with the dog."

James had a thought as they neared a door to what had once been the control tower of the old airfield. Now converted into office blocks, but with part of it set aside as a small museum to the RAF base from the war years. "Sally is actually DS Sally Hansone with the Lincolnshire Police and if I'm honest she will be pretty displeased with me as I did promise I wouldn't go chasing after ghosts again."

Greg stopped in his tracks and James almost bumped into him.

"Sorry, what did you say?"

"Err, my wife is a DS with Lincolnshire Police…"

"No, something about ghosts?"

"Well, as I said, it's a bit of a long story depending on where you want me to start."

"Last time we met, were you following a ghost then?" Greg asked pointedly. James thought about his reply but decided to come clean as they were now quite close to the blue door of the old control tower.

"Well, yes. An airman in a blue-ish sort of old RAF kit that seems to walk from our cottage through the woods to here."

Greg fell silent as he reached the door and opened it, gesturing to James to go in as he brought up the rear. They were in the reception room with a lady at a desk who looked up, smiled at Greg but looked at James a little puzzled.

"Sandra, can you just let Michael know I'd like a few words and say I've got someone with me he might want to listen to."

Sandra nodded as Greg indicated to James to take a seat near the window. He did so and gazed out looking at what remained of the old airfield. Most of the original runway had been taken up, but a few sections remained. He thought he spotted the signs of where a building had stood and realised it was the place where he'd saved Eric Arthurson, or at least he thought he'd saved him. All the while he kept wondering if in reality he was suffering from delusions and had imagined the whole escapade.

In the meantime, Sandra kept looking at him then back down to her desktop screen before stealing another glance at him. He wasn't sure quite what was going on until she spoke up.

"Are you that Hansone man, the ghost hunter of Grasceby?"

Greg looked round puzzled then looked at her questioningly.

"Err, what did you say?" he asked.

James smiled knowing this could help save the day.

"Well, I don't like to think of myself as one. You could say I don't really advertise myself like that."

Sandra looked smug with herself for recognising James.

"I doubt you'd recognise me, but I was at one of the talks you gave at Lincoln University about how you helped discover the original remains of the first Grasceby manor. Really interesting, but when a few people tried to ask you about the rumours of you seeing ghosts that led you to it, you quickly changed the subject!"

"I'm glad you enjoyed the talk."

He was about to continue when her intercom buzzed and a faint voice could just be heard.

"You can go in now Greg. Nice to meet you Mr Hansone" said Sandra and she watched a bemused Greg usher James towards a door with the words 'Managing Director' on it.

The man sitting at the desk looked similar in age to James, whereas Greg was at least a decade or more younger than them both. The man indicated to James to sit and looked questioningly at Greg who cleared his throat.

"Found this gentleman wandering around the grounds again Mike. Turns out he is some sort of local ghost hunter according to Sandra. James Hansone's his name."

"Ahh, yes, I have heard of you. Don't you live at the old cottage down the road, looks good now it's been done up?"

"Thanks, DS Sally and I think we've done a good job doing it up, if I say so myself."

"No need to mention the police Mr Hansone, you're not in trouble, but Greg and I are intrigued."

Greg had taken the seat nearest the window in Mike's office and kept glancing out as he listened to the conversation between the two men. He turned and smiled a little.

"Truth is, we might be in need of your services." he said with a knowing look towards Mike.

"Oh, as I said in reception, I'm not really a ghost hunter." James wasn't sure where the conversation was going but he had a bad feeling about what was coming.

"Look at it like this, that's not what Lord Grasceby said when I mentioned we thought we were being haunted here at the old base."

James heart sank as he had said quite often to his Lordship he didn't want a reputation as a ghost hunter and all the attention it could bring. Looks like he had failed, again.

"If I'm honest, I overheard a conversation he was having with that archaeologist chap a few months back, the one that you helped find out what happened to the original Lord De Grasceby family from France. Seemed that you and several others at the time had seen their ghosts and I've since learned that you also helped his Lordship regarding ghostly sightings at the modern manor. So, by all accounts I think you may be able to shed light on events that seem to be occurring here over the last few months.

There is also the small matter of trespass on our property here at the industrial estate to deal with … "

James was now hooked and was realising that he wasn't the only one who had seen the airman.

"OK, you have my attention. I'll level with you. Since Sally and I renovated Wolds View Cottage we have been experiencing sightings of an airman that looks to be from the second world war. He walks from the cottage through the woods and ends up here, so I figure he is naturally linked to the old airbase, RAF Grasceby."

"So you were following him the first time we met then?" Greg offered. James nodded but Greg continued. "In fact, I knew you were following him because I've seen him a few times myself and so has Mike here. I saw him that day when I caught you with your dog and I had been watching the airman until he vanished before my eyes over towards where the old huts used to be. Then I realised you were following the same route, so knew you had to have seen him too."

"Yes, he'd left the cottage and took the usual route but it was the first time I'd followed him all the way here. He must have worked on the base but question is, what happened?" James decided to omit the odd circumstances of the airman hanging from a tree until he knew more and what Greg and Mike's connection to all of it was.

"Well, now we've made contact, feel free to drop by and let us know if you see him again or find anything out. It's definitely very strange and so far just Greg and myself have seen him. I don't want anyone else being spooked by all this.' Let's keep this to ourselves and ..." he lowered his voice, "...not tell Sandra anything as she is a little free and easy sometimes with the gossip, if you know what I mean."

Greg smiled and nodded. They all shook hands before Greg escorted James back out into reception.

"Well Mr Hansone, good to meet you at last and hope the renovations continue to go well. The cottage does look good since it has people back in it."

"Thank you, Greg. Perhaps have you around sometime. I'll give you a call once we're all done."

James hoped the impromptu conversation was enough to throw Sandra off the scent as he opened the door and headed out to go home. Greg turned, smiled at Sandra and went back into Mike's office.

"Well?" he asked as Mike noticed his name plate had tipped over and set it back upright.

"Interesting, I didn't want to bring someone in up until now but looks like we're not the only ones to have seen the airman. Perhaps Mr Hansone will shed some light on it as it is becoming quite unnerving every time I spot him. Wonder what the connection is with his cottage?" Mike said as he joined Greg to look out the window and watch James leave via the main entrance and turn towards the direction of Grasceby.

"Perhaps it was someone living there who worked on the base? We both had grandfathers working here. I will always be proud of Granddad Sanders, flight leader on this very base for the last three years of the war. Your granddad was in charge of air maintenance on the base during that time, wasn't he?" Asked Greg.

"Yes, Granddad Eric kept those Lancs flying. He's almost ninety-eight now but still pretty sharp in the old mind. Not so much in body though, bless him. Must go over and see him at the care home and have a chat to see if he remembers anything."

Mike stood up and indicated for Greg to follow and they headed out, down past reception along a corridor that led to the small museum that had been set up in agreement with the local history society. They entered and stood near the back looking at several group photos taken of the squadron during the war and smiled as they picked out their respective grandfathers. A range of candid shots, taken by one of the grounds men who was a photographer, had been bequeathed to the museum and some were on display.

One such candid shot taken just before an air raid on the base showed the squadron leader in the distance seemingly talking to a man behind several emergency vehicles racing off to see to a stricken aircraft and its crew. Mike and Greg didn't inspect it closely as they perused the images on the wall then left to continue their work, little knowing that they could have identified the second man in the picture …

#

"Now what did I say?" Sally had her hands firmly on her hips and stood in a commanding pose as James recounted the morning events. Scruff could tell from her tone that James was in trouble and so he trotted away to lay in his basket, keep out of the way and nurse his wounded pride. These humans didn't seem to understand how painful injections were!

"Did you not just hear me? I was in 1940s RAF Grasceby and nearly got killed!"

"Come on James, I've been open minded and had to accept ghostly goings on after seeing things myself, but *time travel*?"

"I know, it actually scares the shit out of me, but you know it's not the first time it's happened. Remember the non-existent toy cupboard in Grasceby Manor? Then the archaeologists, Andrea and Malcolm? When they saw one of the ghostly girls she could see them too and even wondered why they were high up and were looking out of a door at her.

I can't explain any of it but I tell you it was quite a frightening experience. We forget when we see the glamour of war at the movies that the reality was that millions died during the second world war. It was quite a wakeup call I can tell you."

Sally shook her head not really knowing what to think, then sighed.

"All I ask is just keep that bit to yourself, you haven't told anyone else have you? The chaps at the industrial estate?"

"No, only you. I know it's pretty hard to take in so I thought it best just to say I'd been following the airman and that he starts from here and goes through the woods to the old airbase. I didn't even mention that sometimes he's taken a detour and hanged himself."

Sally came over and sat down beside James.

"Let's keep it that way. But we have to find someway of discovering what's going on. This is our home but it is beginning to freak me out.

Oh, in the meantime, Scruff is OK according to the vet and he gave him a couple of jabs so I think for now I'm not his favourite!"

James chuckled and was glad of the change of topic. "No wonder he's gone off in a sulk to his basket. Still, he won't need to go back to the vets now for a while so I bet he will soon be back to his usual self. Anyhow, I'm famished so why don't we go down to the Star and Crescent Moon and get a bite to eat. We haven't been down to see Marcus for a while now."

"Good idea, best let Scruff out into the garden out back to do the necessary and before we go, I'll leave him some food and water so he doesn't go hungry whilst we're out."

"I'll do that, you're in his bad books!" With that James got up and headed out to find Scruff as Sally went upstairs to tidy herself up ready to go out.

9: A most welcome visitor

Sally looked around but although there were several customers in having lunch, there was no sign of Marcus. Sharon, his daughter, came out from the kitchen and smiled when she saw Sally and James.

"Now then strangers, seems ages since you were last in, everything OK?"

"Yes, no problem, busy with work and pest here is often away giving talks about how he single handed discovered the old manor ruins" replied Sally as James turned round and looked at her, puzzled.

"Heard my name, what's up?" he asked innocently and both women just smiled.

"Nothing dearest, best grab a menu for us. You OK if we just choose from the sarnies menu Sharon?"

"Yeah, no problem. Better for me as I'm on my own for a few days."

"That's a point, where is your dad?"

"Scotland, for starters that is! It's your two's fault too. He seems to have won over that there Jenny, took him long enough! They're flying off later today away to Barcelona for a short weekend break. Let's just hope they're still talking when they get back!"

"Ha! Jenny is a tough cookie, but I'm sure Marcus has managed to win her over if they're going away." Sharon handed over the laminated sheet for the sandwich menu and Sally passed it to James. Sally looked at him, nodded over towards a clear table and he obligingly headed over to it to claim it for themselves.

"I'll have a glass of chardonnay but his lordship over there is driving so will have orange juice. Can you put it all on our tab once we've ordered?"

"Yeah of course. Give me a nod when you are ready to order. Looks like I'll be at the back as Charles and Fred over there are looking like they want another round."

Sally looked towards them and turned back shaking her head.

"What's up with them, they look glum as hell!"

"Well, dad is their mate and they think they're losing him!"

"Oh dear."

"Yep. Mind you good for business as they're drowning their sorrows in a few pints."

Sally smiled then walked over to the table James was now sitting at to give him an update on the news about Marcus.

"No wonder they look miserable." replied James. "You know, it was Fred who convinced us to go down to Dreyers' old business to get the table and chairs for the kitchen. Wonder if he knew anything about them?"

"Good point but not worth tackling him now, poor things looks like the world is ending for them. Anyhow, I have something to ask and hopefully you won't mind."

James looked at her puzzled just as Sharon came past and glanced at them expectantly.

"Ham and cheese for me and…?" James looked at Sally who took a final look at the menu.

"Egg and cress please. Two coffees too when it looks like we're nearly finished."

"Side plate of chips?" suggested Sharon and James eyes lit up. Sally glanced at him and he nodded approval. Sharon took the menu and headed back to the kitchen. Ten minutes later she arrived bearing a tray of sandwiches and the chips and the couple tucked in with delight.

Sally looked at James as if wondering what to say.

"I have been in touch with Harriet and she's got a free weekend this weekend and wondered if she could come over from Nottingham and visit until Sunday?"

"Of course she can, mind you she'll have to have the front spare room, Jenny's old room, so hope she won't mind."

"I was thinking that and had mentioned it to her but she doesn't believe in ghosts so isn't bothered. It'll be good to see her, we last saw her at the wedding reception!" Sally stopped and took a bite out of her sandwich as James smiled.

"Yes, she got a bit tipsy didn't she. I seem to remember she tried to snog both of us at some point during the evening celebration. What is she like!"

"Perhaps best to lock away the drinks then." suggested Sally, not very seriously.

"Nah, I'm sure she's embarrassed and probably won't touch a drop. Send her a text and find out what time she is coming over so I can move the cars a bit to give her space for parking."

"You are so thoughtful my love. I'll text her now. Thanks."

James had just finished his sandwich and was taking a drink of coffee when Charles and Fred walked past them.

"Hey, you two, it isn't going to be that bad, I'm sure" he called to them. They came back and joined them at their table. Fred spoke.

"It's your fault! We had a cosy little group going and could twist Marcus' arm for free pints. Even Sharon looked after us with the occasional free beer for being such loyal customers. But when that there Jenny McClacken came over for a week's stay last month she made sure we didn't get owt for free!"

"Free drinks? I'll have to have words with Marcus about that" exclaimed James but Sally was more interested in the other titbit of news.

"You mean she has been over and she didn't even let us know she was in the area. Gosh it must be serious!" she exclaimed.

Fred looked annoyed and seemed to ignore her.

"That's my point, if they hook up and she comes down here to help run things then that's it! The end! No more freebies!"

"Well, seems to me Fred that if Jenny does come down and stay then the profits may recover!" suggested Sally and Charles scowled, got up and turned to leave. He waited for Fred by the entrance.

"So Fred, spill, what do you know about the table and chairs we bought from Dreyers' old place eh?" asked Sally, innocently.

"Why, summat up?" he replied cautiously.

"Maybe. Any reason why you sent us there in the first place?" added James and he could tell Sally was also enjoying watching Fred squirm a little in his seat.

"Well, only that I knew Richard's dad had a table set from your old cottage many years ago so I thought if it was still up there then it might be good if you liked them and they returned to their original home, that's all."

Sally eyed him but seemed happy with the answer. James always liked how Sally showed why she was such a good detective and could get an answer from almost anyone she questioned.

"OK, for now Fred, see you around I'm sure. But I may have more questions for you, so as they say, don't leave the country" she joked but you could tell Fred wasn't sure if she were kidding or not.

He got up and along with Charles left the inn leaving Sally and James to finish up and pay their bill.

Driving back home Sally smiled as she received a reply from Harriet. "Brilliant. Harriet will be with us by eight pm tonight so I'd best get the spare room ready when we get back. Oh, she also says that she hopes we've got a few bottles of wine in!"

"Oh, best be on my best behaviour then and not have too much! At least we haven't been visited by Jenny since we solved her missing persons case. So, as long as the chair in the kitchen behaves itself, fingers crossed we will be OK." James offered as they turned into their driveway and he parked up.

Scruff was barking at the window, pleased to see them back. As they entered through the front door he kept jumping up and down with excitement.

"Tell you what, I'll take him for the W word and you sort the room out, deal?" James offered and Sally waved at him to go ahead. Scruff could sense he'd got his way, wagging his tail as he watched James lift his dog lead from its hook on the wall.

#

"Well Scruff, for once it was nice to head the other way and visit the duck pond in the village again. Better than following that funny airman into the woods, isn't that right boy?" James looked expectantly at Scruff for a simple bark to show they were fully in tune, but Scruff just looked briefly up at him then carried on walking and sniffing the ground every so often completely un bothered by James and his ramblings.

They could just see the tree line dip back into the field and through the trees that had been spared during the renovations of the grounds. Wolds View Cottage stood barely visible, as it always had.

James smiled at how everything had turned out, both with the cottage and with Sally, but his thoughts were rudely interrupted by a blast from a car horn behind startling both himself and Scruff who began to bark as the car approached and passed them.

It slowed and pulled to a halt as they caught up with it and the drivers side window scrolled down to reveal of all people, Harriet.

"Hey ho, fancy seeing you here. Wanna lift?" She said smiling at both of them and grinning like a Cheshire cat.

"We're almost home, just up there as the tree line bends into the field up ahead. Thought you weren't getting to us until tonight? Sally will be sorting your room out but hopefully she's probably got it done now."

"Finished early. Thought to myself that what was left could wait until Tuesday so had a quick sort out, grabbed some things and here I am!"

"Tuesday?" asked James a little hesitantly.

"It is a bank holiday weekend you know."

"Oh, to be honest I lose track of them now I'm retired. Sally hasn't got Monday off however as she has to go into Lincoln for some sort of important meeting, no idea what and apparently she can't say. Guess you'll be going on Sunday then."

"Nah, I'm sure you can entertain me for another day. Sally wouldn't mind, I'm sure. See you at the cottage as I can see a car back in the distance so best not block the road." She revved up and drove further up the road then turned into the driveway as James made sure Scruff stayed sitting on the grass verge to wait until the second car had passed.

"Oh dear Scruff, let's hope she isn't like when she was at the wedding reception. Wish Sally could get out of the Lincoln meeting."

The car passed them and together they made their way back to Wolds View Cottage.

#

Surprisingly things went very well. At Sally's insistence they had the evening meal at the Star and Crescent Moon Inn much to the surprise and enjoyment of Sharon. Harriet insisted on paying for the meals as she was doing quite well as an independent forensics specialist. She regaled them with tales of some of the bodies she had examined, unfortunately in a bit too much detail, causing comments to Sharon from other customers. Suitably chastised but still in high spirits they headed back to the cottage by eleven pm to be greeted by Scruff wanting to go out so James grabbed his lead and they set off, again in the opposite direction to the old airfield but this time with a torch. To James relief, a short journey once Scruff did what he had to do.

As they approached from the front gate they could hear the laughter from inside and James couldn't help think that so far Harriet's visit was quite enjoyable, perhaps he had misjudged her, he mused.

Inside he found Sally and Harriet sitting together on the sofa and Scruff rushed over with his squeaky bone. He jumped up nearest to Harriet who was surprised but quickly grabbed the toy from him and threw it over where James was standing in the entrance to the lounge. Scruff loved the attention so for the next half hour Harriet and he played catch whilst Sally finished her glass of chardonnay and decided they had all had enough for that night.

Tired out, Scruff finally gave up and wandered over to his basket, turning round several times and flopping down as Harriet stood and looked at her two friends.

"I agree with Scruff, time for bed. You didn't tell me he was so much fun, but I'm worn out now and I think those three large glasses of wine are finally taking their toll. I'll go up if it's OK with you two, may I ask what time I should be up by?"

James looked at Sally who just smiled. "Don't worry about that, have a lie in, you've earned it with the work schedule you normally keep. We're not early risers at the weekend unless we need to, so if you're not up by ten in the morning I'll get Sally to haul you out of bed."

"Oo, look forward to that." It was hard to tell if Harriet's eyes lit up or not at that prospect but she smiled warmly and headed out and up to her room.

Sally looked at James but he couldn't quite read her face. She tapped the sofa for him to join her.

"What's up?" he asked.

"Nothing, just good to see she is doing well and enjoying herself. Although all that talk about dissecting bodies almost got us thrown out of the Star and Crescent Moon Inn. Sharon's face was a picture and I'm sure one lady sitting a couple of tables away was going green!"

"Ha! Harriet is a bit loud isn't she, especially when she's had a few drinks inside her. At least she's not made a pass at either of us. But…" James trailed off not sure what to say or think.

"But her last comment was a bit odd ..?"

"You could say that." James said not sure what he was going to discover.

"It's nothing. A long time ago before you and I became an item, she did make a pass at me. End of story and it's you I'm married to and happy with. OK?"

"OK. "

"Ahh, there goes the toilet so time to go up to our room don't you think?" Sally asked looking towards the doorway.

"Yes, mind you that sound reminds me, I do keep wondering if there is room to make the spare room en-suite?"

"Nah, don't think there is enough room without a big change and I thought you'd prefer to keep Jenny's old room as it is except for the decoration?"

"True, anyhow, let's go up as the wine is definitely making its way to my bladder so I bag's our en suite."

However, Sally was already up on her feet and dashing out as she had anticipated him. James shook his head, "Back bathroom it is then!" He headed up after just patting Scruff gently on his head noting he was already fast asleep.

#

There was someone in her bedroom…

Jenny?

He stood and looked in the dark but couldn't tell. The room seemed different from the last time he'd been pulled to it. He didn't have any normal sense of the passage of time but all he knew was that something had changed at the cottage. It had become stronger when he'd been drawn back to his favourite chair and table that were somehow back at the cottage. It had allowed him to retrace his steps into and through the woods but there were two people he didn't recognise when he took his walks during the daytime. One, the man, did seem slightly familiar and always seemed to have a dog with him, but was not Jack, whilst the woman was certainly not Barbara.

Now someone was back in Jenny's room and drawing him to it, but something was wrong.

The person in the bed stirred and looked up a little groggily.

"Jenny?" he called out gently.

"Jennifer, is that you my dear grand daughter?"

"What? Wha.. Who is that?" came the sleepy reply.

He moved closer and round to the side of the bed to get a better look then realised something was amiss.

"You're not Jenny, why are you in her bed?" he asked as Harriet finally came awake, turned on the light and screamed her heart out as the apparition faded away as it backed off towards the window.

10: Harriet's surprise

It was distant and so, so far away but Sally knew a scream when she heard one although it didn't seem to be in keeping with her dream of flying over the sea as a bird on the wing with not a care in the world.

Except the scream.

Very realistic until she realised James was shaking her and jumping out of bed throwing on his dressing gown and she realised the scream was coming from the other bedroom.

Harriet!

Quick as a flash she too was up and had her dressing gown quickly flung over her naked form as James raced across the landing and barged into Harriet's room flipping the light switch expecting an intruder.

The bedside light was on and Harriet sitting bolt upright in a flimsy nightdress taking deep breaths and struggling to speak. She pointed roughly towards the window and curtains but there was nothing there.

"He, he…" Harriet stuttered. Sally entered and sat next to her, cuddling her and saying soothing words as James examined the window but found it locked and nothing out of place. The mention of 'He' rather than 'She' was telling but he didn't want to say anything until he'd heard what Harriet could tell them.

As he looked back at them he realised how skimpy Harriet's nightie was so, as a true gentleman, he saw her dressing gown hanging up on the back of the door and took it over to her. Sally nodded and helped Harriet into it as she started to calm down.

James dashed out and down to the kitchen to bring up a tumbler of water and as he returned Harriet was at last calming down.

"I must have been almost dead to the world but I thought I could hear a man's voice. He was calling to me but it wasn't my name.

Oh god! He was calling out as if I was Jenny! Wasn't that your sister that you found dead all those years ago, James? You put me in *her bedroom*?" She took a swig from the tumbler and took long deep breaths.

Sally spoke up. "Harriet, we said you'd be in here. We've not seen Jenny for a few years now, or at least James hasn't, as I never really saw her properly.

"But I did the autopsy on her!" said Harriet as it dawned on her.

"But you said you didn't see a girl?" asked James carefully and Harriet sat still thinking about that.

"Yeah, you're right, it was a man, a man's voice at first and as I came awake there was a shape, a person, standing over me and he said something like 'I was not Jenny, why was I in her bed' or something like that."

"Well that's the first time that has happened. I wonder if.." James didn't get to finish as Sally shot him a sharp look then turned to her friend.

"For now that doesn't matter. You feel OK now?"

"Yes, it was just a shock." Harriet took a deep breath and sighed. "If I'm honest with you, I have seen the odd thing occasionally but I've always explained it away as a trick of the light, but tonight I think I've joined your little club of seeing ghosts. Any idea who he might be?"

"Well, what I was going to say earlier was that Sally and I have been seeing an airman, of something like the second world war era, since we were about half way through renovating the cottage."

"An airman… Yes, the brief look I got could have been some form of uniform." Harriet's scientific training was kicking in, but Sally had other ideas.

"Look you two, it's almost three in the morning and we can talk about this after a good sleep. Harriet, you come and stay with me in our bedroom and James, you can sleep here tonight."

He knew it was not worth arguing about, but had to agree that was probably the best course. At least if he was in Jenny's old room and the airman returned, James thought he might stand a chance of trying to talk to him.

"OK, love. You two head off and I'll stay here tonight."

"And tomorrow night!" added Harriet quickly. "I don't think I want to stay in this room on my own another night" she said as she looked for support from Sally.

"Come on then, let's go to our room." Sally looked resigned to the situation. Harriet had a twinkle in her eye now.

"You do say the nicest thing, don't you! I'm all yours." Sally gave her a stern look and Harriet ducked her head in deference.

She waited for Sally to get up then got out of bed and together they headed out. James took a final look around the room before turning the main light out then getting into bed and switching off the bedside lamp.

He remembered something Sally had once confessed to, not long after they started seeing each other as a serious relationship took off, but he pushed it out of his mind and hoped that the airman didn't actually come back that night.

Meanwhile as they entered the master bedroom, Sally pointed to James side of their bed and Harriet climbed in after taking off her dressing gown. Sally paused as she was about to take off hers as she was still au naturel but then shrugged and slipped it off causing Harriet to give her a little wolf whistle.

"Oi! You can cut that out." she remarked as she slipped back under the bed covers and Harriet sat up on her side with her hand holding her head up as she looked at Sally.

"Spoil sport. I guess it really was a one off then?" she asked hesitantly Sally turned over carefully and looked her in the eyes.

"Yep, no more to say and nothing happens, right?"

"Yes miss Sally." came the meek reply and Harriet settled down and turned to face the other way as Sally switched off the side light.

#

It was an uneventful night for James and he found he slept quite soundly until his phone alarm chimed to say it was seven in the morning. He'd heard nothing from the 'girl's room' so assumed there had been no more unwanted visitations. He threw on his dressing gown and headed downstairs.

Scruff eagerly awaited him at the door so James led him to the back door and let him out knowing he couldn't get round to the front garden due to the fencing they'd erected a few months earlier, just for this purpose. James wandered into the kitchen but stopped in his tracks then sighed.

The usual chair was out of place again. He knew they'd put them all tidy before they came up to bed, so it had to be the airman again. It was getting beyond a joke now, but until they could figure out what was going on and the connection between the airman and the cottage, James figured they would have to put up with it.

He sorted toast, orange juice and a couple of rashers of bacon for each of them, plus a rasher for Scruff who scoffed it down then looked up for more.

"Sorry old chum, gotta watch your weight eh boy!"

James headed back upstairs with the tray hoping the two women would be awake and stood outside the bedroom door hesitating, wondering if Harriet was covered up.

"Blooming heck James, what am I like? It's our bedroom for heavens sake!" He chided himself and gently knocked on the door.

A faint, sleepy voice, Sally's, answered with an OK. He carefully opened the door and went in to find Sally beginning to sit up in bed whilst Harriet had her arm tangled over her but was now beginning to stir. He spotted Harriet's nightie thrown over to the bottom of the bed, partially draped on it and Sally nodded and put her eyebrows up in despair as she looked to the ceiling. Harriet's eyes fluttered open and she began to turn over as Sally quickly grabbed the bed sheets up to hide her friends modesty.

James set the tray down, picked up his own plate and shook his head.

"I'll go back downstairs to the kitchen and have this whilst you two come down when you are ready."

"OK love, thanks for the brekie. Sleepy head here I'm sure will soon wolf it down."

He left them to it and decided that Scruff was probably right as thoughts of doing more toast and bacon took priority. Along with a large mug of coffee, he decided!

#

"So, be honest, is it like this often?" Harriet looked at them both over her mug of tea questioningly.

"Not really, we seem to have episodes then quiet periods then things happen again." replied Sally who was standing casually looking out of the back window towards the Lincolnshire Wolds.

"So, it's not your dead sister but perhaps another ancestor?" Harriet offered as she looked at James and he shrugged.

"Could be, the uniform would suggest World War Two and he does always seem to head off to the site of RAF Grasceby and he looks the sort of age to be my grandfather. Again, I have nothing about him so it could also be someone not related to me. Rev Cossant was going to see what records she had as we know he appears to have hanged himself an …"

"WHAT?" Harriet was incredulous. "First I've heard of that bit!" Sally came over to the table and pulled a chair out to sit.

"I've not seen that bit but James here has. Tell her then now you've spooked her more," she said looking at her friend mischievously.

"I wasn't spooked last night, OK well, just a bit, it's true." Harriet looked at James expectantly.

"The chair I'm sitting on has a habit of being moved slightly to one side some mornings, but not all of the time. We don't know why. Occasionally I've followed the airman from our front garden, across the road and along it until he reaches the old back entrance to the airfield which takes you through the woods. Twice, however, as Scruff and I have been following, he's turned off the main animal track or footpath and heads to a small clearing with two old oaks. That's when I thought I'd lost him then realised Scruff was looking up to near the top and I could see him hanging there for a split second before he was gone again."

"Bloody hell! I'd never go back there again." Harriet exclaimed looking from James to Sally then back again. "But what started all this? No one mentioned this chap before?" Sally looked into her mug and realised it was empty so got up to make another drink, she looked at the pair and both James and Harriet nodded approval.

"We had nothing before we bought this table and chair set. Turns out they may once have belonged here but were sold. Perhaps we now know why…" James offered. Sally had her head down, however.

"I actually saw the airman a couple of times before we got the table set."

James looked up at her, surprised.

"Why, why didn't you tell me?"

"Well, it was so odd, I first thought it was just me imagining it as we thought we knew the recent modern history of what had happened here. It was only a couple of times, but certainly after we'd finished the main renovations."

James looked at her, but his annoyance at not being told evaporated as he considered events.

"Something we did here started it and then it really took off when we got the table and chairs. I'm sure Fred doesn't know any more as he did seem sincere when we confronted him about it the other day."

"Fred, you've mentioned him before, how does he fit in?" wondered Harriet.

Sally chuckled.

"Fred knew, and was friends with, Richard Dreyer. You know, the boyfriend of Jenny, who accidentally killed her all those years ago. Fred and Charles didn't know anything about *that* until 'ol' ghost hunter sitting there helped me solve her missing persons case. In fact Harry, that's when you met James for the first time, out at the discovery site. Fred knew that Dreyers' father had bought the table and chairs and that Richard Dreyer wouldn't sell them and kept them hidden away on the top floor when he took over the family business. Sentimental reasons I guess. Fred hinted we might find something interesting and basically sent us over knowing we'd probably buy them."

"A set up then. So they must be about the era of the war?" Harriet mused.

"Possibly, or even older, we've not had them valued or dated so perhaps that's something we could do in the near future, eh James?" suggested Sally and he nodded looking quite thoughtful.

A sudden woof came from the front living room and Sally quickly left to see what Scruff was up to. She returned with a few envelopes in her hands. "Postie." and chucked one marked for James over to him which he opened as Sally finished off making them the extra drinks.

"Oo, this is good. I've been invited down to Devon to speak about the Grasceby Manor ruins and how I used modern tech to discover them. Now I like that sum!" James showed Sally the letter and she looked quite surprised.

"Wow, snap their hands off! Three day stay too as it's a long way, all at their expense. You can do a few more like that if they come along! I might be able to take the Chief up on that early retirement he suggested…"

The room fell quiet and Sally realised she'd let slip something she should have kept quiet about.

"Say again?" said James, a little on the quiet side.

"Oh, it's nothing at this stage love, honest. There's more talk of cuts and one of the suggestions was that some of us could either take redundancy or depending on how long we've been in the force, possible early retirement. But it's all so confusing at the moment that I wanted to find out more before I mentioned it. Sorry."

"Okay… for now, but don't keep me, of all people, in the dark. We are married and a team, remember?" James looked her in the eyes but didn't seem angry, more concerned and she gave him a hug.

"Yes, we're both of those and I just wanted to make sure of my options before I asked you for your opinion. Think of it like this, if I did take early retirement, I could be with you more when you get anything mysterious happen."

"Well that's spoilt your fun eh James?" piped up Harriet and Sally shot her an annoyed glance making Harriet look to the floor and avert her gaze.

"Well if we did need any forensic advice I guess we could always ask Richardson over at Notts HQ, I'm sure he'd be up for helping me."

"Oi! I'm not all that bad you know. Plus he's quite a pillock too, so I doubt you'd get much help from him. Plus my rates are quite reasonable!" Harriet retorted but smiled mischievously at them.

"Now my fine ladies, enough. You are both valuable people to me but I really don't go out of my way to find mysterious things like this. I'd like a quiet life to be honest. And if in the near future, Sally, you are able to be with me more without us suffering financially, then personally that would be brilliant."

The sound of padded feet came wafting through the doorway as Scruff wandered in and looked up at them, moving his head from one side to the other.

"It's all right Scruff, Mummy and Daddy are not fighting. You don't have to worry." said Sally as she bent down and picked him up, ruffling the hair at the back of his head. He whined a little but looked towards the door.

"I think he actually needs to go out. Tell you what, why don't we all go for a nice walk into Grasceby?" suggested James and Sally and Harriet nodded approval.

Scruff's canine powers of persuasion had succeeded in getting them to take him for walkies!

11: Once a forensics expert, always…

Sally again had Scruffs lead as they headed out of the gate and turned left.

At least they tried to.

Scruff was having none of it and was determined to once again follow the old route of the airman. Yet there was no sign of him. Scruff tugged at the lead until finally Harriet spoke up.

"You said Scruff seemed to be aware of the airman's presence, I must admit that I'm intrigued too and had secretly hoped you'd head off that way so don't change your route just to spare me after last night."

James looked at Sally who shrugged and turned towards the direction of the disused airfield as Scruff barked excitedly.

They suddenly spotted why as both James and Sally saw the airman further up the road, close to the turnoff into the woods. Harriet saw the look on their faces and looked but could not see him.

At first.

Then, she became aware there was a faint silhouette of a person and she realised she had to be looking at the airman despite a lack of detail. She quickly looked back at James and Sally then back again, excitedly, only to have her excitement dashed.

He was gone.

"Where'd he..?" she stammered, almost lost for words.

"Welcome to our world, Harri!" answered Sally as Scruff pulled at the lead and she allowed him to take her along the road and onto the grass verge.

They walked in silence and at the appropriate spot James indicated to turn left into the rough overgrown entrance. The old gate was still in place as was the original RAF Grasceby MOD sign, but James could see the barbed wire had been removed and there was some signs of trampling of the long grass. On further inspection it was clear the old lock had been removed and now there was no lock at all, so he unlatched the gate and opened it inwards pushing against some of the undergrowth.

"Looks like Mike and Greg have been true to their word as they have made this much easier and safer. Guess this means we can have access now they want me to look into things."

"Mike and Greg?" enquired Harriet innocently.

"Ah, yes, they are on the industrial estate, the old airfield. They caught me, how you say…" started James.

"Trespassing?" offered Sally mischievously and James grimaced.

"Yes, sort of. I followed the airman several times onto the old airfield and they happened to notice my intrusions. But it seems they too had spotted him so the last time I was err, caught, they asked me to see what I could find out about him. So guess that means I've got free reign to explore the area."

"OK, what are we waiting for?" Harriet asked. Sally and Scruff took the lead, then James as Harriet followed on behind him, closing the gate.

They followed the old track, with dappled sunlight filtering through the trees surrounding them until James moved ahead and stopped, turning to look at the others.

Sally suspected what he wanted to do as Harriet looked on a little bewildered.

"Aren't we carrying on, I'm sure the old base is up ahead."

"Yes, but, well, this is where I think the airman's last journey was to rather than the base. He turns off here to my right," he waved to his right and Harriet could just make out a very old animal path. Scruff was tugging at his lead and Sally was being pulled onto the path.

"Oh…" Harriet remembered their discussion earlier. "This leads to the two oaks?" she asked a little more quietly, almost in deference to the fate of the airman. James just nodded and together all of them headed down the path with Scruff leading the way.

The path suddenly opened out into the clearing and there stood the two trees just as James had described. He pointed to a thick-ish branch extending sideways from the nearest main trunk, around fifteen feet above the ground to indicate where he'd seen the airman hanging.

Scruff just sniffed around, this time not looking up at the nearest tree as James and Sally looked about, then back up the path wondering if the airman would appear to them.

A rather unladylike grunt came from behind them and they looked round to see no Harriet.

Until another grunt and they looked up in surprise to see her climbing up the tree towards, then onto, the thick branch.

"Wonders will never cease!" muttered Sally as she shook her head at her friend, but couldn't help but be impressed with Harriet's agility and stamina.

"OK, Harri, what gives?" shouted James and she sat astride the thick branch, pleased she'd put trousers on instead of the skirt she'd originally planned on wearing.

"Give me a moment."

Sally turned to James and chuckled.

"Once a forensics expert, always a forensics expert!"

Harriet was carefully examining the branch and feeling several sections of it as she also fought to keep her balance.

"Careful Harri, it's a bit of a drop!" cautioned Sally, increasingly concerned at her friends antics. Harriet managed to get her smart phone out and took several pictures before carefully putting it back in her pocket. Finally she edged her way back to the main trunk then made her way down out of the tree, much to James and Sally's relief.

Harriet again took the phone out and started to look at the pictures as James and Sally crowded round her.

"See here, and here, and especially here. Rub marks with one fairly shallow but the other quite deep.

I'd wager that there was originally a swing here at some stage which may have been replaced with a single rope, perhaps with a tyre on it instead of a plank of wood for the swing. Hence the other deeper groove, suggesting it lasted longer. Look around to see if there is anything of them left in the undergrowth."

They scattered and began looking round in the undergrowth. Ten minutes went by until Sally gave out a shout.

"Over here!" She picked up and shook loose soil and grass from what looked like a rectangular piece of wood with holes for ropes and one side rotted away.

Harriet examined it as James headed back to the place he was looking earlier, just off the path heading back towards the old airbase. A few moments later he too gave out a shout and the others came running over as Scruff gleefully scratched away in the dirt nearby.

It was a tyre, very worn so naturally ideal to be used as a swing and again indications of rope 'burns' on it around one section.

Harriet surveyed the scene.

"If I was to hazard a guess, local kids came and played here using the tree as a natural stage to put up a swing. I'd say the original wooden swing soon gave way so they improvised with the tyre. If the tyre was discarded later and the rope had been left then that might be what your airman used to ah, end it all."

"Wow, all that from just a few grooves in a branch," said James, impressed. Sally just smiled.

"Well, glad you came along now. You've seen a ghost and examined the last site of the airman so guess you might end up being called a ghost hunter too!"

"You can forget that young lady, I want to keep my reputation as a hard-nosed scientist!" Harriet shot back then made a funny face and grinned at Sally.

"Well, I reckon we've done enough snooping around and time to head back as I'm getting famished," suggested James and Harriet looked at him.

"Couldn't have put it better. My work here is done."

#

He watched them leave noting that the dog kept looking back and he was sure the hound could see him all the time. The lady had been uncannily correct in her assessment.

He'd been born in the cottage and grew up locally, so as an adventurous boy, he and several of the village lads had indeed explored the area in and around their village. One day they had come across a small clearing dominated by the two oak trees and it was if it was calling out to them to make a swing. He had only been eight but in those days they could roam as far as they liked, as long as they were in before dark.

Two of the older boys had scavenged, at least that's what they claimed, some rope and they had nicked a piece of wood ideal as the seat, so very quickly the swing was up and in action. It lasted a couple of years and could have lasted more but they hadn't noticed a split in the wood close to the knot holes on one side until Godfrey Slate suddenly found himself hanging on for dear life when one side suddenly gave way.

Undeterred, they took the wooden section down and Basil remembered that one of the local farmers had a tyre dump the other side of the village, so they'd snuck in and managed to pull one out of the pile that looked good enough.

Yes, they'd had a lot of fun with the tyre swing in those days before they split up as they got older. Edward had caught the eye of one of the teachers as a possible candidate for further study as he seemed very adept at maths and working out problems. Before he knew what happened, he'd become an apprentice to an aeronautical firm down in Cambridge. He met his soon to be wife Deirdre and it wasn't long before they married and just over a year later had Jack. Fond memories indeed. But tragic all the same ...

12: The museum

The rest of the day soon zipped by and on the Saturday night Harriet had a change of heart and braved Jenny's room. More for her scientific, inquisitive side, at least that's what she kept telling herself.

To her relief, nothing happened and Sunday they headed off for a day at the coast. Skegness was too busy so they travelled further up the east Lincolnshire coast to Anderby Creek, had lunch at the local cafe then explored the beach and the world famous Cloud Bar.

"Must be the driest bar I've been too!" muttered James and Sally gave him a nudge in the back as Scruff dutifully behaved himself walking beside them on his lead. Ever the scientist, Harriet had to explain everything.

"It is quite a unique thing really. A place to watch the clouds go by with the wide expanses of the Lincolnshire coast and the grand vista of the sky above. It was opened by the regional weather presenter and set up by a local man. It is highly recommended as a tourist attraction according to the Cloud Appreciation Society."

The what, what society?" asked James incredulously.

"Cheeky devil, mind you considering you spent most of your years *down south*, I'm not surprised you still haven't seen all our fair county has to offer." rebuffed Sally.

"And there really is a society to appreciate clouds?" he asked, not knowing when to give up.

"Yess!" came the joint reply as both ladies shook their heads in desperation.

"Well, how do you know so much about it then?" he added. Harriet looked at him proudly.

"Because I am a member and won't have anything bad said about them." she replied as Sally looked a little sheepishly at him.

"So am I…" she said quietly.

"What! How did I not know that?" he was stunned but impressed that he'd discovered something new about the love of his life, admittedly to add to the ever growing list of new discoveries about her.

"I subscribe only to the email newsletter," she said and Harriet smiled.

"Yep. Same here."

"Saves paper and the environment too," added Sally as she looked down at her feet just as Scruff did a little whine. "I think boss doggie wants to go home now, he's had enough of the 'W' word." she chuckled.

With that they headed back to the car park and were soon back at Wolds View Cottage, home. On entering the kitchen Sally found a familiar sight. The chair was again slightly out of place and she shook her head wondering when they would finally get to the bottom of what was going on.

A faint but distinct rumble could be heard coming from outside and she heard James shout something as Scruff began to bark and scratch at the front door. Something he rarely ever did. She found Harriet just going out into the front garden, joining James as Scruff also made a dash for it. As she joined them all outside, the roar of four throbbing Merlin engines announced the presence of the Battle of Britain Memorial Flight Lancaster in the distance and they watched as it flew a couple of miles away. James estimated it flew over the old airfield before heading off towards Lincoln and being lost in the hazy clouds that were building up.

James couldn't help but think about the ones he'd seen when he had somehow ended up in 1940s RAF Grasceby, instinctively he gave the departing plane a salute.

"Good to see the old girl up and about. Can't mistake those Merlin engines," said Harriet to no one in particular as she watched the plane vanish to a dot then into the distant clouds.

"I remember now, it was on the news that it was going to do a fly over of the International Bomber Command Memorial near Lincoln, that's where it looked like it was heading just now." Harriet added.

They continued peering into the distance hoping to see if it would turn and circle around again, but the sound of the engines petered out. In the cottage the airman sat and stood up from his favourite chair, nudging it to one side as he headed over to the window and looked out forlornly for his Lancaster.

None of the group saw him and he faded from view just as they entered the cottage…

\#

"Now make sure you look after Harri for me and don't get up to any mischief!" Sally said without quite realising what she'd said.

"Don't worry, he's not my type!" quipped Harriet as James shook his head.

"Can't you get out of it?" he asked quietly in a desperate last minute act of really hoping he didn't have to be with Harriet on his own for the day.

"No, sorry, work has to come first and the visit by the Princess to Lincoln takes top priority for all of us in the force charged with her protection. Don't be a sissy," she said quietly then turned and spoke in a louder voice, "Harri won't eat you, will you dear?"

Harriet just grinned with a mischievous look in her eyes and shrugged as if she was as innocent as the day was long.

"I'm sure James will find something interesting for us to do, won't you James?"

"Quite…" he didn't have much to say and just hoped the brief flirtation Harriet had tried at his and Sally's wedding reception was indeed a one off!

Sally picked up her things, grabbed her packed lunch and kissed him on the cheek. "See you tonight, hopefully, if all goes well."

"OK."

"And be strong…"

"OK."

Harriet stood in her dressing gown next to the kitchen door watching them both, then turned back into the kitchen.

"Coffee James?" she called back as Sally opened the door, gave him a reassuring smile then left.

They had a quick breakfast as Scruff lay in his basket asleep, presumably chasing rabbits considering his feet looked as if he was running.

"Tell you what, as it's a bank holiday, why don't we go to the air museum based in the old control tower on the industrial estate. I'm sure it'll be open and if not, I reckon Mike will be happy to open it up for us. We could do a bit of research about the airbase during the war years."

Harriet supped the last dregs of her coffee and nodded.

"Yes, must admit, all my years in the county and I never got round to visiting it, so why not. I'll just go and get dressed. Say about ten, fifteen minutes?"

"Yes, I'll just have Scruff out for a quick walk as we'll leave him here. I'll make sure he's got water and a little food, don't want him to get fat." Harriet got up and went upstairs as James set about finding Scruff's lead and collar before taking him out, much to Scruffs delight.

Once they got back Harriet was already downstairs sitting in the kitchen with her coat on checking out her social media feed and chuckling occasionally to herself. James made sure Scruff had a bowl of water and a few dog biscuits to keep him occupied then indicted he was ready and together they stepped out the front door. Scruff realised he wasn't going with them and he gave out a little bark, almost sounding as if he was disgusted he wasn't included.

He ran through into the living room and jumped up on the sofa pushed up against the front window. He settled down on the windowsill forlornly watching James and Harriet walk up the garden path.

Outside Harriet looked at James as they walked along as he wasn't heading for their cars.

"Is it far then?" she asked and James just indicated, pointing up the road to the right.

"Only about ten to fifteen minutes' walk. It'll do us good. You never know, we might even see *'him'*." As he waved his hands spookily in the air.

Harriet grimaced. "I'd rather not. I like dead people to stay that way, they don't talk back when I do my work on them and they don't usually send you off on wild goose chases!"

"Tell me about it," agreed James as he opened the garden gate and politely ushered Harriet through and out onto the roadside verge. Surprisingly, there was little conversation between them except when Harriet realised they were not taking the short cut through the woods. As they passed the turning she pointed, but James shook his head.

"Thought you didn't want to encounter our mystery airman? If we carry straight along the road we'll come to the official entrance and that seems the better option."

"Oh, good point."

Again they were silent for the rest of the walk and as they turned into the entrance James remembered it was close to where he'd first noticed the airman. It had been when he and Sally had been out walking and she was looking out for butterflies. He was sure now that he had seen the airman in the distance. As they entered the industrial estate entrance road he recognised the view and confirmed that the airman would have been in the right place to be heading towards the old shortcut through the woods.

Greg spotted them and approached from the direction of the old control tower and the site of both the haulage company headquarters and the museum.

"Hello James, ahh, good to meet you at last Mrs Hansone," he said as he extended a hand to shake Harriet's. She smiled but James was quick off the mark.

"Err, no, this is a close friend of Sally's, Harriet, meet Greg."

"Oh sorry for the mistake, easily done however." replied Greg a little embarrassed at his mistake.

"No worries Greg, James here has the job of entertaining me today whilst Sally has to work. Something to do with the royal visit to Lincoln so she can't be here."

"Say, Greg, is the museum open as I'd like to have a look to see if there are any clues to our little mystery in there."

"Yes, Sandra is on the door so I'll just send her
a text to say to let you both through for free. Quiet today so I guess it must be down to that royal visit then, that would explain things. See you later perhaps as I just need to check on the contractors at the far end of the site on the last section of the old runway. We're having new fibre work put in so a local firm are digging out the trenches for us. I happened to mention you and they know you, Phil and Joe are their names."

"Ha! Them two get everywhere. Let's hope they don't dig up any bodies then," chuckled James as Harriet and Greg looked at him, mystified.

"Each time we've come into contact they always seem to discover a body that's connected to what I'm doing. I'd best steer clear of them as they already think they're jinxed every time they see me around one of their work sites!"

Greg shook his head and bade farewell as he texted Sandra as promised. James and Harriet continued on but Harriet kept chuckling and shaking her head, clearly amused by something.

"Go on then, spill. What's funny?" James had to ask.

"But darling, now we're a married couple you should know what I'm thinking." Harriet teased.

"Simple mistake, how was Greg to know, he's never met Sally. Anyhow, I doubt I'm your type."

Harriet looked at him sideways, puzzled and a little concerned.

"Erm, say what?"

"I know...*everything*." he replied carefully as he kept an eye on her reactions. He knew he'd hit a nerve and for a moment did wonder if he was pushing their friendship a bit far.

"Sally told you then about our brief past?"

"Yes. So let us get this clear if we are going to be honest with each other. What's in the past is Sally's and your business. I'm a modern sort of bloke despite my age, so I won't judge you on your choice of partner. But I'll tell you now, I will forgive the early hours of Saturday morning between you two and put it down to the drink and the fact you were scared shitless by what happened in Jenny's room. I was a bit dubious about you two sharing a bed that night so I'm glad nothing else seems to have happened, but don't cross the line again.

Are we clear?"

Harriet looked shocked and knew she had indeed crossed a line putting their friendship at risk.

"You're right, it was silly of me and all I can say was Friday night into Saturday morning I felt vulnerable and you know, one thing led to another.

Did Sally say anything then about this weekend?"

"Yes, she came clean when you had a lie in on Sunday morning. Sounds like she read you the riot act."

"Yes, she did whilst you were taking Scruff for a walk," replied Harriet quietly.

"You're a nice person Harri, we do both love you but not in that way so now I've had my say, let us put it in the past and start anew?"

"Yes. Indeed."

Her demeanour brightened and they stopped walking and faced each other, standing outside the entrance to the old control tower.

"I'd like that very much. Friends?"

"Of course. Hug?"

They hugged as Sandra opened the door wondering why they had not entered but stayed outside, not quite knowing where to look or what to say.

"Hi Sandra, meet my wife's best and dearest friend, Harriet."

Sandra just said hello politely but you could see in her eyes, her mind was busy concocting a cock and bull story about them. She ushered them in and indicted to the corridor leading to the back where the museum was located. Not that they needed directions considering the big sign stating 'The country needs you…to visit our museum'.

Harriet smiled at her inadvertently eyeing her up and for that got a light tap on her shoulder from James to keep her eyes and mind at the task at hand.

"Spoilsport," she whispered to James as they walked down the corridor and he couldn't help but laugh a little which broke the ice between them, and Harriet relaxed.

It was small, but packed with memorabilia, examples of parts of a Lancaster, small parts but all historic. A full flight suit was on display on a mannequin. Unfortunately, it seemed the only mannequin available had been female so the airman's suit had been 'beefed up' in places to hide the fact. Harriet looked at it from a variety of angles then looked at James.

"It'd look good on you. If you ever do fancy dress see if you can borrow it!"

"Cheeky. Mind you when you think what they went through, then I guess it would be an honour to dress up as a pilot. Without people like that, we wouldn't be here today."

"True," she looked at the various photos and maps up on the walls. "Did you know that the Lancaster we saw yesterday fly over from the Battle of Britain Memorial Flight didn't actually see action?" she said as she studied a picture of several Lancasters lining up to take off from RAF Grasceby.

"No, why's that then?"

"It was one of the last batch to be built just as the war ended. It was, if I remember right, going off to the far east but that part of the war also ended before it could be flown out."

"Probably explains why it has lasted so well then if it didn't get shot up. Can't imagine what it must have been like to fly in one."

"Well you sort of can if you go down to East Kirkby as they have one of the few remaining that has running engines but can't fly. They do taxi runs, for a price of course, but they're always popular."

"Strange, I've been in Lincolnshire now about four years, life turned upside down, lost a wife, gained a wife, ended up doing something I never believed in. Plus I didn't know that about East Kirkby!"

"You learn all sorts when I'm around, ask Sally!"

James shot her a glance but then smiled and carried on looking at the exhibits. A large propeller was mounted on one of the walls and on inspection you could see it had been shot at but had somehow survived. Harriet beckoned to him, pointing at the steep wooden stairs and they went up to the next floor where tables held maps of various operational sorties that the base had been involved in. It was all very sobering when they came across a display cabinet that had someone's wartime diary and medals on display.

"They look like the ones Sally and I found at the back corner of our garden when we were getting it ready for the brick wall to be built," James muttered but not really aloud so Harriet didn't hear him.

She joined him as he looked at the notebook and spotted it was a pilot's log book as they peered at it closer through the glass noting it was open towards the end. The pilot had survived twenty five sorties over enemy terrain and incredibly he had applied for a second round but had been shot down only four flights into the second set. He'd been killed when his parachute had not opened but the local French resistance had managed to secure his body and get it back to England where he'd been buried with full honours.

A newspaper was on display from 1944 explaining the successes the Allies were having as the German forces were being pushed back and the role the RAF was playing. A small sub story involved the crashing of a Lancaster on returning to RAF Grasceby where the one of the crew had been considered negligent as all but he had perished in the crash. The story went over to the next page and there was no way to turn it over with it being inside the display cabinet. A tragedy at a time of war, James thought as he moved on from the cabinet.

James saw there were more steps and indicated to Harriet so they headed up, out onto the roof for what was a great view of the surrounding countryside. He scanned around the view and noticed something.

"Look, you can make out where most of the runways were. There were buildings over there and I stood next to one of them the other day."

Harriet looked at him quizzically but said nothing as she knew he and Scruff had come to the industrial estate a few times.

But to James, in his mind he was playing out what had happened to him recently when he'd saved the chap, Arthurson, or something like that. Or had it been a daydream..?

A spot or two of rain struck his face and he wiped the drops away as Harriet too felt the start of the rain so they headed back downstairs to the ground floor room and took a final look at the many photos on the walls.

Ground operational staff lined up for a group photo caught his eye and he spotted Arthurson grinning two thirds of the way along from the left. James smiled.

"Probably in his nineties at least by now, if he's alive at all," muttered James but Harriet didn't hear him as she was chatting up Sandra, until she discovered Sandra was married!

He motioned to Harriet and they headed out as Sandra noted one of the photos was at a slant and she set it right. She didn't recognise the tiny image of two men, one of them looking decidedly like James …

#

"Oh heck, just got a text from Sally. Seems like something has happened to the transportation arrangements for the Princess and Sally and the rest of her officers are to stay in place overnight until arrangements have been made. Could be an all nighter, she says. Looks like we're on our own tonight then," James said as he looked slightly annoyed but resigned to the news.

Harriet wasn't sure what to say although since their little frank chat in the morning things had settled down and they'd got on really well. They'd taken Scruff for another walk and for once he'd been happy to head off towards Grasceby, something apparently they'd not done for quite a few months.

Scruff had been somewhat noisy as they'd passed a house on the outskirts of the village and James explained that the lady who lived there, the postmistress for Horncastle, had lots of cats. There was also a very loud dog behind a wire fence that always barked at Scruff, probably at anything else that went by too. They'd spent a little time at the village pond sitting on a bench watching the ducks as Scruff kept his beady eye on them, before they headed back to the cottage.

James cooked them a chicken and bacon risotto, washed down with a glass or two of chardonnay and he kept a portion in the fridge wrapped up in case Sally was able to get home. Another text said otherwise, so James fired up his console and together he and Harriet enjoyed several bouts of computer tennis, word challenges and watched a movie to pass the time.

Eleven pm came and James sat there a little sleepy eyed.

"Remind me Harri, what time do you need to be away by tomorrow?"

"Oh, I haven't anything urgent on at the moment, but I was thinking about just after lunch if that's all right with you and Sally.

"Yeah, no worries. Look I'm tired so am thinking about turning in."

"OK, I was wondering about that myself. I'll go up to the spare room then and wish you goodnight. Breakfast at seven thirty?"

"Yes, I'll be up, so bacon and eggs OK?"

She smiled and nodded as she left the living room and he heard her go up the stairs. Scruff had woken up and wandered into the room looking up at him.

"OK, but just out into the back garden!" Scruff followed James out as he went to the back door, opened it and Scruff obediently trotted into the garden.

Not long afterwards there was a light scratching on the back door and James let him back in, let him settle in his basket then said goodnight before turning in for the night.

He came awake oddly wondering what it was that had caught his subconscious attention.

A noise.

And again.

A sort of sniffling, faint sound of someone sobbing coming from behind his bedroom door.

It opened as he heard his name called out quietly and Harriet stepped in shaking like a leaf.

He turned his side light on seeing she was ashen faced and trembling.

"Heck Harri, what's wrong?" he pretty much figured it out as she began to talk in a stuttering way.

"He's, he's back. The room, it's so, *cold*. It's like there is someone in the room but, but I can't see anyone. I had to come to you but I didn't want you to be annoyed or angry.."

"Oh Harri, don't be daft, I'm here. Stay here and I'll go in," he hesitated then looked back at her. "Err, can you just turn away, I need to put something on!" She dutifully did so and listened to him get out of bed and something like the sound of clothing being put on. "OK, I'm decent now," she turned around to see James had his pyjamas on and a dressing gown too. He went past her out across the landing and into Jenny's room.

It was almost ice cold and he turned on the light but the room looked normal. He checked the windows but they were closed and the air vent was closed too so there could be no draft from them. He looked around and came to a decision.

"RIGHT! WHOEVER YOU ARE, THIS STOPS NOW! I DON'T WANT YOU HERE, YOU ARE NOT TO COME BACK AND DISTURB US. DO YOU HEAR ME?" he said angrily.

Silence.

But oddly, the room began to warm up so James quickly checked the radiators but, as the weather was quite warm of late, they were off. The room seemed to go back to a more normal temperature as James looked about with no sign of the airman to be seen or indeed felt.

James walked back across the landing and to his and Sally's room. Harriet was sitting on the bed but still looked quite shaken.

"Listen, you know how we stand relationship wise and there is no way I'm letting you go back to that bed. But at the same time, I also don't want to go in there either as it will leave you alone. So, you take Sally's side of the bed and I'll stay to mine, OK?"

She nodded meekly and took of her dressing gown, slipped into Sally's side of the bed and drew the bedclothes about her. James switched the main light off and got into his side of the bed and snuggled down.

"Goodnight Harri."

"Goodnight James. Thank you."

James turned his side light off and hoped the rest of the night would be uneventful.

To their relief, it was.

13: An old acquaintance revisited

They came clean about events both during the visit to the museum and overnight and Sally took it in her stride.

She and James waved Harriet off as she drove away and Sally turned to him.

"Now you see what I mean about her. Best friend you could ask for, but you could say she's a bit on the naughty side. I'm still glad she came. I think in many ways we needed it so that we could lay down the rules, especially after her antics at the wedding reception. I think she's got it. I'm still forgiven for early Saturday morning, right?"

"Of course you are. And I can tell you that last night was quite odd but she was true to her word and let's be honest, when you got home in the early hours, any other woman would have jumped to the wrong conclusion, wouldn't they?"

"Yep, was quite funny in a way to see you both in bed like that. She really did make an effort to keep right over on her side. Any closer to the edge and she'd have been on the floor!"

"So, now what? I would hope you have a few days off after all that extra time, including overnight too!"

"I've got the paperwork to do but I can have today off then it's back to full flow on Wednesday. I err, also had a chance to talk to the Chief whilst we were at Lincoln. It's certainly looking likely I may be able to retire early with a good pension but he did say he would try to swing things for me if I wanted to stay in the force.

I think we should sit down and have a good talk about what I should do and if I did leave what I might be able to do to keep me occupied once I'm not working. But for now I need some sleep as the long day and night is catching up with me."

"OK love. Tell you what, something keeps popping into my head about Jenny so I'm going to play a hunch and go to the graves shortly. I'll drive down whilst you get some rest."

They kissed briefly then Sally went inside and up to their room as James called out for Scruff to go for a quick walkies before he headed out to Grasceby Churchyard.

#

It was peaceful, he thought, as he looked down at the gravestone and reflected on what might have been. A father and a sister he had never known in life. In truth only his deceased sister Jenny had appeared to him on a regular basis. And then only for a while as he helped unravel the mystery about her disappearance all those years ago.

James looked about for any other people visiting the graveyard but as it was a weekday it was quiet, so he looked again at the headstone.

"Jenny? Mum? Dad? Anyone?"

He spotted a familiar sight appear to one side but it was only Mr Shabernackles, Lord Grasceby's daughter Heather's cat. He was clearly on his rambles and presumably keeping out of the way of Heather as she was somewhat controlling. He was fortunate to have got out from the manor, mused James.

Mr Shabernackles looked up at him, did a brief meow, then trotted off away towards the back of the graveyard, disappearing through a hole in the hedge.

James looked about and again called out for Jenny but to no avail. He walked up the path, past the bench and entered the church, startling the Reverend Cossant in the process.

"My, you were quiet, I didn't hear a thing but then I was deep in thought," Sarah said as she regained her composure.

"Sorry Reverend. Didn't mean to startle you. I just wondered if you had come across anything yet?"

"About?"

"Wolds View Cottage and possibly an airman committing suicide in the woods nearby?"

"Oh, yes, err, no actually. I've been a little distracted as one of our most elderly parishioners is quite ill and if I'm honest, may not be for this world much longer. I've been calling in at the request of his family and so have been a bit distracted. I will redouble my efforts for you, however, as I know you and Sally have seen this airman a few times."

"Fair enough, I'd best be getting back, Sally was sleeping as she'd been on duty yesterday and into the night at Lincoln and I'm sure Scruff will be soon wanting to take his usual walk."

"Oh, bet it was something to do with the Princess's visit. Nice seeing you James and if I do find out anything then I'll get in touch."

They shook hands and he left the church pleased he'd bumped into Sarah even though there was no news yet.

The road was now a very familiar and well worn route for James as he headed out of Grasceby, through several bends then the long straight that would pass the cottage. The tree line dipped back into the field and hid the secret that was Wolds View Cottage, unfortunately it also meant a few drivers came hurtling down the narrow road without a care in the world. Speeding past, it was only at the last minute they realised there was a cottage and slowed down. James did wonder how long it would be before there was an accident. Hopefully not to Sally, Scruff or himself, he mused.

Although paying attention to the road, up ahead there seemed to be someone standing on the grass verge on the right, a little unusual as very few people ever walked out their way but as he drew closer James suddenly braked hard and stopped in shock.

The ghostly form of Jenny was standing looking in his direction. Regaining his senses James drove the car onto the grass verge, stopped the engine, got out and cautiously walked towards her as he looked around for any other traffic using the road.

There were no immediate signs of any other cars and as he neared her, Jenny smiled at him.

"Hello brother," she said, as if it was the most normal thing in the world for the ghost of his sister to greet him.

"Hello Sister. Erm, why didn't you appear at the graveside?"

"Hard to explain but better for you if we follow this rough path, you might remember it?"

He looked about then realised where they were. The cottage was a few hundred metres further along the road but there was a gap in the hedge and tree line. He realised it was the original path Jenny used to take when she was a lost soul, following her final walk towards the woods on the other side of the field.

She headed through and continued along almost echoing the walk they had taken only four years earlier and James felt a sense of déjà vu. She walked, or rather seemed to glide along and James rushed to keep up.

"Why this path? Why can't we just stop and talk?" he asked quite puzzled about her motive.

"For now let's go into the wood, just past where I came to my unfortunate end. For me, I have to follow my original path, I don't know why but I feel it calling to me. But you can use the new bridge over the drainage ditch that replaced the old one I used to walk over with Richard…" her voice tailed off as her own memories flooded back but she kept her emotions in check.

James took the new bridge then re-joined Jenny as they passed the site where Joe and Phil had accidentally discovered Jenny's remains only a few years earlier. She ignored it, carrying on a little further into the first of the trees until they could no longer see the road behind them. Just ahead, James could make out the archaeological excavations site that was still exploring the original De Grasceby Manor. Out of respect they had not excavated in the direction of the old tunnel but had concentrated on the main building and the extensive gardens they had uncovered the other year.

Jenny stopped and looked at James. She now seemed sad and he wasn't sure what to say.

"I couldn't appear or talk to you at the graveside as it would have upset our parents. I also don't like to come back to our home now due to *him…*"

James froze at this last nugget of information and a chill ran down his spine. He looked at her warily and motioned for her to continue.

"It is very complicated, but I think you have been seeing an airman from the war at our home, haven't you?"

"Yes, but how..?"

"James. He's our, he's our *grandfather…*"

"*What!*"

He stood there shocked, but at the same time a dawning realisation that all along something deep inside was telling him the airman had to be related to his family.

"But, but why now?"

"You and Sally have disturbed something or brought something back into the house that has allowed him to come back."

James eyes widened in realisation.

"The table and chairs…"

Jenny looked at him. "*No,* you didn't?" she asked but quickly realised he would not have known their history.

"What is it with them?" James asked not knowing if he really wanted to hear the answer.

"From my vague recollection and what our mother used to say to me, they were Grandfathers pride and joy. They were old, hand made and handed down over several generations. He always sat in the one opposite ..."

"…the window." James finished for her and she nodded slowly.

"I can barely remember it but Grandfather did something bad in the war and several of his crew died and he was to blame. Mother said he had brought shame on the family. She said he left us but when he came to me when I was little, I realised I could see through him.

Mother saw me talking to him several times and she couldn't stand it, so had the house visited by a reverend who exorcised Grandfather's ghost and made him leave. I never saw him again. She sold the table and chairs to someone in town and we never saw them or Grandfather again. But now he is back…"

"He's my Grandfather…" James was still taking the information overload in.

"Yes, our Grandfather, but I wasn't allowed to talk about him. Ever."

James stood in shocked silence as he tried to take in what he had just discovered. It was almost too much.

"So..so what did he do that was so wrong?" he asked, as much to himself as to Jenny's apparition.

"I don't know, I was too young, but what I can remember is that he wanted to tell his side to me but wasn't allowed to do so, mother made sure of that."

"Then that's it, my job, to dig into his past and find out what on earth made him get to the point of ending his own life."

Jenny looked aghast.

"Sorry, what, what do you mean?"

James felt guilty as it dawned on him their mother had probably shielded Jenny from the truth.

"Through the woods, on the way to the airbase, there's a small clearing with two oak trees and I saw him hanging from one when I followed his spirit. Much like I did with you when you first began to appear to me."

Jenny clasped her hands to her face in shock and James felt sad that he couldn't hold his sister to comfort her. She stood in silence for a few moments.

"I, I remember it now. Somehow I had forgotten but the last time I saw him was when I was almost six and he led me into the woods and then off to the left to a clearing. It was very strange as I saw two of him, one next to me and another up the tree with a ..." she paused, as that awful memory came back. "...a rope around his neck. But there was something odd, I don't think he meant to go through with it. The grandfather standing next to me wanted to see if I saw anything unusual. I think something startled him from behind us and he slipped instead. But I wasn't allowed to give my side to mother and father, they didn't want to listen.

That is why I was always forbidden to go into those woods. Mother was so adamant, that I never did, although one time Richard... Well, Richard and I did follow the path through to the airbase, but he didn't believe me when I said I thought we were being watched. I never went on that path again, I refused and Richard couldn't change my mind. That's when we walked the other way and found the old path and eventually the old tunnel from the buried ruins that Richard turned into a love nest for us."

"And where he felt he had to hide your body after the accident."

"He really never meant me any harm, we were in love. I think, well, it's doesn't matter now, what's done is done. But he was very kind all the while to me, he doted on me and I think we'd have had a good life together…" Her voice tailed off as she wondered on what could have been.

"Jenny, I had better get back to Sally and Scruff, so what shall we do, meet up here another time?"

"Scruff?"

"Long story, tell you another time but he's our dog."

"I always wanted a puppy but mother always said no. I think if you can come back here tomorrow at the same time and call out for me I will come and tell you what I know and remember if there is anything else. If we come here no one sees you talking to no one and it won't look odd."

"Ahh, that's why we came into the woods."

"Yes. It would look odd to others if you were talking to thin air, as very few can see me."

"You know, I really wish we'd known each other in life, instead of death. I reckon we'd have got on well considering brothers and sisters usually fight all the time."

"Me too. But at least we seem to be linked and can meet up. Bye Brother, see you tomorrow, and James …"

"Yes?"

"Bring Sally, she should know what happened to me and your Grandfather all those years ago too." Jenny faded from view as James started walking back along the rough animal track, onto the path and headed for his car, deep in thought.

#

Once home he filled in Sally with events.

"I had a suspicion, but kept an open mind. But James, what did your Grandfather do all those years ago?"

"I don't fully know but it sounds like it led to the death of several crew members so I wonder if he was a pilot flying Lancasters from RAF Grasceby during the war?"

They sat in the living room as Scruff wandered from one to the other with his toy bone in his mouth, no one paying him any attention. He finally gave up and trotted back into the kitchen and lay down in his basket, somewhat disgruntled.

Meanwhile the doorbell chimed. He pricked up his ears and sat up alert and ready to run to the defence of his family.

Sally reached the door first, opening it to find their pizza finally had arrived.

"Huh, quite a way out really, we don't normally deliver out in the sticks," came the gruff voice of the delivery rider. He handed her a card machine and then scowled as he realised there was no internet signal. "It'll have to be cash then Miss".

"Mrs, and be careful, you might find a smile somewhere and it'll catch you by surprise. I'll just be a moment." She turned and yelled out for James. "Hey James, thought they'd sorted better signals out here? Bring my purse will you!"

She looked at the rider who had to be only just old enough to ride a motorbike but she decided not to do a check, not this time.

James poked his head around the door, gave her the purse and the rider was dispatched on his way leaving them to head into the kitchen to sort out hot drinks.

The chair was out of place again. They both looked at each other, sighed, abandoned the idea of coffees and grabbed a bottle of Chardonnay out of the fridge instead. Sally picked up a couple of glasses for them as James grabbed plates and his novelty pizza cutter.

Dropping down onto the sofa it didn't take long to munch through the, by now, lukewarm pizza and James finally spoke up.

"I find it odd that he doesn't say anything to us."

"Well I did give him a bit of a look of disdain at the poor service."

"No, the airman!" James chuckled and Sally smiled at him as she reached for her wine glass.

"Perhaps it's like what you found with Jenny. She couldn't say anything until you had discovered the truth about how she died. Once you had solved her disappearance and 'freed her', so to speak, she could communicate. So going by that, once you find out more about why your granddad committed suicide, he might be able to talk to you."

"Pity he can't just tell us now - would save time and us looking here, there and everywhere for clues."

"Welcome to my world, Detective Ghost Inspector Hansone! Hah! DGIH! You should put that on any letterheads or emails from now on," laughed Sally and James just gave her a withering look.

"Well, I'm finished and that's the last of my wine so I'm going up to bed. Care to join me DS Hansone?"

"Yep, but you're forgetting someone …" Sally nodded towards the living room door and there stood Scruff who knew it was about time for the last walkies of the day.

"Oops. Coming boy!" James got up and Scruff barked then rushed out towards the front door. Sally finished off her wine and collected the glasses and plates, piling them in the dishwasher as she heard James take an excited dog out for his constitutional.

#

Next day, Sally walked along the grass verge, following James until he pointed to a small gap in the hedge and tree line, memories of four years earlier flooding back.

She'd been called out to the site of a body discovered by two workers digging out and improving the drain, until they found what they would later discover to be the body of the missing teenager of fifty years earlier, Jennifer Portisham.

So much had changed since then when James and her old mentor, Mike Freshman, had approached. She had been shocked and a little wary when James knew all the details of what Jennifer had been wearing and on first impulse she'd have suspected him. Yet she worked out he hadn't been born at the time of Jenny's disappearance so she had to put up with Mike convincing her that James had seen Jennifer's ghost.

And that he had walked this very path with the ghost and she had led him to the spot where she was located.

So as James walked along the faint animal path ahead of her, Sally couldn't help but wonder what it must have felt like to James at that time. At least it had meant they met and amazingly, were now married, living in the original cottage no less. Who'd have thought it?

They crossed over the newer bridge that had been put in place by Lord Grasceby once the drain had been widened and dredged out. She noticed a little plaque and stopped to look at it.

"Hey, James, did you know about this?"

"About what?" came the reply and she motioned for him to come back to the bridge. They looked at the plaque and James felt a tear in his eyes.

This bridge is dedicated to the memory
of the missing teenager, Jennifer Portisham,
whose body was discovered nearby after
fifty years lost and all alone.
Rest in Peace
The Grasceby Estate

"I knew a small bridge had been constructed to replace the old small rough one that used to be there. But I had no idea, no one at the estate told me about it. A really nice gesture by them." he said. Sally put her arm about his waist and nodded. They set off and entered the wood. At the right spot, James came to a halt, looked about then called out.

"OK, we're here Jenny." They stood and waited for a few minutes and James began to wonder if she would show.

A cool light breeze drifted over them and a familiar voice announced she had arrived.

"Hello James, hello Sally. I hope you are looking after my brother now his ex wife has passed on?"

Sally was still not sure on what to believe but there in front of her stood Jenny, smiling.

" I try my best," was all she could think of saying.

"Well, we're here, Jenny. So can you fill us in on why our grandfather is haunting our home?"

"I'm not fully sure but perhaps it is best to tell you what happened to me when I was very young. He had already passed away but mother said she saw him several times and he approached me too. So this is what I remember…"

Part II

Jenny's story

1949

14: First encounters

She loved the new bedroom. It was at the front of the cottage just across the landing from her parents' bedroom. Now she had her very own room. At only six years old, she knew that this was special and it was to do with her Daddy being able to get something called a morgarage or a word like that. Daddy and Mummy had bought their half, and now the other half of the home she had been born into and they had spent the last year, or was it two, making it into a full home, whatever that was. She thought she knew all there was of her home until they'd shown her the large living room and said that she no longer had to sleep in their bedroom.

Yes, she was very lucky, now she had all her toys strewn across the floor from the upturned box she kept them in and she had to make a decision:

Dollys or horses.

Undecided, she took the easy option, she bundled all of them into her bag, or rather the bag her Mummy had given her to play with. In went the cups and saucers, teapot, teddy bear and of course the wooden dollys and horses that were her prize possessions. They were very old, something from her grandmother, but she didn't fully understand who they were or where they were, she'd never seen them as far as she could remember. She only knew a grandma but no granddads as they had already gone away to somewhere called heaven.

Her dolls were going to have a grand day out. Mummy had finally relented and said she could play in the front garden as it was a nice sunny day. She hauled the bag up, trying to lift it but realising it was quite heavy. Nonetheless she managed to drag it down the stairs, bump, bump, bump, until she was standing at the foot of them near to the back door. Well, the only door actually to get in out out of her home, but she wasn't to know that a lot of homes usually had a front door as well as a back one.

Mother peered around the doorframe that joined the kitchen to the hallway. "You be good now poppet and remember, don't go out the gate and stay in the garden at all times. Oh, and no talking to strangers neither or else you'll have to stay indoors." For a moment Barbara did think that seeing someone else outside would be rather unlikely as they were "*out in the sticks*" so to speak but it was always worth reinforcing the message.

"Yes Mummy, teddy is taking the dolls out to meet the horses and they will all be having tea and meeting the King too!"

"Yes dear, I'm sure they will have a lovely time but you just be careful now won't you poppet," she smiled as Jennifer grinned and waved at her before dragging her heavy bag out through the open door and into the sunshine.

An hour later and still not tired of playing and rearranging the dolls and horses, she lined them up once again for King Teddy to look them over. Jennifer was paying little attention to the rest of the , being lost in her wonderful imagination and was talking to the dolls as if she was King Teddy.

"Now we all need to be very smart and dressed up for his majesty to look you over." she proudly announced.

She shivered, took no notice and carried on then sat puzzled as she felt really cold, as if the sun had gone in.

It had not and it continued to blaze down from an almost cloudless sky. Something caught her attention from the corner of her eye and she looked back towards the path.

He walked past silently in his blue uniform and didn't look at her once, but as she was about to call out she remembered what her mother had said and so kept quiet. As she watched, he strolled along the path and reached the gate, turned and looked up at the cottage. An odd thing happened. The gate was closed yet she could have sworn that a see-through gate had opened and he stepped through it but passed through the 'real' yet closed gate.

A bird was disturbed from the trees across the road and as it flew behind the blue clothed person she blinked quickly as she saw the bird through him as it passed by. He stopped outside the gate and for all intents and purposes, he looked really sad as he looked up and down the road before walking off towards the right and beyond her sight.

She sat for a few minutes completely forgetting about her toys, but curiosity got the better of her and she stood up and wandered over to the closed gate. She could just about peer over the top but the blue man was nowhere to be seen and she turned to look back at the cottage.

Giving out a big sigh, she decided it was nothing and so went back to her teddy to make sure he inspected the dolls and horses to make sure they were all very good, well behaved and lined up ready for inspection.

But her thoughts kept wandering back to what she had seen. Finally, she picked everything up, pushed them into the bag and dragged it back around along the path to the back door and stepped inside. She could hear her mother humming away in the kitchen so Jennifer wandered in, looked up at her and waved.

"Oh, hello dear, did you enjoy playing outside with your dolls?" asked Barbara.

"Oh yes, but some of the horses and dolls were very naughty and did not line up very well. Mummy, who was the blue man that walked along the path to the gate from our house?"

Caught off guard Barbara was briefly lost for words but quickly composed herself.

"Oh, no one dear, no one to worry about. Now do you want some ice cream as a treat for being a good girl?" Jenny's eyes lit up and all thoughts of the odd blue man evaporated as she eagerly nodded and waited for the treat.

After just a few minutes she was wandering back up the stairs to her room enjoying the ice cream. She dumped the bag with the toys in on her bed as she sat heavily on the floor licking away at the dribbles of ice cream before it could drip all over the floor.

Downstairs in the kitchen, Barbara Portisham sat with a small glass of sherry in her hand, white as a sheet, as if she had seen a ghost. She had come into the kitchen and there, his favourite chair, was slightly ajar from the table.

#

It was a lovely bright sunny day. Jenny had her small bucket and spade with her as she wandered off the path towards the wooden lean-to shed that acted as a makeshift garage for her daddy's motorbike and sidecar. She wasn't allowed into the garage but daddy had made a large sandpit nearby at the corner of the garden just off the path and it was there that she was heading.

She just loved getting dirty as she played in not just the sand, but the wetter patch that was quickly becoming a mud pit! She knew Mummy would probably tell her off but for some reason Mummy had been a little odd recently when she had asked to go outside and play and Jenny couldn't work out why.

The clouds came and went and occasionally she could hear her mother singing to herself as she cleaned the house. Jenny felt happy that Mummy seemed happy again.

She filled the bucket with sand and scowled as she spotted her skirt was getting dirty, but she put it out of mind. Tipping the sand out along the rim of the small pit she was making she was pleased but now she needed to fill the pit with water to make a little pond. She hoped she might get some froggy spawn in it and could watch them like Daddy had told her a few weeks earlier. It was at that time she had decided to make the pond herself and impress him. She loved Daddy. She did love Mummy as well but Daddy played more with her and would often swing her around and throw her up into the air so that she came down giggling all the time.

The sun appeared to go in and she looked up briefly as she thought she heard her name called out faintly.

There it was again.

'Jenny'.

Jenny stood up and turned round in a full circle looking for the voice.

'Jenny'.

She stopped in her tracks and stared.

Mummy was smiling at her through the window and calling to catch Jenny's attention. Her mother waved then went back to her work, busying herself with the chores. Mystery solved. Jenny waved then went to sit down in the sand.

'Jennifer.'

She spun round quickly as it almost sounded as if her name had been spoken quietly into her left ear.

Nothing.

No one.

'Jennifer.'

She spun round again, now alarmed that someone had got into the garden and was spying on her. She trembled a little her mouth began to dry up.

'Don't be afraid, I won't harm you. Not you. You are special to me.'

A few minutes later, Jenny suddenly screamed as she wildly looked around.

Instantly Barbara heard her and looking up out of the window and her heart jumped into her mouth as she saw the blue suited man standing looking at her daughter.

Barbara screamed and raced for the back door, running round along the path shouting frantically.

"Don't you dare, don't you dare touch her. Get away from her get …"

Barbara stopped abruptly as Jenny looked up at her with a puzzled expression on her face as she sat quite content on her own next to the makeshift garage.

"What's the matter Mummy?" she asked innocently.

Barbara looked round and glanced towards the road.

The blue suited man was nowhere to be seen.

#

"Jenny, now tell the truth my love. What did you see to make you scream like that?"

Barbara knew there was more to what Jenny had already said and needed to know if it was the person she suspected. Jenny just looked innocently at her mother as if butter wouldn't melt in her mouth.

"I was playing and imagined a monster grabbing my toys in the sandpit. Sorry Mummy. I didn't mean to upset you." Jenny put on her most tearful face and it worked as Barbara took her in her arms and gave her a little hug.

"That's okay, my love, but try not to do it again, it was quite worrying for me and I'm sure you don't want that, do you?"

Jenny looked down and nodded.

"Good. Remember, you only scream out like that if something is really wrong such as someone talking to you that shouldn't or if they have come into the garden without us knowing."

"All right Mummy. I'll remember."

"Good girl. Off you go, are you going to play in your room now?" Jenny looked round as she skipped towards the kitchen door and stopped.

"Yes, I'm tired of playing in the sand so will get my dolls out instead." Jenny continued through the door and turned up the stairs, running up them and into her bedroom. Throwing herself on her bed she lay there thinking about what she had done and briefly re-lived what had really gone on at the sandpit …

The sun appeared to go in and she looked up briefly as she thought she heard her name called out faintly.

There it was again.

'Jenny.'

Jenny stood up and turned round in a full circle looking for the voice.

'Jenny.'

She stopped in her tracks and stared.

Mummy was smiling at her through the window and calling to catch Jenny's attention. Her mother waved then went back to her work, busying herself with the chores. Jenny waved then went to sit down in the sand.

'Jennifer.'

She spun round quickly as it almost sounded as if her name had been spoken quietly into her left ear.

Nothing.

No one.

'Jennifer.'

She spun round again, now alarmed that someone had got into the garden and was spying on her. She trembled a little and her mouth began to dry up as she looked up at him in his blue suit.

'Don't be afraid, I won't harm you. Not you. You are special to me.'

"You look funny," she said as she looked up at him.

"Well you would look like me if you had died!"

"Are you a ghost then?"

"Yes. Are you frightened?"

"No, I think I saw you before. Along our path then out through the gate."

"Yes, I am fated to walk my last steps, perhaps forever. I don't know when it happens, it just does."

"Are you frightened, being dead?"

The airman looked solemnly down and Jenny felt a pang of sorrow for him.

"Children always ask the best questions. Yes, yes I am frightened. But you make me happy."

"Why?"

"I am your grandfather. I thought I would never get to see you again but something keeps me here at the cottage. Perhaps it is you?"

Jenny looked around at the garden and makeshift garage, thinking carefully.

"Does Mummy and Daddy know you are here?"

"They may do. Your mummy doesn't like me so it is best if she does not know you have been talking to me. Oh, quickly, scream, scream your heart out as she is looking through the window again and might see we are

talking. Don't tell her about me will you? Scream Jenny, Scream!"

Jenny did as she was told …

#

Barbara felt uneasy after Jenny had gone up to her room. She had spotted the airman talking to Jenny and her replying back to him yet Jenny had clearly lied about it. She knew she would have to have words with Jack when he got home from work that evening. She didn't have a clue as to what to say or do about the matter and wished the old git of a father-in-law would leave them be.

He was a disgrace in life and now too in death, and she wasn't having it. She stood up and went to walk towards the kitchen sink but caught her hip on a chair that was just at a slight angle to the table, again. She glared at the chair and set it straight, her patience was beginning to wear thin.

Nothing was going to spoil her Jenny's childhood …

15: Unnerving times

Jack was away in Lincoln with a potential employer, so Barbara busied herself with the usual chores and hoped he was going to have success this time. First the master bedroom, now they had a decent one she was determined to keep it clean and tidy. She carried the large rug downstairs, hung it up as best she could on the clothes line and began to beat away to rid it of the dust and anything unpleasant that might have accumulated over the last few weeks.

She checked the wind direction holding her wet finger up in the air and adjusted position as the first few beats had sent dust straight into her face. It was a consequence of the outbuildings nearby, including the water closet, that channelled the wind in a different direction to what it should be according to the sky.

She coughed and cleared her throat.

"Are you alright Mummy?" a little voice piped up from behind Barbara who was briefly startled. Jenny had come to the back door when she heard her mother coughing.

"Yes my love, now what are you going to do, play in your room? It's not a nice day for you to be outside as it looks like it could rain," she smiled at Jenny who nodded her head and went back inside, much to Barbara's relief. She carried on beating the rug as she watched the clouds darken a little and the wind picking up a bit more, sending the clouds of dust scurrying away with each beat of the rug.

Meanwhile Jenny headed back to her room and wandered around it thinking of what to play with next. The three dolls on the floor seemed to beckon to her but she wasn't feeling in the mood to set up a tea party for them. Not this time. No, the toy rocking horse felt like the right toy and she dragged it to the middle of the floor between the bed and the window overlooking the front garden.

She looked up at the clouds and saw they were getting quite dark but putting any worries to one side, she began to rock the horse back and forth as she tried to remember the simple rhyme she had been taught.

"Rocking Horse, Rocking Horse, stay with me.

Don't go running away to the sea.
Gallop, oh gallop, come to my aid,
Before I become a sad old maid.
Rocking Horse, Rocking Horse, stay with me.
Don't go running away to the sea.
Come to my aid where ever you be,
Away from the rocks beside the sea.
Rocking Horse, Rocking Horse, stay with..."

She stopped suddenly, aware she was no longer alone in her room.

"Jenny…"

Jenny looked round the room but couldn't see *him*.

"Jenny…" said the disembodied voice. *"It's Granddad."*

Jenny smiled broadly and, as she looked over towards the window, he appeared to her in his smart blue uniform.

"Hello again Granddad. Better not let Mummy see you. She doesn't want me talking to you and would smack me or even worse tell Daddy."

"I understand. That is why I try to see you when she is busy. Your mummy is only trying to protect you and that is a good thing. But she doesn't understand what happened to me and won't let me explain it to her. You are different, young and open minded and perhaps my best hope for salvation.

Jenny, will you take a walk with me, even if it is outside and into the woods?"

"I, I don't know, Mummy and Daddy have always said I can't go into the woods as they are dangerous and something bad may happen to me."

"Yes, I understand, but you are not afraid of me are you?"

"No, I like you and you look like Daddy but older so that must make it alright."

"You are a clever little girl. One day you will make your mummy and daddy very proud, I'm sure. I want to show you what happened so you must be very brave. Are you a brave little girl, Jenny?"

"I, I don't know." She said quietly as she pondered the question.

"We need to hurry Jenny as your mummy is using the outside toilet and won't be long so we must go now or not at all. So, are you brave and coming with me?"

"Well, if you want me to, is it very far?"

"No, not far. I will meet you at the gate, hurry as we don't have much time and you need to get out of the back door before your mummy is finished."

Jenny nodded and headed for the door as the ghost of her grandfather faded away.

Considering that for the last couple of weeks she'd been holding conversations with her dead grandfather, she was not the slightest bit fazed by that thought. But she knew her mother and, to a lesser extent, her beloved father, were for some reason against Granddad so she knew she had to keep quiet.

Well for now anyway.

#

He stood next to the front gate as Jenny approached. She had managed to slip out before her mother had finished and returned to beating the rug out at the back of the house. He glided through the gate causing Jenny to giggle quietly as she always thought it funny and, in some ways wished she could move through things like that. She reached up and managed to lift the gate latch and was through, out onto the grass verge next to the road but couldn't reach to flip the latch back. But she didn't think she would be away very long so left it.

Granddad was a little further up the road to her right and she did a little sprint to catch up with him as they crossed the road together to the other grass verge. She began to whisper the rhyme to herself, partly because she did like it but also as it helped calm her down. This was an adventure but she was having misgivings. She knew she had always been told never to go out of the gate on her own, but, but she was with Granddad and she felt that had to be alright.

He smiled at her.

"I know that rhyme, my mother also taught it to me when I was close to your age.

> *Rocking Horse, Rocking Horse, stay with me.*
> *Don't go running away to the sea.*
> *Gallop, oh gallop, come to my aid,*
> *Before I become a sad old maid.*
>
> *Rocking Horse, Rocking Horse, stay with me.*
> *Don't go running away to the sea.*
> *Come to my aid wherever you be,*
> *Away from the rocks beside the sea.*
>
> *Rocking Horse, Rocking Horse, stay with me.*
> *Always be around to play with me.*
> *Rocking away but never to flee.*
> *Always my companion, forever with me."*

"But you wouldn't be a maid would you?" asked Jenny as they seemed to slow down close to an entranceway with a wooden gate and sign.

"Oh no, but it is just the way my mother, your great grandma, told it to me. We have to go over the gate, I can go through but you will have to climb it. Do you think you can manage to do that?"

Jenny smiled and remembered how she had managed to climb up the banisters once, before Daddy spotted her and stopped her. He had said something like she was fearless and she knew she could climb this gate as she could see it was locked so there was no choice. She reached up and grabbed the wood, hauling herself up and over but did fall a little heavily on her feet causing her to grunt a bit. A small part of the hem of her dress had snagged and a tiny piece tore off, but in her haste she didn't notice.

"Are you alright little one?" Granddad asked as Jenny stood upright and just smiled at him, nodding.

"Follow me then. It is only a little way and on the left. I promise there is no danger but I want to show you where things ended for me. I need you to understand so one day I will be set free from this form and go to heaven."

Jenny just nodded as she took this all in and followed him as he seemingly glided along the grassy path between the trees of the wood. He slowed, then turned onto a smaller less well defined path off to the left and she dutifully followed him as she began to hum the rhyme again.

A short while later they emerged into a small semicircular opening in the woods with two large oak trees to one side. Granddad moved over in front of it yet still a respectable distance away and Jenny stood next to him on his right.

"Any moment now, don't be scared, I am here but it will look very odd to you. Look up into the tree…now."

She did so, then gasped, not knowing what to believe.

High up in the tree, she could now see a second Granddad on one of the larger branches, then she spotted the rope.

If she could have held his hand then she would have, she did hold her hand up to her side without thinking. Naturally, the Granddad that had led her here couldn't take hold of it but did stretch out his hand to meet hers and she felt a slight cold tingling sensation as they stood there looking up.

Tree Granddad didn't seem to know they were there and was busy making sure the rope was secure round the thick branch. Then he made a loop and as Jenny watched in horror, he placed it around his neck. He looked so sad, resigned to his fate. She was mortified, rooted to the spot. Ground Granddad whispered to her.

"Be ready as I remember this last bit, but keep an eye out for anything else as he can't see me down here. I only know that this is the right time and your reactions they tell me you can see me up there, can't you?"

"Yes, but you're here. That can't be you!" she said in a hushed tone.

"Yes it is, but you are seeing a glimpse of the past before I died, which is why Grandfather can't see myself if I understand things correctly. I am hoping you will see what really happened. Call out 'Granddad' and you will see."

It really felt so strange, but she summoned up her courage from deep inside.

"Granddad!"

Incredibly Tree Granddad stopped and looked down in surprise and puzzlement. His eyes looked straight at her and something changed about him just as Jenny thought she could hear something in the bushes behind her. She briefly looked back but couldn't see anything.

Tree Granddad continued to look down in her direction and something changed. A ray of hope passed over his face and he paused in what he was doing and began to fiddle with the rope, attempting to take it off. He had changed his mind but then…

A shout from behind Jenny startled Tree Granddad who lost his precarious seating on the branch, slipped off and fell writhing about, hanging on to the end of the rope, desperately trying to take it from around his neck.

Jenny screamed her heart out…

#

Barbara was almost finished with the rug and was thankful the sky had lightened a little with a chance it wouldn't rain. She pulled the rug off from the line and folded it as best she could, walked round to the back door and entered into the small hallway with the stairs on the left. She put the rug over the banister and called up to Jenny's room.

"Jenny, I'm making a drink so do you want some apple juice?"

No reply, but then Jenny could have fallen asleep, so Barbara grabbed the rug and climbed the stairs to wake her.

Popping her head round the door Barbara stood still, puzzled as the room was empty and everything was still. Her toys were lying on the floor and some on the bed which was not like Jenny at all. Barbara walked to the other side of the bed but Jenny wasn't hiding either.

She went across the landing into the master bedroom but again, nothing.

"Jenny? Jenny, it's not funny, where are you?" A rising tide of uneasiness began to take hold. She quickly checked the bathroom then the solitary storage room next to it at the back, but to no avail.

Rushing downstairs Barbara kept calling out as panic began to set in. She dashed into the kitchen expecting something to be out of place but for once the chair, his chair, was neatly tucked under the table. She turned and raced out of the back door and around to the front of the cottage but there was no sign of her little one at all.

Then she noticed the gate was unlatched and a feeling of dread came over her as she rushed out and looked up and down the road.

Which way…

Instinctively something drew her to the right and she began to run down the road keeping an ear and eye out, not just for Jenny but for any traffic that may be coming.

"Jenny? JENNY?" she kept calling until she reached the gate that led into the MOD property and she spotted something.

A tiny piece of material caught on a wooden splinter on the top of the gate.

The same colour and type of material as in Jenny's dress.

She quickly climbed over the gate and carried on calling out then stopped in her tracks.

Jenny was screaming …

Barbara ran as she realised where Jenny must have headed. She turned onto the smaller path and moments later came out into the clearing to see Jenny sobbing her heart out, standing looking at the tree. Barbara rushed over and embraced her, gently rocking her as she tried to calm her little girl down.

She led her away and back to the gate where she stopped and bent down to look Jenny in the face.

"Sweetheart. Mummy has to go back and do something so it is very, *very* important you stay here and don't leave until I get back. I won't be many minutes. You will do that now won't you? Cross your heart and say you won't move from here until I come back for you?"

"Yes, yes mummy, cross my heart." Jenny said still sobbing at what she had seen.

Barbara turned and headed back to the clearing. She stood there, so much anger was rising that it was time to release it.

"NOW LISTEN HERE YOU GHOSTLY GIT. THAT DOES IT. I'M DONE WITH YOU AND YOUR VISITS SPOILING MY LITTLE GIRLS LIFE. I'M DONE WITH YOU AND YOUR DAMMED CHAIR ANTICS. I WILL DO EVERYTHING I CAN IN MY POWER TO HAVE YOU DRIVEN OUT, NEVER TO TORMENT MY FAMILY AGAIN. DO YOU HEAR ME?

THIS IS THE END OF IT. DON'T EVER COME BACK TO WOLDS VIEW COTTAGE. YOU ARE NOTHING TO US ANYMORE."

Barbara turned and running back, joined up with Jenny and together they headed home to the cottage.

16: Extreme measures

"Jack, we need to talk."

"There's nowt to talk about. I've said it once and I'll say it again, there's no such things as ghosts!"

"Jack Portisham, stop being a stubborn silly old bugger for once and get yer head out of the sand. Our lass wasn't just asking about him over and over now. HE LED HER AWAY!" she lowered her voice to a hush. "To where he hanged himself from shame. It's not good I tell yer, not good at all. She's young and doesn't understand what's wrong and why I struggle to talk about it. You need to do something, say something to her."

"Like what? What am I to say? Oh, by the way Jennifer, sounds like you're seeing the ghost of grandpa as he died close by when you were but a bairn! How do you think that'd go down with a five and a half year old!"

Barbara sat down on the kitchen chair then realised which one it was and moved to the other side of the table and sat again.

"He's still here, this chair keeps moving of its own accord and it's going to get worse, I tell you. How do we explain to her what happened to him? What's more, I think he's talking to her. She says he's not, but I've *seen it*! Jack, it frightens me, what's it going to do to her over time? She stood there traumatised for God's sake! What does it take to wake you up to the truth?"

"Look Bar', I won' go along with this ghost malarkey, but, well, I'll sit down with her and have a chat about Dad and try to put it over as best I can. I can't do any more." Jack hoped that would do the trick and he looked expectantly at his wife almost pleading with her to now let it go.

Barbara nodded. "Thank you love. I know it is hard and it's still very painful. But she doesn't have to know all the details, that can come when she's much older. I do think however, we should ask the Reverend if he'll come over and perhaps see if he can do something to sort out this business."

"That's out of my hands. You can ask him but I don't want to have anything to do with ghosts and spooks and the what 'ave ya." Jack sighed as he really did dread the thought that his disgraced father was haunting their little girl. He got up, tucked the chair under the table and smiled grimly at Barbara then headed out of the room.

Upstairs Jenny was playing with her dolls and had them all lined up on parade. Jack gently opened the door and stepped in, smiling as best he could to try to settle Jenny and not tip her off he was about to have a serious conversation.

"Now then Jenny, having fun?" asked Jack a little lamely.

Jenny looked up and smiled.

"Yes, Daddy, I have everyone on parade ready to be inspected."

"That's nice my little poppet. All ready for me then."

"Oh no Daddy, this is for Grandpa."

Jack stopped dead and quickly looked round the room then down at Jenny.

"W,wh, why do you say that?"

"Oh he thinks I'm a nice girl and wants me to grow up big and strong and to look after you and Mummy."

Jack felt something strange inside, a tear welled up but he fought it back.

"But poppet, Grandpa is dead, you know that, right?"

"Yes Daddy, but that doesn't stop him from seeing me. I like him. Why did he die? Did he do something wrong? He looked like he'd changed his mind and wasn't going to do it."

"Er, do what?" Jack was nervous now, not knowing what to think.

"Hang himself…"

Jack sat down on her bed a little lost for words. He motioned for her to come and sit on his lap and she did so whilst still looking at him with her innocent eyes full of questions.

"You could say that. Something happened in the war and people with him died due to him. So yes, he did do a bad thing and he couldn't face the truth. That is why we don't talk about him in our family. Sometimes people both alive and I guess dead too, do things that can't be forgiven and that is the case with Grandpa. I need you to promise me poppet that you'll not speak to him anymore as we don't know what he is trying to do and Mummy and I are frightened for you."

Tears welled up in Jenny's eyes and she began to cry as she flung her arms around her beloved father.

"Daddy, Daddy, I won't, I won't speak to him again and I'll tell him to leave me alone. Don't leave me here tonight, please, please let me stay in your room?"

Jack cuddled her and whispered gently in her ear.

"Poppet, I'll not let anyone or thing scare you my love. Come downstairs as your mother is worried sick about you."

He stood up, held out his hand and Jenny took it as they headed downstairs.

#

Three days later Reverend Samuel Stoneham arrived at Wolds View Cottage looking serious with a purposeful manner about him.

"Good day Mr & Mrs Portisham. I know this is quite hard for you Jack, not being much of a believer in the faith, but rest assured this will clear the house of any evil spirits. I can feel it now, a presence, lingering nearby so if you will just allow me to get on with my job, I'll soon free you of this unholy burden."

Jack grimaced and looked at Barbara.

"This had better work." he had a heavy heart. He had never fully accepted that his father was to blame for the deaths of his colleagues in the doomed Lancaster but the evidence had seemed conclusive. Perhaps now their lives could get back to something more normal. It pained him to even consider there really was such a thing as ghosts but things had gone too far and so it was time to do the right thing.

Reverend Stoneham smiled at them and gently nodded, he had seen many times before how frightened people could be when confronted with such things, so he knew they were doing the right thing.

"Please, it is important for me to have you both and your daughter present, we shall walk to each room as I perform cleansing prayers. If you have any items that are particularly associated with the deceased then please gather them up as we go along as we will need to bless them and ask for the spirit to leave them and the rooms in peace along with the inhabitants of this cottage. Agreed?"

Barbara nodded and Jack grimaced but also nodded ascent.

They followed the Reverend as he moved from room to room sprinkling holy water here there and everywhere as he muttered his prayers. They reached Jenny's room. as they went in there was a distinct chill in the room The Reverend stopped in his tracks almost making Barbara, Jack and Jenny bump into each other. Jenny didn't know whether to be amused or frightened and didn't really understand why Grandfather was supposed to be evil. She knew, however, her mother in particular was anxious to rid the cottage of him so he'd no longer try to talk to Jenny which she felt was sad.

"There is a strong presence in this room, is there an item that may be allowing him to linger here?"

Barbara looked around the room quickly but couldn't think of anything but surprisingly it was Jenny who spoke up.

"Wasn't Teddy Grandfather's before Daddy's?" she asked. A dawning realisation came across Jack's face as Jenny fetched the teddy bear from her toy cupboard and gave it to the reverend.

"Ahh, I feel it, it is cold, mournful in fact. Add it to the medals you have downstairs." Reverend Stoneham seemed pleased and sprinkled the holy water in an arc across the room. Barbara couldn't help but think she was going to have to do a lot of changing of bedclothes and sheets after the reverend had left.

"Begone from this room and never visit young Jennifer again for she is of our Lord Jesus Christ and under his protection. Amen."

Without waiting the Reverend turned and walked out of the room and they all quickly followed as he walked into the master bedroom.

He performed the same prayers as they went from it to the rest of the rooms on the upper floor before heading downstairs, into the living room, then finally into the kitchen.

Again the reverend stopped in his tracks but the others were ready this time.

"It is strongest here. There is a presence here with us now, over in that direction. Without looking the reverend pointed towards the chair that Edward always sat in. He walked over to it, staring at it intently.

Reverend Stoneham muttered a prayer over the bowl of water he had been carrying and sprinkled, nay splashed it around the kitchen but in particular over the offending chair and the table too.

"Let the mighty power of his Holiness, the Lord God our Father be present in this place, to banish from it uncertainty and unclean spirits. May it be cleansed and made a secure and peaceful habitation for all who dwell in it, in the name of Jesus Christ our Lord. Amen" He turned and looked at the Portisham family. "Please recite the Lord's prayer with me." They did so in unison and as they came to the final amen, all of them felt something surreal happen.

The room warmed a little.

Reverend Stoneham smiled and put the, by now empty bowl down on the table top.

"There is one final thing, although I believe I have been successful, I feel that something helps link his spirit to the cottage, and indeed to the kitchen in particular. I believe it may have something to do with the table and chairs, one in particular as you may well have noticed."

Reverend Stoneham indicated the offending chair and Barbara recognised it as the one that was always out of place.

It had been Edward's favourite chair.

"I highly recommend you remove it and the items we have collected as they appear to have the strongest connection with the presence. The smaller items can perhaps be buried somewhere on the boundary of your grounds, well away from the cottage. The table and chairs I am sure can be stored elsewhere or even sold, I'm sure old man Dreyer would be happy to take them off your hands. Once gone they will not cause any further problems, but left here they could act as a conduit back for his lost spirit and I am sure you wouldn't want that now would you?"

Jack didn't know what to think but Barbara, as always spoke for them both.

"We will do as you say your Reverendship, I can't thank you enough for this."

"I do hope I shall see you at Sunday worship from now on?"

"Oh yes, of course, we are really most grateful."

They saw the reverend to the back door and he put on his hat and coat. As he walked away he couldn't help be pleased as he always got a cut from any dealings he was able to pass along to his old friend Dreyer and he thought about the high quality workmanship that had clearly been taken in the furniture's construction.

Meanwhile, Barbara motioned to Jenny.

"Now young lady, off to bed with you and not a word of this at school, understand?"

"Yes Mummy. Does this mean I won't be able to see Grandpa again?"

"That is the last you will see of him my love. We will be at peace. Now off to bed!" Jenny ran up the stairs but was sad. She wouldn't get to see her grandfather ever again. Plus she had lost King Teddy and she wasn't sure which she'd miss most!

Barbara walked back into the kitchen and looked at the table and chairs.

"That does it then. They have to go."

But Bar, they've been in my family for several generations…"

"You heard the reverend. They are the link and could allow *him* back. I'm not having it and neither should you. We have to throw sentimental thoughts and feelings out of the window and get rid of them."

Jack knew she was right but it was going to be tough for him.

"Very well, perhaps old man Dreyer in Horncastle will take them as the reverend suggests and give a decent price. We'd best not mention anything about the funny business with them to him in case he is put off. I'll put Dad's medals and his teddy into a tin box and bury it at the far corner of the garden bordering the field, deep enough so it won't be found again."

"Thank you Jack. I know this is hard but we have to think of Jenny and her future." She kissed him lightly on the cheek. I think if you go into Horncastle in the morning and see old man Dreyer he may come out and have a look. Hopefully he'll bring his van and can take them away for us. Once that's done we can get something to replace them from Lincoln eh? A new kitchen dining set for a fresh start. We can just say we wanted a new set for the kitchen now we've finally got the two sides joined up as one house.

Jack knew she was right.

#

The next morning, when Barbara came down and tried to open the kitchen door she felt it move slightly but hit something.

"Jack. JACK! Get down here, we have a problem."

Jack hurried down the stairs and tried to push the door open but it wouldn't move. He barged the door and it burst open as the table and chairs were forced across the tiled floor. Jack looked at them astonished that they had somehow been pushed up against the door.

That was the last straw and Jack took his motorbike into town to see Dreyer, determined that the table and chairs would not spend another day in their cottage.

Arnold Dreyer was a little puzzled and drove over in his van following Jack. After much haggling over the price, he loaded up the chairs and table into his van and left the couple with a little less money than they had hoped for.

That afternoon Jack and Barbara drove into Lincoln, purchased a basic kitchen dining table and a set of four simple looking, quite plain, chairs and set them up in the kitchen. They fitted surprisingly well with the décor and that made Jack feel a little better but it still cut deep that a cherished family heirloom had been lost, probably forever.

Over the coming months and years, life settled down to normality, Jenny blossomed into a fine young girl and of all people fell for Arnold Dreyer's son, Richard. Little did either know how fate would treat them.

Meanwhile, the haunting of Wolds View Cottage became but a distant memory…

James and the Air of Tragedy

Part III

Unravelling the truth of 1944

17: An interesting development

"So, it's our fault, we've disturbed the cottage and brought back the table and chairs and it's enabled your grandfather to return. But why stay and haunt us? What have we done to deserve his attention?"

Sally sat in their living room on the sofa as she tickled Scruff under his right ear, much to his delight.

James sat across from her deep in thought.

"From what I have learned over the last few years, the reason Jenny was haunting this place was she didn't understand what had happened and that her body had not been found. So her soul, for want of a better word, was restless and wandered, going over and over her last moments. It wasn't until I passed the cottage that something clicked and gave her hope that someone was close enough to find out the truth.

With servant Annie and Master George at the manor, neither could find peace until their bodies were also found, properly laid to rest and their murders uncovered," he added.

"And of course, that's what happened to Helen and Craig, Helen was connected to you and so she appealed to you to find her body and again, be laid to rest properly," Sally offered thoughtfully.

"The original lord of the De Grasceby Manor and his family were murdered, buried in the cellar, but they were so far off the beaten track that it was almost sheer luck we found them and again, helped lay them to rest."

Sally indicted to the wine cabinet. James nodded and continued with his train of thought.

"Yes, I think we need to know something else about him after hearing what Jenny had to say. No wonder she doesn't appear here anymore, she's afraid of her grandfather. That's a real shame. I don't think he understands or accepts that I am his grandson, but then again, the age difference is so great I'm not really surprised."

Sally poured two glasses of white wine and brought one over for James who took it eagerly.

"Then surely there are three parts to this puzzle. One, we need to find out what he did that was so awful his own family turned against him. Two, we have to find out if there was a mistake and he is innocent or not."

"And three?"

"Three, we need to find out where he is buried." she replied.

"That's a good point, if he committed suicide then he probably wouldn't get a Christian burial, would he?"

"No, but he has to be buried somewhere. I think you should check with Reverend Cossant and ask what would likely to have been done with his body under such circumstances."

"Great idea, love. Anyhow, a certain doggie looks like he wants to go out, so I'll just take him out for a short walk before we go to bed. I'll give Sarah a call in the morning and see if I can meet up with her again."

Sally looked deep in thought. "You know, if it comes to it, we could always sell the table and chai.."

She didn't get a chance to finish as the usual offending chair suddenly was hurtled across the kitchen making both of them jump out of their skins and Scruff to bark angrily at one side of the table.

James recovered but was having none of it.

"Hey, Granddad! Listen up. We'll not sell them, but you can cut that antic out for a start! We'll do what we can to help you but stop disturbing us for the time being. If you know where you are buried then guide me to it in the morning, OK?"

Silence, then slowly the chair lifted up onto its feet and slowly moved back and settled under the table, neat and tidy. They both watched in silence with mouths open in astonishment and listened for anything else, but Scruff stopped barking and went through to the front door expecting to be taken out.

"You OK?" asked James as Sally looked at him somewhat ashen faced.

"Yes, but that was pretty frightening. I've only ever seen that in horror movies."

"I think the message got through. I'll let Scruff into the back garden to do his business then let's get to bed. The sooner we get to the bottom of this the better."

They both looked about the kitchen but nothing stirred so, taking their empty glasses and putting them in the sink, Sally followed James out, then up to their room as James called for Scruff to go to the back door.

It was to be a sleepless night ahead for them both, thinking about what had happened over the last twenty-four hours.

\#

Surprisingly the kitchen was undisturbed when they came down, much to their relief. Sally picked up her work briefcase, looking very smart and official.

"Shame I have to be out all day but I've got to call in to Horncastle Police Station and pick up several outstanding case notes then go to HQ, so when I fill up with fuel I'll grab a sandwich to keep me going until tonight. What are you going to do, give Sarah a call?"

James looked at the chair, still in its rightful place parked under the table.

"Yes, I think I'll give her a call and see if I can meet up with her at the rectory. I'll sort out food and water for Scruff, take him out first and try not to be too long away."

"OK, love, see you later." she gave him a quick kiss on the cheek and headed out as James took another sip from his coffee. Scruff had heard his name and had come into the kitchen to sit next to James right leg, looking up at him with the eyes that said 'walkies'.

"You're persuasive aren't you!" so James got up and took him for his walk. For once Scruff didn't want to go the direction of the airbase, instead they did a short walk roughly in the direction of the village.

Or so they thought.

They didn't get far as they reached a spot James recognised and Jenny appeared to them, indicating to take the field path towards the woods again. Scruff didn't seem at all fazed by her and she smiled at Scruff who just cocked his head from one side to the other as if trying to figure out why he could see through her.

"He's a nice doggie. I always wanted one but Daddy wasn't keen and Mummy felt pets were too much work. He can see me too but doesn't seem bothered by my presence."

"Well dear sister, Scruff probably can sense that we're OK but he does bark if Granddad is about. In fact last night we let it slip we might sell the table and chairs and his chair was thrown across the kitchen. I had to read him the riot act! It was quite something to see the chair carefully put back in its place, neat and tidy."

"I wonder if because he was in the RAF, he appreciated a commanding tone? The last time I saw him at the tree when I was very young, Mummy did the same in a very loud voice and after that once the table and chairs were out of the house he didn't come back. Not until you brought them back into the cottage."

"True, but the odd thing is that Sally saw him before we bought them so there has to be something else that drew him back."

"If I remember right … have you dug anywhere near the back of the garden, towards the right hand field?"

"Err, yes, I think so, when we were putting in the brick wall for our boundary. Oh heck…"

"You found a tin with things in it?" Jenny asked, leading James expectantly.

"It had medals and a..."

"Teddy bear! King Teddy, that's what I always called him. He was granddads originally then handed down to our father who passed it on to me. We had a reverend do something odd in the house, sprinkling water about and saying strange prayers.

He asked Mum and Dad to collect together anything that was connected to Granddad and the main items were his medals and the teddy that had been given to me. Our father buried them thinking no one would dig so close to the boundary. You found them?"

"Yes, that explains it as we found them several months before we bought the table and chairs and Sally admitted she'd been seeing his ghost before we got the kitchen furniture. So had I and come to think of it, it was after we'd found the tin. It's put away for the time being until I had time to research into what the medals were for."

"There is also another possible connection."

"What?"

"Not what, *you*?" suggested Jenny as they passed into the woods. Once again they were obscured enough so that it wouldn't look like James was talking to himself to anyone driving along the road.

"I don't understand, he never knew me."

"Perhaps he doesn't need to know it consciously as you are family. Now you live in the cottage and are there all the time he was drawn back to a 'new' member of the family."

James nodded as he thought about this. "Yes, that's a good point and may be right. Guess we won't know the real reason but it all does seem to make sense. You don't happen to know where he is buried?"

"No," she replied looking sad. "I was too young and I can't remember Mummy and Daddy mentioning his funeral."

"They wouldn't as he wouldn't get a normal Christian burial because of committing suicide. But he has to be buried somewhere."

"Our parents spirits won't get involved and even I am not happy that for some reason I am still here, perhaps it is because he visited me on several occasions when I was little and so that's my link to him?"

"Well, I had best get this little chappie back to the cottage and fed and watered so I'll leave you for now Sis and if somehow you do find out any more then you know where to find me."

"Sorry, but not at the cottage," she replied solemnly.

"Understood. Bye for now. Come on Scruff, let's get you back."

With that James and Scruff walked back along the path towards the road as Jenny faded from view.

#

"Good to see you again James." Reverend Sarah Cossant sat in her chair as James took a sip of the cup of tea she had offered him. He glanced around, admiring the main living room of the rectory and wondered how old the building was.

"Good to see you too. It's quite a place you have here, I'm guessing it must have come much later after the second manor was built?"

"Perhaps, but I'm not much of an historian so couldn't tell you. I am just the current caretaker here but it is a pleasant place to be in, trust me I've been sent to worse places before coming to Grasceby, I can tell you."

"I have some news for you," James said as he put his cup down. "I now know that the ghost Sally and I have been seeing is of the grandfather I never knew. I assume he has to be a Portisham but don't yet know for sure. Perhaps you have had some success?"

"I can tell you that name is no surprise to me. I was going to give you a call but you beat me to it. I found several old diaries and one, by the Reverend Samuel Stoneham will be of particular interest to you."

She stood, went over to a small cabinet on top of which lay a small booklet which she picked up, then brought it over and sat down. Sarah leafed through it until she found the small bookmark she had put in and smiled.

"There is a paragraph here, dated to late spring of 1949. This is what it says:

'I had the unusual request to attend to the Portishams of Wolds View Cottage on the outskirts of the village of Grasceby. They had an urgent request for me to perform an exorcism on a troubling spirit that they were worried could have an ungodly influence on their young daughter, Jennifer. She, being almost five and a half, was susceptible to the evil presence in the cottage. Mr Jack Portisham and his wife, Barbara, explained that Jack's father, Edward Portisham, had begun visitations to Jennifer earlier that year and had led the impressionable youngster to the site where he apparently committed suicide, a sin in the eyes of our Lord. He also acted in what can best be described as poltergeist behaviour with the moving of a particular chair without warning or reason.

Having entered the cottage I was immediately struck with a strong feeling of a presence not of this world and so I performed the exorcism and noted that there was a strong connection with one and possibly all, of the kitchen dining chairs. I recommended they be removed from the property to fully exorcise the malevolent presence.'"

Sarah paused, looked at James who was fascinated by the account, then she continued. "There is a footnote to this entry: 'I am delighted to report that the Portishams did indeed sell the afflicted kitchen dining chairs and table and that there have been no more sightings or activity of a poltergeist nature since I preformed the exorcism. Young Jennifer appears to be non for the worse for wear and no longer sees her grandfather.'

That is all he writes as Reverend Stoneham soon left due to retirement. Sadly he passed away about ten years ago so we can't talk to him about the exorcism, but it seems clear to me that it was indeed your grandfather and that for some reason he haunted young Jennifer until her parents, err, your parents, brought in Reverend Stoneham."

"And they of course took his advice and sold the offending kitchen dining set. So without Sally or I realising we helped bring this onto ourselves. Do you have any clues as to where he might have been buried?" James asked as he shuffled in his seat.

"Not directly. The Church views suicide as an affront to God and so for several centuries, such people were buried close to or at the side of crossroads as they could not be buried on consecrated ground. They also had a stake pushed through their heart, the idea was supposedly to pin them to the location to prevent them wandering or even trying to get to heaven. That's why so many crossroads have stories of wandering spirits unable to pass on.

However, in 1820 a law was passed stopping such bodies being buried at crossroads and so the Church had to find somewhere to bury them that did not constitute acceptance of suicide. You often found such burials took place in a forlorn corner of the churchyard, as far away as possible from the actual church and normal graveyard.

It is possible he is buried somewhere in the Grasceby churchyard but it may not be a marked grave, so hard to find."

"Gosh, it would be a shame if we can't find the actual site. Do you mind if I take a look?"

"Not at all. Indeed if you don't mind if we go now then I would like to accompany you. This is an interesting case to me too and I'd like to see if we can resolve it."

Sarah motioned to James and they stood as she lead the way out to the porch, grabbed her coat and handed James his, then they headed out along the path around to Grasceby Church.

#

James smiled as they walked round in silence and he spotted a familiar figure ahead of them, almost leading the way. Mr Shabernackles had once again escaped mistress Heather's clutches. Once he'd spotted the man called James who had helped free him of the ghostly cat, he felt an urge to keep ahead of James and the lady who was always, it seemed, dressed in a large dark gown with a white frill.

Something took Mr Shabernackles off the main path amongst the gravestones and memorials that had been erected over time and he realised he was close to his usual sunny spot where he liked to lie down and sleep.

James and Sarah followed the main pathway until Mr Shabernackles turned, noticed they were not following him and he gave a little meow. James was curious.

"You know, that's Lord Grasceby's daughter's cat, Mr Shabernackles, it may seem odd but I think he wants us to follow him."

"Oh Mr Hansone, you are always full of surprises, a cat now leading us to the burial site? Come now, I've seen the cat often and he has a nice quiet spot where he lies out sunning himself and I really think that's what he's up to, don't you?"

"If you say so, but it is interesting he's taking us away from the main graves and off towards the fencing towards the back of the graveyard. Didn't you say that is the sort of place where they would bury someone who has committed suicide?"

Sarah just shrugged but James stepped between the graves, carefully avoiding treading on them and Mr Shabernackles continued on his way. Sarah looked on and shook her head but followed.

Sure enough Mr Shabernackles came to a halt close to the rough fencing that had seen better days and James noticed there were signs a little further on of stonework, a wall that had long fallen into disrepair. The cat stretched a couple of times before settling down but not before giving James a stare making him feel a chill pass over him.

He looked about as the reverend joined him, looking a little smug that there was no clear signs of any sort of burial and James had to admit there was every chance Edward had probably been buried elsewhere. Perhaps they would never know the actual location. He turned to go as Sarah began to walk back the way they had come when a soft voice spoke quietly in James' right ear.

"He's here…" whispered Jenny but she remained invisible.

James turned around and there, only a foot or so away from an annoyed looking Mr Shabernackles, stood Edward.

He looked sad, nodded then faded from view as the cat hissed at where Edward had been standing. Sarah, who had not seen Edward, looked questioningly at James, then at the cat, then back to James.

"That's the spot, he's just appeared to me. Mr Shabernackles must have known somehow," James said in a quiet tone of voice as both he and the reverend walked over to the spot and began to examine it. Mr Shabernackles, quite annoyed, stood up and walked away briskly, his afternoon nap having been so rudely interrupted.

18: A close call…

"Oh my god, really?" Sally was stunned at what James had just recounted.

"Yep, the grave had a thin layer of soil and that rough grass that always seems to get everywhere, but once brushed aside it has a small slab that covers where he was laid to rest. There would have been no prayers and according to Sarah there was little likelihood of anyone attending it. There is a faint set of letters that look like his name and that's all. How sad is that?"

James sat on the same chair that always moved and without thinking he shuffled it slightly so it was at a slight angle and he could face Sally better. She noted the irony of it and looked thoughtful for a moment.

"So, one of our three questions is now solved, but it still means we have no idea what he did and if it was a mistake and he was innocent."

James nodded. "I feel I need to 'get inside' the mindset of such a person, he must have flown on the Lancasters that operated out of RAF Grasceby. I wonder if Mike at the haulage firm will let me put on the airman's kit that's at the museum?"

"You'll be lucky, there can't be many examples in that good a condition left. I'd really be surprised if he let you." she looked him up and down and smiled wryly. "Not sure if you'd fit anyway!"

"Cheeky devil, you haven't even seen it."

"Yes I have, don't forget that I had a case there a while back so got to see the museum in person without visitors hanging around. Still, worth going back there tomorrow. I can't as I'm seeing the Chief in the morning. I might have more news on if I'm part of the selected ones to be either made redundant or can take early retirement."

"Oh heck, which one would you prefer?"

"Neither…" Sally said, her face saddened by both prospects. James stood up and went round, gave her a hug and whispered in her ear.

"Think of it like this, you'll be seeing more of me, whatever happens."

She gave him a smirk and cocked her head to one side.

"And that's a good thing?" she cheekily asked but then relented. "Yeah, I can help you more with your investigations, you might do better then with the help of a pro."

"No comment." he replied as Scruff wandered into the kitchen wondering why he hadn't been taken for his bedtime walk yet.

"OK, Scruff, hint taken." Sally smiled and went out into the hallway to fetch his lead.

Next morning, James woke up and realised he'd slept through Sally's alarm. She wasn't in bed but he could just hear her on her phone somewhere downstairs.

It didn't sound like the conversation was going well so he quickly got up, dressed and headed down not sure of what he'd find.

Sally wasn't actually dressed but still in her nightie and dressing gown. She held her hand up as James came in to the kitchen and he took the hint to stay quiet. Scruff just kept looking back and forth at each of them wondering if he was being taken out or fed. It didn't matter that it was a little early, he didn't mind being taken out or fed at any time.

Sally tapped to end the call then looked at James quizzically.

"Err, well, what's happened?" he asked as he sat in what was becoming his favourite chair and pulled it slightly out to one side. Sally noticed and chuckled a little.

"You do realise you are now sitting in *that* chair and doing the same as your grandfather used to do?"

James looked at her surprised then looked down at the chair and shrugged. "I had no idea!"

"Anyway, seems the Chief is off with this flu virus thing that's going around so meeting is cancelled this morning. The good news is I'm taking the day off in lieu of the Lincoln Princess time owing so you've got me with you today, isn't that fun for you!" she made a funny face and James had to laugh.

"Well now, I'll have to put that detective expertise to good use then. But first, we can have a lie in then, fancy going back up to bed?"

"Well I would, but looks like someone else has other ideas," she said as she nodded towards the kitchen door where Scruff sat wagging his tail excitedly.

"Typical, thanks Scruff!" James' shoulders slumped and he walked to the kitchen surface to put the kettle on. "But first I need a wake up coffee!"

"Me too, make it strong as well, not weak like last night, I reckon you only put a few granules of coffee in the cup!"

"Ahh, didn't want to keep you awake all night dearest!" he quipped and dropped four slices of bread in the toaster much to Sally's approval.

Scruff just looked at them then turned and walked to his basket, turned around several times then settled down, resigned to not going out.

Fifteen minutes later he got his wish when James drew the short straw and in the light rain took Scruff up the road. As it began to fall more heavily they were soon back at the cottage, somewhat soaked after what for once was an unsurprising walk.

The rain abated and the sky began to break up into scattered clouds with a few decent blue sky breaks so Sally, James and Scruff all went out, but this time with a purpose. James had Scruff's lead in hand as Sally spotted a white butterfly and began to chase it with her smartphone at the ready to photograph it. She exclaimed at her success, looking at her pics.

"Wood White, haven't seen one for a while so good to see it back," she proudly said as James just nodded and Scruff tugged at the lead. For once there was no sign of James' grandfather and they carried on along the roadside verge instead of taking the shortcut through the woods until they reached the official entrance to the Grasceby Industrial estate and a sign stating that Arthur and Sons operated from there.

The public gate was open at the side of the main gates for larger vehicles with a sign saying the museum was open until 4pm during the weekdays, for visitors to keep to the prescribed path and to watch out for haulage vehicles.

"I'm pleased to see they appear to be busy, I thought there was a chance they could have been taken over by now by one of the larger national firms," said Sally as they walked along the path.

"Well, it must be difficult keeping costs down. I wonder if the visitors to the museum help financially?" offered James as they approached the door to the old control complex. It opened on Greg standing in the doorway smiling at their approach.

"Hello there James, Sally, I see your doggie has dragged you out here again, or is it a certain other person that's brought you here?"

"Not him this time but I'd like another look in the museum if I can, plus I'd like to ask Mike a favour too if he's in," replied James as Scruff looked around and without any of them noticing, spotted the airman in the distance watching them.

They all shook hands as Greg motioned for them to enter and he indicted to the seated Sandra to provide two tickets for the museum.

Sandra looked at Scruff then broke into a smile.

"Ohh, he's gorgeous, I'll get him a bowl and some water if you want. What's his name?"

"Scruff," both James and Sally chimed together.

"Aww, fancy calling you that, you don't look scruffy to me you handsome little boy." Sandra started fussing Scruff who loved the attention. Greg left them for a moment as James and Sally took the proffered tickets from Sandra and they headed along the corridor to the museum with Scruff in tow. Meanwhile, Greg knocked and then entered Mike's office.

A few moments later both men joined them as James stood looking at the airman's flight uniform. Sally looked him up and down as she considered whether or not James would fit into it. Mike shook their hands warmly.

"So James, any news?"

"Yes, it would seem the ghost is of my grandfather who died in the nearby woods between here and the cottage."

Mike was interested but a little perplexed.

"Well, that seems to fit with the route he always seems to take, but I'm puzzled, I don't recall any mention of a person by the name of 'Hansone' being stationed here. I've been through the records for your surname and nothing came up."

"Ahh. They won't probably know will they love?"

Sally realised what the problem was as James nodded.

"It's a complicated story and one that I don't tell to many people but Hansone is not my original surname, or rather it was and it shouldn't have been." Mike and Greg looked confused and Sally indicated for James to explain a little more.

"You see my mother moved away from Grasceby before I was born to give us both a better life after a family tragedy in the early 60's. The sister I didn't know I had, went missing and it was only a few years ago that her case was solved, partly by me and partly by Sally and her former mentor."

"Good grief, the Portisham case?" asked Greg and Sally nodded.

"So, let me get this straight, you should actually be a Portisham?" wondered Mike as he stroked his chin.

"Yes, Jenny was my sister but she had disappeared almost a year before I was born. I never knew my father, Jack, but my mother was Barbara but she changed her first name to Mary and changed her surname officially to Hansone so when I was born I was christened James Hansone, not James Portisham."

"Well I'll be…" muttered Greg as Mike looked deep in thought, then spoke.

"Portisham, Portisham, I'm sure there is a cutting from a local newspaper about a Portisham being based here during the war who was going to be court-martialled but committed suicide before the hearing could be convened. Locally I believe. I'll see if I can find it but there are no digital records, all are paper files locked away in the bomb shelter that lies below us."

"Wow, didn't know there was a bomb shelter here!" Sally exclaimed.

"Yes, sadly used quite extensively during the war but now a good air-conditioned place for keeping the old war records safe for posterity. I'll go down now. You want to come along?" Mike offered.

"Actually, I wondered if you'd do me a favour. I want to get in the mindset of an airman such as my grandfather so for just a short time, would it be possible for me to try on that flight suit, if it fits that is." James looked quickly at Sally but she didn't make a sarcastic remark, just smiled sweetly at him, mainly to humour him, he figured.

Mike looked at Greg and they seemed to be almost in telepathic mode before Mike nodded slowly.

"It's such an unusual situation and in normal circumstances I wouldn't even consider such a request. But as long as it is a one off and you will stay nearby then I'm sure Greg will give you a hand. Mrs Hansone, Sally, do you want to come with me and we can have a bash at searching the records?"

"Yes, certainly, as long as Greg gets a picture of wingman Jamsey here for fun. Make sure we get to see you dressed up as I wouldn't want to miss it for the world. Is Scruff OK to come down with us?" she asked as Scruff looked up at them wondering what was going on and why they weren't walking outside for him to get his exercise.

"No problem, I'm sure he's well trained. Follow me then." Sally gently pulled on his lead and Scruff dutifully followed her and Mike out into the corridor where Mike fished out a set of keys to a door they had not noticed. "As a rule the public are not allowed down here but on occasions I do get enquiries from historians and sometimes students to take a look at the records. One day we might even get round to having them digitised but it would be a big job I can tell you."

"I'm sure James could help you with that as he is a whiz with computers and writes his own software and apps. I bet if you ask him nicely he'd be all too willing to help you out. Especially as you've been so helpful lately."

They headed through the door but as they did so, Scruff looked back along the corridor and for a moment almost growled as he spotted James' grandfather standing at the end of the corridor before he faded away.

Meanwhile, Greg had unlocked the glass cabinet and was trying to help James fit into the flying suit.

"To be honest James, I'm surprised Mike has let you do this and it is a tight fit. Don't go running about in it for heavens sake."

"Are you saying I'm fat, Greg?"

"I don't know you well enough to make such a personal comment. But your wife was close in her assessment!"

"Cheeky! I see there's a bit of ventilation in the left leg near the thigh. Must have seen some action then?"

"Odd that, we've always wondered about that and there was some dried blood on it too so we had a small sample sent away for DNA analysis. When we got the results back, Mike had a friend at Lincoln Police HQ check it against their databases but nothing showed up. It is a bit odd as, according to the date of manufacture it was one of the last made and shouldn't have seen action. Probably got ripped more recently as it has been used a few times in the past for filming various movies. Especially not long after the war ended.

Now listen up. This has an inbuilt heated element as the mid upper gunner and rear turret gunners were in a section of the Lancaster that was not heated. It makes it a bit more bulky than some of the others, we're pleased we've got one as there are not many surviving. This is your oxygen mask but neither device works unless plugged in to the aircraft so you may as well leave the face mask off as they wouldn't have used them on the ground."

"Well, how do I look?"

"Not bad, I have to admit. Take a stroll outside, I'll just open the fire escape for you without setting off the alarms, go round and see if you can give Sandra a scare walking past the front windows. She's a bit of a loose tongue, much as we love her, but she doesn't half like to spread gossip. Let's see what she says when a World War Two airman walks past the window!"

"Ahh a sneaky side to you then Greg, right ho, off we jolly well go."

Greg looked at him and shook his head. "They only said that in the movies, James!"

"Oh. Thought I was getting into the spirit of things. See you in a minute."

James walked out the emergency exit and turned left, walked around following the wall until he was close to the front. Then he decided to stroll out a few feet towards where the runway had been, based on what he remembered from his strange encounter with the past a week or so earlier.

Up ahead he suddenly became aware of his grandfather standing over towards the entrance to the path through the woods and he was shocked to see the ghost suddenly wave at him. He turned to look back but felt giddy and closed his eyes for a moment, wondering if the belt was too tight. Then he felt a rush of wind and someone was shouting at him frantically.

He opened them and stood stock still in shock.

The Lancaster had to be just thirty feet from him and an airman was frantically shouting at him.

"Hey, you, yes you man, we're a flight crew down, get here immediately, that's an order."
James stood in shock. The man shouting was his grandfather and he was back in wartime Grasceby.

19: The raid

"For heaven's sake man, don't just stand there, get over here and get in." shouted Edward in frustration.

James stumbled forward not knowing what to think or say as the officer climbed aboard the Lancaster and offered his hand to James. As James was bundled into the airframe Edward shouted forward.

"We're good to go," he turned back to James and looked a little oddly at him. "Do I know you?"

It caught James by surprise and left him a little lost for words. He was still taking in that he seemed to be aboard an actual Lancaster bomber that was now taxiing along a slipway and he felt a surge of terror as he realised they were going to take off.

"Listen, what's your name, sorry to have to have pulled rank on you but our mid turret gunner 'Bondy' broke his leg only half an hour ago and we almost had to stay behind and we can't have that. Where's your name tag?"

James had to think fast despite his growing fear.

"Name, err, Mike, Mike Barracks. I've somehow lost it sir."

"Very well, I can sort a temporary one for you once we're airborne. Good, now Mike, get up into the mid upper turret, make sure you have your radio switched on and check out the gun in case any of the ground crew have screwed up. Not that they're likely too knowing our lives are at stake. Got that?"

"Err, yes sir. Wilco!" James said lamely as Edward looked at him oddly and shook his head.

The Lancaster reached the end of the runway, turned around and lined up along with the last few Lancasters getting ready for the raid. The engine noise was almost unbearable as suddenly all four Merlin engines roared into life. The Lancaster raced down the runway and James heart felt like it launched into his mouth as they took off.

The radio buzzed as James watched them climb above the clouds. Far off in the distance he could see Lincoln Cathedral as they turned and headed off towards the coast. He thought back to what he'd read online about the Lancaster and its gun turrets but reading was one thing, actually sitting there with the controls in his hand was another. For a brief moment he remembered a scene from a sci fi movie where a newbie in his situation was put in charge of a space gun, and the words 'they're coming in too fast' played through his mind. He was brought back to reality as the radio came to life.

"Right chaps, let's get the job done and get back in one piece eh? Oxygen masks on and radio silence from now on unless we hit any bother." James assumed it was the pilot and he wasn't sure, as they climbed higher if his bowels would hold out due to the overwhelming sense of impending doom. That and how he could be on board an active duty Avro Lancaster heading out on a sortie over occupied Europe. The radio fell silent and there he was, in the mid upper turret of a Lancaster crossing the coastline and heading into occupied territory as they joined up with an uncountable number of other Lancasters and what appeared to be a few other types of plane he was not familiar with. High up he thought he saw smaller aircraft on patrol, protecting them and he wondered if they were Spitfires and Hurricanes which gave him a little reassurance. It was one thing to watch a movie from the comfort of a cinema seat or from home but this was surreal and James kept pinching himself to make sure he was not hallucinating.

Suddenly underneath him came a voice.

"You OK up there Barracks?"

It sounded like Edward's voice but it was difficult to tell over the sound of the engines throbbing away.

"Yes Sir. Will we be away for long?" James knew it was probably a lame thing to ask and braced himself for the jocular onslaught.

"OPS reckon about eight or nine hours tops. That's assuming we get back of course. Hang in there old chap, this OP is a biggie! Here, I know it's only temporary but it's the best I can do for now. Pin it on with this and hope it stays on." Edward handed up a small fabric rectangle and it had a very rough stitched text saying 'BARRACKS M'.

James was about to ask something else but realised he was now on his own as Edward quickly dropped out of sight. He struggled to think back to his own research about Lancaster flights and dearly wished now he had managed to get over to the East Kirkby Aviation Centre. He remembered Harriet had said that they did taxi runs in their Lancaster and he now wished he'd done one before this happened.

Something caught his eye as the evening twilight deepened and he turned to face roughly behind, which he assumed had to be looking westwards. There was a bright-ish star above the horizon with a fainter one to its lower right. Thinking back to his old school and former work friend and boss, Mark, who was an amateur astronomer and often spoke about when bright planets could be seen. James figured the bright star had to be Venus. Perhaps the other was Mercury, he wondered as he looked around. East had to be roughly ahead of him towards the front of the aircraft which made sense if they were flying into occupied Europe. Off to his right the moon was rising looking as if it was almost a full moon, a dull reddish colour whilst it was still low down, just above the horizon.

"Guess that explains why they're flying tonight, moonlight would surely help..." He shivered and realised there was no heating. That was what he was going to ask earlier but had stopped in time. He remembered the mid upper gunner turret and rear gunner turret were in the unheated section of the aircraft.

Trust his luck!

He pulled back his aircrew jacket sleeve and looked at his watch then realised it bore no resemblance to the time or date in the Lancaster. A thought struck him and he went to fish out his smartphone but then realised he was in the aircrew trousers and the phone was back at the museum in his own trouser pocket. His heart sank.

It was lonely where he was and he thought about all the men who had done this and lost their lives defending the freedom of their loved ones back home from the tyranny that was right wing fascism. The world had pulled through then, but he wondered if it could recover in the so called modern information age where so much false information and pseudo science seemed to dominate modern era social media. He spotted brief flashes from below and shivered as he realised they were searchlights being turned on and upwards briefly catching a few planes in the light. Tracer fire raced up from the ground and way off to his left a ball of flame erupted as, in the near darkness now, a Lancaster and its crew perished. Sadly, he knew it would likely be one of many.

He was shivering now and knew that he should have done something with his suit but Greg had not shown him much about it. For heavens sake he had only been trying it on to see what it was like. He hadn't expected to literally be thrown back in time to experience things first hand.

Noise from below and Edward again appeared, frowned and shook his head.

"You're suit playing up? You look like death warmed over!" he looked about James' person then shook his head and spoke with an angry but muted tone. "What are you up to, do you want to die of exposure?" he plugged something in and suddenly James felt parts of his body slowly revive as the suit's heaters began to work.

"Who the hell trained you Barracks, that was stupid to say the least. If you'd left it like that you'd be dead before we got to our target, let alone getting back."

"Sir, I'm, I'm not really air crew…"

Edward stared at him aghast.

"I was asked to wear the flight suit to check it out but then you saw me and I didn't have much choice. I've never flown in a Lanc' before…" James admitted and Edward looked down shaking his head in shock then looked back up at him.

"You poor sod. My fault I guess. Should have checked but there was so little time. You warming up now?"

"Yes sir."

"Good. Do your best. I'll not tell the others for now but do what you can. Your country needs you and we don't have the luxury of giving you flying lessons or gunnery practise. It's for real so don't let me down."

"Yes sir, I'll try my best."

Edward dropped out of sight and James sat looking out as more stars appeared.

He felt all alone.

More intense tracer fire lit up the sky then the radio bust into life.

"Heads up, incoming trouble, looks like the Luftwaffe have woken up. Look sharp lads. Newbie in the mid upper turret, keep 'em peeled."

James found the controls and moved the turret around just as he realised fire was shooting out from the rear gunner and he looked to where it was aimed. But things were moving too quick for him and something dark shot past before he had time to react.

He scanned around and something caught his eye. He aimed the sights, remembering the odd computer game he's played many years earlier and pulled the trigger.

The sheer violence of the gun caught him by surprise but he held on and tried to follow the shape, disappointed he couldn't keep up with it. The front gunner took over and suddenly a ball of fire erupted ahead and a cheer went up from the cockpit that even James could hear over the noise of the engines.

Several more bright balls of fire erupted on both sides but his heart broke when he realised they were Lancasters and not Messerschmitt Bf 109s. The radio spluttered into life again.

"Keep your eye on the ball lads, we're on the final run, keep them off our backs and lets get the job done. Ackers, you're in charge now."

James had no idea what that last bit meant, he had to trust that whatever it was, 'Ackers' was doing it as the Lancaster seemed to slightly change course. James realised it was probably the navigator and bomb aimer who was relaying instructions to the pilot.

There was a lurch from somewhere below and the Lancaster lifted slightly as if it had shed weight and James knew their bomb load had been dropped.

A shout came from below but not aimed at him this time.

"Skipper, something's wrong."

James recognised it as Edwards voice and it was fraught. The radio came alive again.

"Chaps, we're not as light as we should be, Teddy reckons we've still got about a third of the buggers still on board!"

There was silence for a few moments as more fire from below raced up to catch them out and the right hand wingtip was blown off, losing around two feet. The aircraft shuddered but the pilot was a veteran and stabilised the plane after a short while. Then James realised they were banking round and for a moment he thought they'd bought it but the

Lanc completed its turn, though James could now see stars he was completely disorientated in the turret.

He had no idea how long it had taken them as he'd not even looked at his watch at the start. When he had done so during the flight he'd figured it was at least three or four hours into the mission, but he couldn't remember what time it said, as it was out of sync with his reality.

He listened to the roar of the engines as he spotted dark shapes against the light sky. He suspected it had to be summer time, maybe June or July. A couple of Lancasters joined up back in formation with them again but their numbers were seriously depleted attesting to the danger of the mission.

Suddenly more searchlights hit them and ack ack fire erupted from below. The ground fire abruptly stopped and then he realised why. Several German fighters came up from underneath and sprayed the formation with gunfire. As one shot past, instinctively James tracked and opened fire and it erupted into a fireball.

"Gottacha!"

Suddenly he heard another commotion and everything seemed to happen at once. The Lancaster was again strafed and suddenly the radio coms went haywire, then dead. A searing pain shot through his thigh and one of the turret panes of glass was blown out as James grabbed his thigh and held back the tears. He could hear shouts from below and what seemed to be from the front, which didn't bode well and the Lancaster swerved a little before settling down.

He saw one of the remaining Lancasters off to his right catch fire with an engine ablaze but valiantly it carried on. Gradually they fanned out as the skies slowly began to brighten but he could tell they were still over mainland Europe and so over enemy territory. The other Lancasters had to be from different airbases as they changed course and slowly shrank into the distance before vanishing.

They were now alone and a disturbance from below brought his attention back to reality as he gritted his teeth against the surge of pain. Edward pushed up from below.

"Bad news, Chappers, our pilot, says one of the engines is losing oil and we're likely to lose it shortly. Worse is the bomb bay. It's difficult to tell but seems like we may have up to a third of our load still on board. What's more I've managed to use a mirror and think that several of the incendiary devices are hanging just out of the fuselage and we can't close the doors for fear of setting them off. If we can get across the Wash and do a wide circle most of us are to parachute out and Chappers is going to try to bring it in but we all think he's bonkers as it's likely to explode on landing.

Our nav and wireless chaps have bought it and we can't raise Jackers in the rear turret so we think he's bought it too. Chappers was also hit in the arm by shrapnel but he can still fly the old bird so we're in the lap of the gods now.

We've got about an hour yet before we have to make a decision so I'll keep you informed. If we make it of course, without another surprise like that. Oh, looks like you've caught something too. Hold on, I'll see what I can find to stem the blood, doesn't look too bad so probably a flesh wound. Hang in there Barracks."

Edward disappeared but was back a few minutes later and James felt his leg being tied up with something but he had no clue as to what.

"There, best I can do. Hang in there and we'll make it, haven't failed yet and I don't intend to start now."

Edward disappeared again and James couldn't help but wonder how on earth he could have done something so bad that his own family would disown him. From what he'd seen so far Edward was an exceptional person and dedicated to his crew.

He wasn't sure how long it was but all he knew was that a while later they were crossing the coast and the sky was getting lighter by the minute. He was still chilled to the bone and felt the first signs of a cold developing as it seemed with the last attack the heating had packed in. How would he explain all this when, *if*, he survived and got back to his own time? He'd only had brief time slips before and indeed often wondered if he'd imagined them, but this was going to be hard to explain away.

There was a change to the engine sound and as he listened carefully, the only thing that he could think of was another engine had failed. He couldn't help but wonder what else could go wrong when a single engine fighter drew up from below and flew parallel alongside the stricken Lancaster off to his right. He smiled then saw the swastika and he felt ice cold with fear. It was a Focke-Wulf 190.

#

The pilot radioed his colleague, "Ja, ich nehme das eine und du fängst das andere, (Yes, I take one and you catch the other)."

He caught up with the stricken Lancaster from below but as he approached, he noted they'd already lost an engine and a second now had smoke drifting out from a nacelle. He was about to open fire when he noticed the bomb bay doors were still open and intrigued, he flew up closer. He knew they had no rear turret as it had been blasted to smithereens so as long as he stayed below them they would have no idea he was there. He was strangely fascinated as he closed in and then spotted several bombs hanging loosely still attached to the stricken aircraft.

They were doomed anyway. There was no way they could land with those hanging down, they'd detonate as soon as they touched down because they would touch the ground first.

The pilot actually felt sorry for them. Did he finish them off or give them a fighting chance of getting back, perhaps not all in one piece? He was aware that the notorious RAF had indeed spared a few German bombers in similar situations, knowing full well they would likely not survive the landing and he hesitated. They were after all human beings, but it was a difficult decision for him to make.

He slowly flew up and to the starboard side of the Lancaster drawing level with the cockpit, catching Chappers attention. Fredericks in the front turret immediately swung round but abruptly stopped with the guns lowered, as the German pilot was canny and held back just far enough that the turret couldn't sight on him. He was however in full view of the upper turret. He saw it move round and the guns aim straight at him.

But they didn't fire.

The German indicted to them as best he could that there were bombs hanging down below them from the bomb bay and his efforts of trying to show them landing and exploding met with a little mirth from the Lancasters remaining crew. Chappers and Edward however got the message and knew it was confirmation of their worst fears.

James watched all this fascinated and couldn't help thinking of the World War One Christmas truce when both sides engaged in a game of football, only the next day to blast each other to bits. He noted the serial number on the tail fin and something in German on the front fuselage which he couldn't quite read.

Then the FW190 peeled away and headed off behind them back to Europe.

They were stunned.

He had spared them.

But the question remained, would they be able to land…

Another half hour or so it seemed to pass and James heard something from below. Edward again appeared below him, ashen faced.

"I knew something was wrong up front when Fredericks didn't get fully turned. He must have been hit and didn't realise how bad it was, looks like he bled out. There's just us two and Chappers left. Another thing, shrapnel has torn through my parachute and it looks like yours is no good either so I've got to come up with a plan for us to get out safely. Chappers is in a bad way but can still fly, he, he …

…he'll not make it, but is going to try to fly as low over our base as he can without hopefully setting off the bombs and we're to jump for it and hope for the best. He reckons another ten minutes until we reach Grasceby so unplug and get down here with me so we can do whatever we can to prepare.

Barracks, I'm sorry I dragged you into this. If I'd have known you weren't aircrew then it's likely we'd have had to sit the mission out and our mates would still be alive."

"But Mr Portisham, it's worse than that I'm no.."

Edward was looking at James oddly. "How did you know my surname? I never mentioned it once since we met… My badge is on my jacket that's been hung up since we left."

"That's what I'm trying to say. I'm your grandson, James and I'm from your future ..." James knew it was risky but surely he had to warn his grandfather?

Edward dropped out of sight and James did as he was told, wriggling his way down into the main fuselage. Edward was looking at him warily as they felt the Lancaster lurch a little and a voice shouted back to them.

"Chaps, we're almost there. I'm going to bank round slowly so as not to jostle those bombs and line up not quite on the runway, just to the side, parallel, so you fall onto the grassed section. I'll do another fly round then try to come down in old man Hatcher's field to the north of the base so if it does blow up then we don't put the base out of action. Good luck.

Teddy, it's been a pleasure and an honour to fly with you. Newbie what's yer name, Barracks, yer did good, keep with Teddy and you'll go far. Now get ready I'm starting the bank."

They felt the Lancaster tilt ever so slightly to the side and Edward looked at James.

"I'll deal with you once we're down but enough nonsense for now as we're out of time." Edward didn't flinch or see the irony of mentioning time as he opened the portside hatch for it to fall away. "Now look, this is important. We're close to the tail plane as we can't use the front pilot, bomb aimer exits. So you have to drop quickly or the tail plane will slice you in half. Get down on your stomach and when I shout, shove yourself out. Don't hesitate, I'm behind you and come what may I'm getting out before Chappers has to climb to go around again so if you hesitate I'm going to push you out regardless. Got it?"

"Yes sir. If I survive, I'll not forget you. You have my word."

"Don't you worry about that as I'll be filing a report on someone impersonating an aircrew member and putting the crews lives in jeopardy.

GO! NOW!"

James fell onto his stomach, pushed himself out the hatch and fell to the ground rolling over and over onto the main runway. Edward followed suit and hit the ground hard, but his training had prepared him and he rolled to take the sting out of the fall. He looked up and watched the stricken Lancaster and his flying buddy of twenty four sorties manage to climb up and begin to turn but as he recovered from the fall Edward knew in his heart it was the end of the Lancaster.

As it began to bank round a third engine spluttered and fell silent. The Lancaster began to pivot as one wing dipped, caught a tree top and the Lancaster tipped over and came crashing down, just outside the airbase boundary. The ball of fire engulfed the plane just as Edward lost sight of it and he heard what remained of the gunnery ammunition explode as the fireball erupted into the sky with a dark billowing plume of thick smoke. Edward stood shakily up and felt a lump in his throat for his lost crew and friends.

Battered and bruised Edwards looked back towards where he figured Mike Barracks had fallen but to his shock, there was no sign of him.

Mike Barracks had vanished.

Edward collapsed just as the sound of sirens from the emergency vehicles raced towards him with a couple heading off to the site of the downed Lancaster and he passed out.

20: Back from the past…

Phil and Joe felt lucky. It had been almost a year and a half since they'd had the unusual experiences at the Grasceby archaeological site when Joe and the digger he was operating had uncovered and nearly fallen into an unknown cellar.

The fact they had also seen what could only be described as a ghostly little girl run away into the nearby woods had unsettled them so much they were almost ready to quit. But once the mystery of the original De Grasceby family had been solved things settled down. Since then, other work had come in with no paranormal events much to their relief.

Now they were contracted to dig the main trenches ready for fibre optic data cables to be laid down as exciting things were happening at the old RAF Grasceby airbase museum. Outline planning permission had been granted to create a virtual reality centre where the public could experience a realistic VR of an operational airbase and even fly in a Lancaster without ever leaving the ground. But it did require significant improvements to the site and with the nearby Grasceby Estate helping with funding, things were looking up.

Joe and Phil sat on the small seats Phil had bought for them for when they had lunch and tea breaks scoffing their sandwiches. Once again Phil's wife had provided Joe with a packed lunch too. Joe's life partner, Steve always insisted on the latest healthy food fad, which for the most part Joe actually detested although he didn't have the heart to tell him so.

Joe looked around and back towards the remaining buildings including the control tower and the last remaining runway. He smiled knowing he was helping in his own small way to get the project working.

"So is it tomorrow that Hamptons will be here to do the tunnel under the runaway?" he asked as he looked at his boss and friend, Phil.

"Yes, it'll be interesting as it's like a mini version of the one that used to be in that kids TV programme when I was a lad, Thunderbirds. It'll drive down into the ditch we've dug out and then burrow down from there. Then they'll guide it down to about ten foot, cross under the runway and emerge, hopefully, where we dug out the first part that connects to the main buildings. Should be fun to watch."

"Let's hope it meets up with our trench then!" quipped Joe. Phil smiled and nodded.

"Actually it's all state of the art tech and so far I hear they've had a one hundred percent success rate in similar situations."

Joe was impressed but still a little sceptical as he looked all around, stopping abruptly to look back again.

He stared in disbelief, not believing his eyes and grabbed Phil's arm causing him to wince in pain.

"Oi! Stop that you daft bugger what's..."

"Back there, there's a body on the runway!" shouted Joe as he stood up and began to run towards it. Phil stood up, stunned, then ran after him catching up as Joe reached what looked like an airman lying on his side, out cold.

Joe looked carefully at the airman, then gasped.

"Bloody hellfire, it's James Hansone!"

Phil whisked his phone out.

"I've got D.S. Hansone's number." He tapped the number, it rang briefly then Sally connected.

"Hey up, long time no chat Phil, what's up?"

"Sally, we're at the old airbase at Grasceby, it's James he's in a sort of airman's uniform but he's lying unconscious on the runway." Phil spotted Joe hurriedly indicating to something on James' leg. "Oh heck, his leg is bloody and there's a tourniquet on it."

"WHAT! I'm in the museum, we'll be right out."

It only took a few seconds for Greg, Mike and Sally to race out from the main building and rush over to where Phil was huddled over James trying to wake him.

"Good god, what's happened to him, he looks like he's been through a hedge backwards," Mike said as he looked on in shock. Sally was on her phone again. Then turned back to them.

"Best not to move him yet as we don't know what injuries he's got. I've called for an ambulance but they say it'll be a while. However, they have managed to get hold of a paramedic currently in Bardney and she's on her way." Sally knelt down and got as close to James as she could.

"James, James, it's Sally, love, can you hear me?"

He stirred slowly then opened his eyes but winced in pain and grabbed his leg near the thigh.

"Oh shit, that's so painful." He seemed temporarily oblivious to them all as he sat up holding his sides, then thigh, head and back to his thigh again. "Sally?" he said, wondering if it really was her voice he'd heard.

"Yes love, I'm here."

"Oh thank god for that, I thought I was going to be there forever."

"Where James? You're at the old RAF Grasceby airbase. We were visiting the museum as you wanted to wear the airman's flight gear to get the feel of what it must have been like."

"Never again. Never again," was all he could say as a vehicle with sirens came in through the entrance then turned as the driver saw them and headed in their direction. The vehicle stopped and a lady in a green paramedic uniform got out, grabbed her kit and came over as all but Sally stepped back to give her room.

"Hi Sally, didn't realise it was your James, just got an odd report of an airman injured here and couldn't for the life of me work out how, no one has flown from here in the last forty years!"

"Glad it's you Julia, don't ask as we have no idea what happened either. Mike, Greg and I were in the museum and Phil and Joe were digging away somewhere over there."

Julia quickly assessed James, asking him questions and checking various vital signs. She held her finger up and asked James to follow it with only his eyes then used a small light to look at them more closely. Finally she took a look at his thigh, much to his embarrassment as she helped him peel down the trousers to his knees. A quick look at the wound was all she needed and she indicated he could pull them back up to cover his modesty.

"Well Mr Hansone, all in all, I can't find anything broken, just a lot of bruises as if you've fallen and tumbled over from a height. The gash on your thigh is superficial and looks worse than it is so I don't think a hospital visit is really needed unless you want to be checked out at Lincoln County A&E. I'll tell you now that it's pretty busy and you'll have a long wait. I can call it in if you want but I think they'll be pretty miffed if they found nothing serious."

Sally took her gently by the arm. "Bed rest for a few days?" Julia nodded in agreement.

"Yes, a bit of antiseptic cream on that gash, it's not deep enough for stitches and will heal over in time as long as you keep it clean and covered up," Julia replied and Sally shook her hand.

"OK, thanks Julia, must catch up sometime eh, down at the Star and Crescent Moon one evening?"

"Yes, when shifts allow. See ya!" Julia walked back to her emergency vehicle and went on her way as Mike and Greg helped James to his feet.

"As they used to do in the old days, time for a debrief and get you out of that uniform," said Mike wondering why he'd let James borrow the uniform in the first place, considering the condition it seemed to be in now. He noted the fresh blood now covering the original blood stain and shook his head, wondering what could have happened in such a short space of time.

As they got inside, Sandra was holding Scruff's lead. "He's been going frantic. He must love you both very much." She looked at James, saw his discomfort and kept quiet but knew instinctively she would have some gossip to tell later down at the inn.

Phil and Joe said their goodbyes and headed back out to continue their work muttering to each other that at least they hadn't seen a ghost. The rest headed into Mike's office and sat James down on the office chair facing Mike's desk.

"So, care to tell us what happened?" asked Mike as they helped James out of the uniform, being careful in consideration of the pain he was still in from his thigh. James was only too happy to put his own clothes back on. Mike sat down in his chair opposite, Sally and Greg drew up chairs of their own and they all waited for him to speak.

"Trust me, you won't believe me and I am still trying to get to grips with it myself," James replied but Mike gave him such a look that he began to recount to them what had happened.

#

Later back at the cottage, Sally stood in the kitchen whilst James sat on his favourite chair looking glum.

"Well, that went well didn't it?" she didn't want to sound sarcastic but it came over loud and clear to James.

"Sally, you know I've told you I've had a couple of similar experiences in the past, but I can tell you this was the most frightening thing that has ever happened to me. I was *there*!"

Sally took another sip of her coffee and sat down across from him.

"You have to understand how strange and downright silly it sounds. I know you and well, I am struggling, but you saw the looks on Mike and Greg faces. I don't think you'll be allowed back there again!"

"I know, their faces told a million thoughts, all disbelief. But you have to believe me. Come on, you heard Julia, I have loads of bruises all over, how did I get them?"

"So, as Mike asked, why didn't you break something? If you'd fallen from a height then you should have done more damage."

"But Chappers got the Lancaster as low as he dared and made sure we slid out and rolled to try to avoid serious injury. It worked. Edward was a hero, although I probably shouldn't have told him I was his grandson and from the future."

"WHAT?"

"Err, yes, forgot to mention that bit. He wasn't convinced but he had noticed something familiar about me."

"If it really did happen then you know what that scientist chappie said, something about meeting your grandfather and changing history, or something like that."

"You mean Einstein and he said if you met and killed your grandparents or parents then you'd instantly cease to exist. Well I'm still here and you seem to know me - we're still married, right?"

"No, we're not married, just living together."

James froze and his face must have been a picture as Sally suddenly collapsed with guffaws of laughter.

"Seriously James, you should see your face. Of course we're married, but I can't accept the thought you have somehow travelled back in time, taken part in an air raid on Germany in a World War Two Lancaster bomber with your grandfather and he saved you. You have to admit, it is pretty far-fetched and no one would believe you."

James looked at her a little disheartened. "Well, for the first time since we met, I can honestly say that for the first time ever, you and my ex have something in common. She didn't believe me about Jenny, yet look where we are today. You've even met and spoken to her, a ghost.

I'm tired and sore all over so I'm going up to bed for a few hours if you don't mind." James got up and walked out of the room leaving Sally to ponder the events of the day. Scruff sat looking at her knowing something was wrong and he wondered if it had anything to do with the airman standing behind his mistress looking puzzled. The airman faded from view as Sally turned around and walked over to the cabinet. She needed a drink and it wasn't going to be coffee.

#

Mike and Greg stood in the museum laying out the airman's uniform as Mike contemplated the best way of cleaning it.

"Bit of a tall story, wasn't it?" he said to Greg and his friend and colleague nodded solemnly.

"I really don't know what to make of it or Mr Hansone. His wife didn't seem too enamoured of his story either but ..."

"But what?"

"Well, I examined the flight trousers and showed him the blood stain and tear."

"And?"

"Look at it. Here, and here." Greg pointed out the tear and the blood stain. "There's no change to the tear or the blood stain. They both match, *perfectly*. The blood is fresh that's all."

"Come on Greg, you've been watching too many horror shows, that's impossible, you have to be mistaken."

"I wish I was. Didn't the previous keeper have a DNA test done on the blood?"

"Yes, a few years back, but there was no match anywhere so it drew a blank."

"You may think I'm daft, but there's a private forensics expert over in Nottingham that I could send a sample of this blood to - worth a shot as this is too uncanny for my liking." Greg said, still trying to come to terms with what he was thinking and proposing.

"Go on then. But let's keep this to ourselves. You know what Sandra is like!"

Greg nodded and set to work looking for the right contact on his phone. He knew they would have to come over and do the sampling as they didn't have the technology locally, but what he'd say to them was a different matter. He hadn't mentioned the cost to Mike either but he would cross that bridge when he came to it.

#

Sally left him for over three hours and then took a coffee up as it was late evening and he'd missed having a meal. She'd just done a couple of rounds of toast but was feeling a little guilty about earlier. Indeed she was still smarting about being compared with Helen, James, ex, now of course deceased.

She carefully opened the door. "James, you awake yet love?" she called out gently and she heard him stir and turn over in their bed.

"Yes, Sal." James rolled over, flicked on his side light and sat up in bed. He screwed up his eyes, closing the lids then opened them again as the bright light briefly affected his vision. Sally came round to his side, sat carefully on the bed and offered him the coffee which he took gratefully.

"I'm sorry…" They both started to speak at the same time and then chuckled. James indicated he wanted to speak first and Sally motioned for him to go ahead.

"I shouldn't have compared you with Helen. You are nothing like each other and I'm lucky our paths crossed when they did. I'm not sure I could have coped the last few years without you beside me."

Sally took his hand. "You don't have to apologise, I was struggling with what has happened and should have reserved my comments. It's clear you've been through something awful, there was nothing at the industrial estate that could have given you bruises like those." She pointed to his partly bare arms. He lifted his PJ top and Sally shook her head in shock at all the bruises he had.

"I've had Scruff out and he's settled in so ..." She got up and walked round to her side of the bed, taking off her top then bra before removing her trousers and panties and putting her PJ's on. She slipped into bed and snuggled up to James gently, carefully putting her arms around him as she nestled her head into his chest ...

21: Revelations

James sat in his, by now, usual chair and looked towards and out of the kitchen window. You couldn't see the Lincolnshire Wolds from any of the downstairs rooms, you could make out that the nearby woods had a gentle slope to them, hinting that beyond lay higher ground, but the trees themselves hid the horizon.

Sally was at work at the Police HQ in Nettleham for the day so it was him and Scruff alone together in the cottage for the day. It was almost a week after his 'incident' as they'd taken to calling it and at last he was feeling a lot better. They'd not heard from Mike and Greg at all and James felt it would be wrong to go back to see them. He'd already looked like a fool for claiming he'd been on an air raid into Germany and clearly had lost credibility with them and to a lesser extent, Sally, which cut James deeply.

He took another sip from his, by now, lukewarm coffee and thought about putting it in the microwave to heat up. He shivered and noticed the view outside darken a little, indicating a cloud had rolled across the sun. It brightened up again but he still felt cold, indeed colder than usual and he frowned. Scruff came trotting in and sat down, looked up at him and moved his head to one side then the other. It was always funny to watch Scruff and James couldn't help be glad that Sally had suggested they adopt him after Bridget had passed away so suddenly.

James smiled and was about to call him over so he could fuss him, but then he noticed Scruff wasn't looking at him, but off slightly to one side. The voice caught him completely off guard and he turned around stunned.

"You are in my chair."

Edward Portisham stood looking at James with an air of authority about him despite being a ghostly figure. James was lost for words as he'd not heard the airman speak up until now.

"So, are you, or are you not, Mike Barracks? Are you really the grandson I never knew I had? Why the name change? Why did you disappear?" continued Edward as James stood up and proffered the chair. Edward appeared to sit down in it.

"It's pretty complicated…"

James proceeded to do his best to explain about his past, although he decided to miss out how Jenny had been killed and skipped what he could, if he felt it wasn't relevant.

"So, you really are my grandson. But I sense you are the only one alive. Why is that?" Edward was clearly able to know things were not right with the Portisham family and that the rest of the family seemed to be missing.

"Well, I didn't want to upset you as I gather you were exorcised from here and don't know fully what happened. I don't like to break it to you but, Jenny died. She was killed by her boyfriend when she was sixteen, by accident we discovered. But she has appeared to me a few times. She seems afraid of you and won't come back to the cottage now that you seem to be back."

"Jenny? Died? She was just a bairn when I last saw her!" Edward seemed shocked and almost in denial.

James explained, filling in the gaps he'd left out earlier and Edward looked sad.

"All I tried to do was get someone to listen to my side and believe me. So you called yourself Mike Barracks in a panic?

"Yes, it was the first time. The second time was when I had tried on the air crew uniform and suddenly found myself standing close to your Lancaster. You saw me and the next thing I knew I was on board and scared out of my skin. It was a terrifying experience, but you saved my life."

Edward appeared to mull this information over.

"The bomb release didn't fully work and we came back under heavy artillery fire with several bombs and incendiaries still onboard. We should have been dead. You saw the FW 190 as we crossed over Belgium? He should have shot us down, finished us off. But he didn't. Seems our luck held out. Chappers did his best although the others had bought it. Our parachutes had been hung up and were shot through so at the last minute as we flew low to the port side of the runway and at Chappers command, we rolled out of the plane."

"Yes, I know, I was there. But I must have been knocked out as when I came around, I was back in the twenty first century."

"There was a well known German scientist who fled to the United States of America before the war, Einstein, who said time travel was impossible. How did you do it?" asked Edward sceptically.

"I have no idea, it is still considered impossible, but it has happened to me a few times, always at random. I never know when it will happen and it occurs fairly rarely."

"Hmm. So when I rolled out of the Lancaster, I managed to stand up and watch it crash, Chappers didn't stand a chance. But when I looked around, you were gone and I could not convince anyone that you were real. That and the fact that something was wrong with the bomb release mechanism. The crash mangled what was left of the Lancaster so badly there was no way to tell if something was faulty at the time. The ground crew clammed up and swore there was nothing wrong with the Lancaster before we took off and I was supposed to check things over before we flew."

"So how come you didn't spot anything?"

"Watch your tone with me laddie. I didn't have time as we had two things go wrong from the start. Firstly our mid upper gunner, Bondy, broke his leg so couldn't fly, that's why when I saw you I just grabbed you for the mission and hoped for the best. Well you were in flight gear!

Secondly, our original Lancaster developed engine problems and the ground crew refused to let it fly as they were pretty adamant we wouldn't even get to France, let alone Germany. We were told the spare Lancaster was just serviced, fully loaded and ready to fly and we were allowed to take it for the mission. Stupid mistake, but can't change anything now.

So, you're the son that not even Jack knew about? It's really sad that Barbara left our home county and had you down south. A southerner of all things! I can't say I fully accepted your mother as we didn't always see eye to eye. But Jack loved her to bits and that was good enough for me.

Until of course she wouldn't listen to my side of the story and insisted I'd brought shame on the family. Of all things, it's partly your fault for vanishing. No one, but no one, saw or met you so, to the authorities, it looked like I was making it up to cover my own mistake. I was blamed for the loss of the aircrew and it was only because of my prior exemplary record that I was allowed back here to put my affairs in order before I was to be court martialled. Next morning I walked back towards the base but took a diversion to my childhood haunt, a clearing with two old oak trees. That's where I committed suicide."

James listened intently then something struck him about what Edward had said a few minutes earlier.

"But at least two others did see me and actually talked to me on the first occasion I found myself on the base during the war. One was a high ranking officer type and the other was involved with the ground crew. Then an air raid on the base took place and I saved the second, rather lanky chap, when a large bomb lodged itself in the front of a Lancaster and before it exploded I got him to safety.

In fact he gave me something to take back to the service hanger but before I could take it I found myself back in my own time."

"Good Lord! What was his name, did you get it?"

"Err, yes, Eric something, Eric Arthurson."

Edward was clearly stunned.

"Arthurson! He was the one who said the second Lancaster was airworthy. He swore an oath that it was and his crew all backed him up. It didn't help that there was no record of a Mike Barracks in the personal records of RAF Grasceby."

"Sorry."

"Guess it couldn't be helped laddie. You look just like I remember you except with no flight kit on. I see you have my chairs and table. That's good. They're family heirlooms."

"So how come you can talk to me and come back to the cottage?" asked James as Scruff began to look bored and occasionally stood up, trotted around then sat back down again looking between the ghost and James.

"Perhaps these." Edward motioned at the table and chairs. "The family heirloom. Handed down for over two hundred and fifty years. Hand crafted, so family tradition has it, by the woodsman to the De Grasceby Manor that was lost. Oliver Portisham and his son, Thomas, are said to have built the new manor, rectory and church, with help of course from other local tradesmen. It was said that the lord of the manor at the time was so pleased with what they'd done he gave them both a plot of land. Oliver's was his original woodsman home that he got to keep and Thomas', well his plot was here. He and his wife are said to have built this place from scratch although we reckoned it must have been rebuilt at the turn of the century, well, I guess the start of the twentieth century."

"So, this is effectively the family estate then?"

"I guess you'd say that. But sometime when it was rebuilt it was taken back into the Grasceby estate and as for Oliver's place, that's been lost to time as no one knows where it was really located."

James was fascinated but a thought came back to him. "But the records will show that you were considered responsible for the loss of the Lancaster and crew back in 1944 so somehow we, err I, need to find a way of exonerating you. I'll find out if this Arthurson is still alive but first, I think a family reconciliation is in order. Stay here I'm taking Scruff out and I hope I'm doing the right thing."

Edward looked puzzled but faded from view as Scruff had stood up excited as he'd heard his name mentioned.

"Yes Scruff, it's time for a little trip!" said James as he headed towards the hallway, grabbed his coat and Scruff's lead and motioned for the dog to follow him.

#

They stood in the woods and James called out, not a shout, but not a whisper either. "Jenny? Jenny? I need to speak to you, its urgent."

A few minutes went by and he began to think she wouldn't show but then Jenny materialised and looked at him slightly pained.

"He's at the cottage, isn't he?"

"Yes, but Jenny, don't leave. He's innocent and I know it now." Jenny looked at James warily.

"Go on then." James took a deep breath then explained all that had happened since their last meeting.

After he'd finished James looked at her imploringly.

"Come to the cottage, see and talk to him. All he ever tried to do was explain to someone who was most likely not biased and would listen. That's why he visited you when you were little. He'd lost the argument with your parents but not with you. You were young and more open to what he had to say. Come back to the cottage. I'm leaving now so I really hope you can see it in your soul to give your granddad, our grandfather, a chance."

James turned and, with Scruff happily in the lead wanting to go home himself, they headed back towards Wolds View Cottage.

22: Reunion and a trip

James stood, nervously waiting to see who would appear first. Scruff didn't care as he'd been fed and fresh water in his bowl so after having scoffed his dog biscuits he wandered back into the hallway and to his basket, turned round a couple of times then settled down and went to sleep.

James sat down, carefully avoiding Edward's favourite chair, beginning to think it was a lost cause, when, out the corner of his eye he noticed something.

Edward appeared in the kitchen and smiled, seeing his favourite chair was empty. But he didn't sit down. Instead he looked around nervously but then looked sad.

"I'm not surprised really. She was a good little girl and very faithful to her parents, especially her mother at the time Barbara realised I was visiting Jennifer, even though I was a ghost. It was when I was drawn to the cottage a few years after I died that I realised the little girl I had seen just before I hung myself was actually Jennifer."

"Sorry, you've lost me a bit. You saw Jenny? But if I'm right she was barely a year or so old when you died and she wasn't a ghost until much later."

"Yes, odd that. On that fateful day when I took the other path into the clearing I was going to do it. It was an old play area we had found when we were village youths. We used to climb the oaks and even made a couple of swings, but when I went back on that fateful morning there was little sign of the old tractor tyre we used when I was a boy.

I was going to take the coward's way out, had a rope, climbed up quite high and swung the rope around the thick branch. I was going to do it too when an odd thing happened. I saw a little girl all ghostly like, looking up at me and I could have sworn she called out *'Granddad!'* It made me stop and think of the future, my future and that I would miss out on seeing baby Jennifer growing up. Something inside told me it was her, somehow from the future, come to save me. A little angel of hope.

But then I heard a shout from somewhere near to where the path branches off to the clearing and I lost my grip and fell. I didn't mean to hang myself, I'd changed my mind, all because of Jennifer. I wanted to live … to see my granddaughter grow up."

Edward looked up with ghostly tears in his eyes then looked shocked. James spun around and there just peeping around the door from the hallway was Jennifer Portisham.

"Granddad?" she said softly then rushed over and embraced him, both bursting out in ghostly tears. James felt a lump come into his throat. He let them have their moment of reconciliation and felt proud that he had managed to bring them together. Whether that would also be possible for Barbara and Jack, only time would tell.

James cleared his throat.

"Listen you two. It's clear now that you had changed your mind Edward but the question remains, who was it that shouted and startled you so you ended up falling and hanging yourself by accident? I think we three should retrace your last walk and see if anything happens that gives us a clue. Agreed?"

Edward and Jenny looked at him and smiled, nodding assent. James went through into the hallway and grabbed his coat. Scruff stirred, looked up and instantly was awake ready for his walk.

"Well all right boy, come on then," James attached Scruff's lead and led him to the front door. "You two coming?" he called out and Edward, followed by Jennifer, came through looking at him oddly as he opened the front door.

It was Jenny who explained.

"For us, it is you who looks like a ghost. To us we see the old cottage and it looks like you are about to walk through a brick wall. We can see the ghostly outline of a door but it is quite strange to us to go through what is a brick wall. I guess we need to stick to old habits." They turned and took the old route back through the hallway to the original back door James and Scruff walked outside, locked the door then waited as both ghosts came round the side of the cottage. Scruff didn't seem at all bothered that two ghosts were accompanying them on his walk.

All three then walked up to the gate which James used the remote control to open whilst the two ghostly figures just glided through and stood on the grass verge waiting for James and Scruff to join them. They walked along the old familiar route as Jenny and Edward talked about when he visited her as a youngster and Edward reiterated that he never, ever meant her any harm. She in turn defended her mother who had only tried to protect her and Edward had to agree he would have done the same thing if roles were reversed.

Edward remembered something and began to say their favourite rhyme as he and Jenny held ghostly hands, she joined in.

"Rocking Horse, Rocking Horse, stay with me.
Don't go running away to the sea.
Gallop, oh gallop, come to my aid,
Before I become a sad old maid.

Rocking Horse, Rocking Horse, stay with me.
Don't go running away to the sea.
Come to my aid wherever you be,
Away from the rocks beside the sea.

Rocking Horse, Rocking Horse, stay with me.
Always be around to play with me.
Rocking away but never to flee.
Always my companion, forever with me."

They both smiled at the memory shared and then fell silent. James wondered if there was any meaning to the rhyme. They reached the old side entrance to the airbase grounds but just as they headed in, a car drove past quite quickly, pipped at them then carried on without stopping. James didn't have time to look round before it was gone but just shook his head.

"Quite a few locals know me well now so it was probably one of them. I figure they didn't see you two. On we go." He was about to warn them regarding about barbed wire on the top of the gate then realised Greg had removed it. It also dawned on James ghosts didn't have to worry about that, as both glided through the gate with ease.

They carried on as Scruff led the way, completely unperturbed about having two ghosts walking along with them. He knew they were friendly and that the ghostly man was accepted by James now, so it no longer bothered him when he appeared. They reached the turn off and took it, before long they walked out into the old clearing and once again there stood the two mighty oak trees.

"I have mixed feelings about this place now. On the one hand, happy memories of being a boy and exploring the woods, making the swings with my friends, then sadly growing up and leaving the area to join the early RAF. We flew biplanes in my early years with the force. They were open cockpits, freezing, yet exhilarating at the same time as being fully exposed to whatever the elements were going to throw at you. Then there's my last day alive…"

Jenny held his ghostly hand, then she stared at the tree.

"Something is happening. I can feel it. A strange sensation." she whispered.

James stepped to one side , puzzled as the air was turning quite cold, positively frosty in fact, yet it was a gloriously sunny day and should have been quite warm for the time of year. As he watched, movement from behind caught his attention and he found himself lost for words.

A second Edward with a very young ghostly Jennifer walked up to almost the exact same spot that the modern ghostly Edward and Jenny now occupied and James watched as both sets of ghosts merged. Modern Jenny gasped as she remembered the day Edward's ghost in 1949 had brought her as a young girl to the same spot. Both sets of ghosts were completely oblivious to each other yet stood there looking up at the nearest oak tree. As James too looked up, suddenly he saw a third ghostly Edward getting ready to hang himself.

This Tree Edward paused and looked down directly at the spot where the two Jenny's stood iand James saw the little girl see Granddad up the tree. Instinctively James and the modern Jenny both began to look back as young Jennifer's ghost cried out *'Granddad.'* Tree Edward paused then, appearing to have changed his mind just as a shout came from the direction of the original path.

Scruff began to bark as he was looking back in the same direction and pulled on the lead in James hand. Modern Jenny and James looked back to see a man shouting, then standing in shock as Tree Edward lost his grip and slipped off the branch, hanging himself in the process. Little Jennifer's ghost screamed then vanished as did the second Edward. Modern Edward had now turned and just caught sight of the man rushing away and he felt a cold hatred, realising who it was.

James too recognised the man and in sync they both said: *'Arthurson'!* However Arthurson vanished from view.

Edward and Jenny both faded away leaving James reeling from the revelation. Recovering his composure, James motioned to Scruff and they headed back to the cottage with a lot on his mind. James kept replaying over and over what he'd just witnessed as he walked back in a daze.

#

Sally had arrived home early to find the cottage deserted but as Scruff was also not present and James car was parked in the driveway, it was logical he'd taken Scruff for a walk.

When the twosome returned home and James recounted what had happened, she was a little sceptical, that is until Edward and Jenny appeared in the kitchen and startled her. Calming down she tried to make sense of what she'd been told.

"So, let me get this straight. You said on your first so called 'time travel' slip, whatever it was, you met someone called Arthurson and he was one of the ground service personnel at the airbase. And he's the same chap who startled Edward who had changed his mind, but then accidentally hanged himself because of this Arthurson chap?"

"Essentially, yes," answered James as Edward nodded. Sally noted he had sat down in his favourite chair and was suddenly aware of the family resemblance between James and Edward. Indeed, she had spotted a few facial features about Jenny that could be taken as signs she was a Portisham.

"Wow! Guess this chap Arthurson must be dead by now, so we can't question him. Plus, who'd believe you anyway? I have to because there are two ghosts here and I know what you must have felt like a few years back when I was so sceptical about you seeing Jenny. You being able to describe her exactly was spooky, I can tell you." Sally looked at James and shrugged.

James' smartphone tinkled into life, startling both him and Sally and he motioned to everyone he wanted quiet when he saw who was calling.

"Yes, good to hear from you Mike. Sorry, say again? Err, OK, we'll be right over. Bye."

He put the phone back into his pocket and looked slowly up at everyone.

"That was Mike at the museum. He wants me and you, Sally, down there right away, no questions asked. He sounded really odd and almost I'd say in a daze."

Edward and Jenny faded from view and Sally stood up as they both went into the hallway, grabbed their coats and headed out.

Scruff sat in his basket a little forlorn as he thought they were taking him back out for another walk.

#

Greg met them at the door and let them in before closing and locking it.

"That's a bit worrying Greg, locked in with you, what's going on?" asked James and Sally gave Greg a wary look as much to say she was a police woman so no funny tricks.

"Nothing to worry about but something incredible all the same. Come through to the museum section please" he said and walked ahead of them down the corridor towards the museum part of the old control tower building.

"No Sandra, I see?" noted Sally and Greg called back.

"No, half day today so left at lunchtime. Just as well really!"

They entered the museum where Mike was standing just inside. There was enough room for them all to get in but for some reason he stopped James moving further into the room.

"I have to say Mike that your call was a bolt out of the blue considering you weren't taking my calls during the week, after last weeks incident. I sensed urgency about it?"

Mike shuffled on his feet and looked at Greg, then Sally and finally at James.

"Greg and I wish to apologise for how we've been since the other week. It was such a shock and an unusual, yes, to be truthful, such an unbelievable story that it felt like we were being taken for a ride by your good self.

However, at Greg's suggestion we did something which, well, it has blown our proverbial socks off, to say the least. There is someone here who can explain better than I and I believe you are well acquainted with her."

With that a middle aged woman walked round from behind one of the display cabinets.

"Harriet!" exclaimed James and Sally at the same time.

"Hello you two. You do have some fun and games out here still without me, don't you."

"But.." James was lost for words so Harriet took up the story.

"Greg and I have been friends since schooldays and dated when we were in our late teens, but we drifted apart. However we kept in occasional touch and last week he asked something odd from me. It sounded intriguing and until twenty minutes ago I didn't know you two were involved.

Anyhow, he and Mike arranged for a DNA sample to be sent to me along with the results of one done around nine years ago. The original DNA test was on a blood sample from a flight suit that was from near to the end of the second world war, but the new one was from last week with fresh blood. I was puzzled but as they were paying for my services I did the tests.

The recent one, I was told today, was from you James, from an incident last week when you were wearing the flight suit. The first odd thing is that there was no sign of the original blood stain on the thigh area of the trousers as the new blood stain matched it perfectly. The result was conclusive, and as I have access to a national database including hospital and doctors records I could confirm that it was indeed your blood. No mystery there as you were wearing the flight suit."

"And the second thing ..?" asked James warily.

"Mike asked me to recheck the original sample results as the DNA database has only recently become available for professional access. At that time, nine years ago, there was no match with anyone known.

But now with that access, I can tell you that the old sample from World War Two is 100 percent yours. There is no doubt. It's not 95, 98 or 99.5 percent, it's uncanny but a 100 percent match.

It's your blood from 1944."

23: Confrontation

Harriet looked around at them all then continued, having stunned James and Sally.

"So, if Mike and Greg are to be believed, you said you had somehow found yourself back in 1944 on a bombing raid and had been slightly wounded. Well, I don't believe in time travel, but I can't explain it as you had no access to the flight suit until last week and I'm guessing you didn't even know it existed until then, so there can't be cross contamination."

Sally stood there, taking in the implications but James now had a smug face.

"And you lot didn't believe me. Good old science. Nice one Harriet. Good work. Question is, where does that leave us?"

Sally looked thoughtful. "Well we could ask about Arthurson?"

Mike and Greg looked at each other and back at Sally.

"You're kidding right?"

James and Sally in turn now looked puzzled as Mike continued.

"Have you not noticed the entrance sign? I'm Arthurson, Mike Arthurson. My grandfather set up this business just after the war once this base was decommissioned."

"Ahh." Greg muttered. "Told you it should be updated. Mike's family name may be Arthurson but when his granddad set up the business and sent off the paper work for tax purposes, the clerk at the tax office got the name wrong and registered the business as Arthur and Son, not Arthurson."

"So what about Arthurson?"

"Your grandfather, was he by any chance Eric Arthurson?" asked James carefully not sure of what reaction he'd get.

"Yes…Why?" Mike was indeed wary.

"Well, in my first, err, trip back I met an Eric Arthurson just as an air raid took place."

"This is uncanny… Granddad always said he met an odd chap who …"

" …saved him when a bomb landed in the cockpit of a nearby Lancaster and didn't explode straight away. But other nearby blasts had dropped us to the ground and Eric was dazed, so I dragged him behind a brick wall and the bomb exploded. We'd have been killed instantly if we'd stayed where we had fallen."

Mike stood looking stunned.

"That's… That's impossible. That's exactly how he describes it. Hold on, if it was you why does he call you a different name? What was it, if it really was you?"

"You mean, Mike Barracks?"

If Mike had looked pale before, he turned even whiter, walked to the other side of the room and pulled a chair out and sat down heavily.

"Granddad always said that a Mike Barracks had saved him, but he also said that the same person condemned a Lancaster to crash whilst still carrying some of its bomb load after a mission. He said he gave the chap a part to take to the maintenance hanger but he didn't discover it had not been delivered until after the crash. He also said it was a mystery because the chap disappeared never to be seen again."

It was James turn to become pale as the implications dawned on him. Sally became concerned as he looked blankly around the room.

"What is it love?" she asked as he looked into her eyes.

"I, I killed Edward. Sort of. Well, I remember Eric giving me a piece of equipment and asking me to take it to the hanger, but before I could do so, I was back in the present. It's at home in my other jacket pocket. If I had got it to the hanger then the faulty part would have been replaced and they wouldn't have all died. I killed that crew on the Lancaster I was with the second time. They needn't have died. It's my fault that Edward got the blame as I vanished leaving him to take the rap. He wouldn't have been up the tree trying to commit suicide if I had just got the item back to the hanger."

"Granddad mentioned the last survivor committed suicide because of the weight of the loss of his colleagues and because he was going to be court martialed." Mike stood and a resolve came over him. "We need to go see him."

James was surprised but it was Sally that said it for him. "You mean he's still alive? He must be, what, in his nineties by now?"

"He's ninety nine this year," replied Mike proudly.

"I guess you and your parents must be very proud of him for his service during those hard times?" asked James, but Mike looked sad and down at his feet.

"Both my parents passed away, Mom about fifteen years ago and Dad just last year. That's why I now have the business. Granddad is pretty tough but I still think we should be careful when I take you to see him. I'd hate the shock of seeing you to finish him off after all this time."

"OK, we'd best be off then so let me know when you have arranged something." James looked at Harriet then Sally and back to Harriet. "Are you staying over or going back to Nottingham?"

"I have to get back so best be setting off. I'll give you a call Sally and perhaps might be able to get over this weekend if you want?"

"That'd be good, call us so we can have your favourite room ready."

"Oh fun, can't wait for that then."

James, Sally and Harriet said goodbye to Mike and Greg and headed back along the corridor, then outside. A thought struck James as Harriet headed over to a car he thought he recognised.

"Ahh, it was you that came past and pipped earlier today as I was taking Scruff for a walk. Changed your car?"

"Yes, I saw you and Scruff as I headed here to give them the results. I already knew about it being you, but Mike had sworn me to secrecy and considering he was paying I couldn't break my word. Changed the car to something bigger so I can take my portable equipment around when I need to. I'll hopefully see you both at the weekend then, bye."

Harriet got in and drove away followed by James and Sally who were glad they'd driven up, even if it was just under a mile from the cottage. There was a lot to discuss when they got home.

#

Two days later, on the Friday, Mike phoned to ask them to meet him at the care home where Eric Arthurson had a room.

Mike was standing outside on the gravel driveway in front of the impressive, almost stately home like, care home and greeted James who could tell he was apprehensive.

"I've told Granddad that I've found someone who he's not seen since the war so he is expecting a visitor, but he's not always lucid. He rambled on that as far as he knew, all his friends and colleagues from the war years were long gone so I don't know how he's going to react. Just thought I'd warn you. I didn't mention any names in case he reacted badly."

"I was thinking that I'm concerned he might have a heart attack when he sees me."

"Yes, the thought had crossed my mind too. Well we won't find out anything standing out here will we!"

Mike ushered James in through the door and motioned to the receptionist who smiled and gave James a visitor's badge. He realised Mike was already wearing one which he hadn't noticed until now. They went along a corridor, then turned a couple of corners before reaching a door.

Mike knocked gently on it and entered indicting to James to wait until he was called for. James listened intently as muffled voices drifted through the close door, then suddenly it opened.

"Come in, I'm not sure what to expect as he does suffer from memory lapses. We're not sure if it is dementia, we're awaiting results." James stepped through the door into a basic, but nicely furnished, room and despite his age, recognised Eric Arthurson sitting at the table in front of the window.

Eric looked at him and a flicker of recognition drifted across his face. He looked intently at James as he studied his features.

"You, you're, you're Mike Barracks …"

"Yes, sir, well sort of err n.." Eric cut him off as if he wasn't listening.

"You saved me, in the war, you saved me from that bomb. But you can't have done.

You haven't changed. Why? Is this a trick? Sonny, what's going on. He can't be Barracks, he should be *old…*"

Before Mike could intervene Eric turned nasty as a flash of memory struck him.

"You KILLED THEM! You! You KILLED THEM! You were supposed to deliver the replacement bomb release gear for me but you didn't. YOU KILLED THEM!

YOU KILLED *HIM*! He wouldn't have done it if you'd done your bit. YOU KILLED HIM!

YOU KILLED HIM!
YOU KILLED HIM!
YOU KILLED HIM!
YOU KILLED HIM!"

Eric was all in a rage now and James backed out of the room as Mike tried to calm his grandfather down. Staff came rushing to see what was going on and James ran outside not knowing what to do or say. He felt sick and saddened at the same time.

Several minutes later, which felt like an eternity, Mike stepped outside and joined him.

He was ashen faced.

"They've managed to sedate him and he's fallen asleep for now but he was really worked up. I don't know whether to be angry with you or feel sorry for you. Granddad is absolutely adamant that you are the same person he met all those years ago. Sort of goes with what the DNA results gave us. I'm confused and mystified as to how it is possible to travel backwards and forwards in time iwith no control over it."

"You and me both. I do need to talk to him so if there is any way you can convince him to let me come back and have a chat to explain what I know then I would appreciate it."

Mike didn't look too impressed but sighed.

"Give me a day or two to let him settle down and I'll talk to him to try to smooth the way. I'll be in touch, hopefully soon but I'm not making any promises."

With that they parted company and both drove away from the care home wondering how life could have got so complicated.

#

Harriet arrived late Saturday morning and quickly settled into her room having been assured by both James and Sally that she wouldn't be visited by any ghostly manifestations.

The three of them were sitting in the living room supping a glass each of a nice Chardonnay when her curiosity finally got the better of her.

"OK, so according to Einstein, time travel would likely cause a paradox. Even the slightest change could have dramatic ramifications, probably changing the future. So come on James spill, how come your DNA was in the original blood stain that was sent off, oh, about nine or so years ago before you even knew of this place's existence?"

James put his glass carefully down on the glass coffee table and sighed.

"Seriously Harri, I have no idea. I swear to you both, on my life, that I'd never known about the flight suit until you and I went over to the museum just the other week. I really don't have an answer and it does my head in trying to figure it out! You're the specialist here, you tell me?"

Sally kept quiet as she knew James was a bit touchy about the subject, but Harriet wasn't put off.

"So, based on what you know, has anything changed here since you got back?"

"Yes, you used to be a bloke!" James joked but Harriet grimaced at him, narrowing her eyebrows, not impressed.

"Now come on Harri, you asked for that. Trust me when I tell you that James was pretty beaten up when he was found on the old runway by Joe and Phil. They said that they'd only looked at the spot a few moments beforehand then suddenly when Joe looked again, there was James, lying unconscious on the concrete." Sally said as she took another sip from her glass.

Harriet sighed.

"Sorry, but it's really hard to accept it. Pretty much any scientist will tell you time travel is not possible regardless of how much science fiction you read or watch!"

James looked at her with sympathy.

"Don't you think I know that? I agree with you, on the whole, but there has been a group who have managed to teleport information from one place to another so who's to say if one day we will also crack time travel? Two things have happened to me in the last few years that have completely unravelled my own world view. One, I see and communicate with ghosts which you can't deny. You saw Edward the last time you were here and that currently has no official explanation.

Secondly, I have several times now suddenly found myself back in another time. The first time it was a toy cupboard from the mid nineteenth century. I found myself in it when, what I thought was the library in modern times suddenly became little George's bedroom with a built in toy cupboard.

I didn't know at the time that the second floor had been reconfigured. To stop being seen by the woman who entered George's bedroom I hid in the toy cupboard. But then all of a sudden I was back in the present and on the second floor landing where Lady Grasceby nearly bumped into me. She was startled and swore I had not been there a second earlier. Isn't that right Sally?"

"Well I wasn't there at the time but Lady Grasceby did confide in me much later that it truly scared her and for a while she had nightmares about James suddenly appearing in front of her." Sally took another sip of her wine and looked at Harriet imploring her to accept everything and not push any further.

"OK, change of subject, well slightly, have you been on the International Bomber Command Memorial site to see if your Edward is listed under their database of lost aircrew?" Harriet asked and James' interest picked up.

"No, hang on, I'll do a search for their site now." He picked up his tablet and linked it to the wall screen and before long they were all looking at the IBCC web site. "Wow, quite impressive, we should go over and have a look, pay our respects. There's the Losses page." He clicked on the link and then put in Edward Portisham but a 'no result' was displayed.

"I'm not there..." came a sad voice from behind Sally. Edward had materialised behind them, Harriet just sat and stared incredulously at him.

"My apologies, ma'am, for frightening you the last time we met. I thought you were my granddaughter, Jennifer. I think you can safely say that you can indeed see ghosts and that we exist, even if I myself don't understand it.

This, wall picture, changes as you tap on that odd slate you have in your hand, James?"

"Must be hard to come to terms with our modern technology, but we call it a screen and I can show images or access news or any information from around the world. There is a site that has been built near to Lincoln, just south of it, that now has a memorial to all those who flew and died in Bomber Command."

Edward's ghostly face was amazed and astounded as James showed the VR walk around view and zoomed in on the various large plaques that held so many names.

So many names...

"Around fifty eight thousand listed, but as we have found, you are not one of them. However, I have found your fallen flight crew." James went to the losses list and brought up the list. Edward looked sadly at the names and looked down again as he said a silent prayer for them.

"I suppose it is not that surprising I'm not listed as I took my own life and it is a sin in the eyes of the Lord."

"True, but as we now know, you had changed your mind and that it was Eric Arthurson that startled you, making you fall before you had removed the rope. Admittedly it was an accident so if I can get him to see me without going into meltdown then he might be able to say something that we can use to exonerate you."

"I do hope you are correct. I will leave you in peace now and hope for the best. Jennifer is hoping to reconcile myself with her... your, parents but it will take a miracle to achieve that."

With that Edward faded from view and James turned to Harriet, but didn't say a word.

She in turn was also lost for words and looked a little sheepishly at James and Sally, knowing she couldn't very well challenge James about his time travel experiences, not after seeing a ghost that actually talked to her directly. Sally noticed her demeanour.

"You OK, Harri?"

"Err, yes, guess so. Not everyday that you have a ghost talk to you, challenging your most cherished beliefs."

"And that's what James has had to live with for the last few years." Sally pointed out quietly.

Harriet looked over to him.

"Sorry for earlier."

"No problem Harri, I struggled for quite a while when I first saw Jenny, before I met Sally. My own background in computer sciences told me it was impossible. Somewhere along the way in the future someone will work out what is going on but for now I have ended up just accepting that it happens. Both for seeing ghosts and somehow finding myself back in the past. The good news on the latter is that somehow I come back and don't get stranded! I actually now dread that happening sometime in the future."

"You won't as you dare not leave me behind! Anyhow you two, it's getting late and personally I'm tired, so time for bed, eh?" suggested Sally and James nodded as Harriet smiled and yawned.

"Yes, hopefully a peaceful night seeing as I have been promised!" she said and got up, gave a little wave to them both then headed out and up the stairs.

"Time for bed then Sally, I'll just have Scruff out for a quick walk then will be right on up." James barely got the words out when Scruff came trotting into the room wagging his tail.

He certainly had good hearing.

24: A package and visitation

His phone chirped into life as they were almost finished walking around and exploring the Bomber Command Memorial south of Lincoln, a sobering experience it was indeed. James tapped to accept the call.

"Hello? Yes, oh hello Mike, wow, that was quick. I thought it would be well into next week. Yes, I can be there this afternoon for three thirty. We're at the Bomber Command Memorial and I've had a talk with the people here, but it's doubtful Edward's name could be added to the plaques now, the names are laser cut. However, if I can provide concrete proof then he could be added to the online losses list which at least would be one good thing.

Yes, I'll see you later then, bye."

He put the phone away into his pocket as Sally and Harriet looked at him in anticipation. "Mike has convinced his granddad to see me later today so if you two are happy now that we've seen most of the memorial, I'd like to get back so we can have lunch."

Sally nodded then had an idea. "Why don't we stop off at the Star and Crescent Moon Inn on the way back?"

There was a general chorus of agreement and they headed back to the car, setting off for Bardney then onto Grasceby. As they parked up and headed into the inn they were pleased to see Marcus was back, his face beaming when he saw them.

"Well now, nice to see you all again." he said then continued in his usual style, "What is it you are having then?"

"Good to see you too and that you appear to have survived the trip. Let's have the menus as we'd like to have a meal if you are serving hot food Marcus."

"Yes, we're serving, soup of the day is minestrone, home made too and tasty it is I can tell you." Marcus was in a pretty good mood and handed over the menus to James.

"I'll get the drinks then as you have been so kind in having me over for the weekend," offered Harriet and took their orders for the drinks as Sally headed over to the far table next to the window, noting it was a bit quiet for a Sunday.

They settled in and Marcus came over after a few minutes with their drinks, "Orange squash for you James, sensible chap as I see you are the driver, small white Chardonnays for the ladies. Err James, can I have a word with you at the bar?"

They all looked a little puzzled as James nodded and got up, following Marcus back to the bar which he went behind, looking at James a little sheepishly.

"This is a bit odd as I had no knowledge of it until the other day, but I have a package for you. It's from my dad of all people but he had no qualms about telling me what it is when he handed it over.

When your mother changed her name by deed poll, I'm sure you know it had to have been witnessed. Well, because she didn't want anyone looking her up, she apparently only trusted my mum and dad. They were the witnesses and sworn to secrecy.

Inside here is the paperwork. She didn't want you to find out whilst she was alive, but dad received a letter the other week from a secure deposit firm down in London. They'd been instructed, on news of her death, to forward the package to either my mother, father or a descendant for safekeeping and to pass on to any relative of hers if they knew of their whereabouts.

The firm only discovered this when a recent routine check of their records turned up details of her death a few years back. For some unknown reason your mother had not updated the records to have it delivered to you up here in Lincolnshire.

They haven't charged for their service as they were remiss in their duties in keeping up to date. Apparently it was down to changing over from written records to digital and some got missed. Sounds like they need your IT expertise! So here you are."

Marcus handed over not just a small official looking letter but a somewhat large parcel wrapped in brown paper.

"Blooming heck, must be more than just the paperwork, any ideas?"

"No, not my place to open it up but if I had to guess then it may be family records or letters from your parents to each other. People used to do that you know when they were courting. Before all this social media malarkey took over."

"Oh heck, not sure I want to read my parents love letters to each other. OK, many thanks for this and thank your dad too. Must have been quite a shock when he found out my mum had me after moving away?"

"No, your mother had only just found out she was pregnant before she decided to move away and change her name so mum and dad knew she was going to have a baby, but once she moved she never got back in touch."

James shook Marcus by the hand and headed back to the table where he ended up being quizzed to death about the package. He opened the smaller envelope and took out the papers.

"Well it's all here, the official documents and the signatures of Marcus's parents." he said as he showed Sally and Harriet the papers.

"Yes, but what's in the large package, that's what we want to know" asked Sally as Harriet nodded in agreement with her.

"Look, for the moment I don't want to open it here. Especially if it is intimate letters between my parents. Let's get the meals over and done with, that's when Marcus decides to collect our orders." Luckily James caught sight of Marcus on the way over and in no time he went off happily to sort their lunches out. Despite their curiosity, Sally and Harriet didn't press any more and over lunch they discussed recent events before finishing and heading back to Wolds View Cottage.

#

It was almost four in the afternoon when James arrived at the care home, apologising to Mike for the delay.

"We got carried away with lunch at the Star and Crescent Moon Inn, sorry I'm so late."

"Ahh, haven't been in for a while, must pop in sometime, is Marcus still in charge? I remember his parents running that place before him. Always thought Marcus would go off and do something else, but he seemed to take to running it like a duck to water."

"Oh Marcus is still there. Plus his daughter, Sharon, too. Anyway, how is your granddad? Calmed down since Friday?"

"Yes, I think so. He was in shock but I had a long talk with him this morning and explained that you had no control over events and he was really pleased to see you again after all these years. Fingers crossed it worked, but we'll only know once we're in with him." Mike led the way and once again they signed in, received their visitor passes and headed down the corridor until they reached Eric Arthurson's room. Mike went in, then opened the door again to let James in. He approached Eric cautiously with a hand outstretched in greeting and Eric stood up, using his walking frame to keep steady, then shook James by the hand whilst watching him intently.

The next twenty minutes or so James patiently went over what had happened and explained how he had somehow ended up on the fateful flight of Edwards Lancaster.

"But, you are so young yet you look exactly how I remember you. You should be in your hundred and thirties by now, it's extraordinary. I'm sorry I lost my temper but it brought back so many bad memories of the war especially towards the end.

We lost a lot of crews and we got hit several times at the base itself. It was during one of them that you dragged me to safety before that bomb blew a Lanc to bits nearby.

I gave you a part, a section of the bomb release mechanism. No one realised after the raid that it had not been delivered and so we gave the Lancaster the all clear to fly when Edward's Lancaster developed engine problems and he needed an aircraft for the big op."

James fished into his jacket inside pocket and brought out the mechanism Eric had described. Eric had tears in his eyes at the sight of it. Mike looked on in astonishment but didn't say a word.

"I didn't get a chance to take it to the maintenance hanger as you had asked because I suddenly found myself back in the present. I found it was still in my pocket and had no way of getting it back as I never have any control of when these things happen to me. Tell me, that day I met you briefly, I saw an officer and got told off by him just before I met you. I had to come up with a name for him as to who I was otherwise I thought he was going to shoot me. I looked around and saw what I took to be barracks and just came up with 'Mike Barracks' as my name, but I didn't get his. Surely he was the other person who could have vouched for Edward's story that there was a Mike Barracks on the base, even if it was for a short time?"

Eric looked down at his feet thoughtfully.

"I think I remember, it was Squadron Leader Harris. Oh, he was killed soon after that air raid we survived. That's why he couldn't testify that you did, or rather had, existed."

James knew his next question could cause an unsavoury reaction but now he had Eric talking he felt he had to probe Edward's suicide attempt.

"Edward Portisham was blamed for the death of his crew in that Lancaster crash wasn't he? Without any evidence of the missing part or the testimony from that Squadron Leader chappie, he must have felt pretty isolated and hemmed in if no one would believe him about my existence?"

"Yes, the investigator couldn't find any record of you anywhere and concluded the maintenance crew must have done their job otherwise the Lancaster wouldn't have been cleared for operational duty. But it was a rush all the same. I, I was concerned for Edward as he was an upstanding person, but it didn't seem he had a leg to stand on and it looked like he was going to be formally charged. He was allowed home for a few days to put his affairs in order but sadly never lived to face the trial."

"Is that why you called out when you saw him in the clearing up the tree?"

Eric looked up sharply, staring at James as Mike watched both of them warily, not sure what was going on.

"How did you know..." stuttered Eric as tears appeared and began to trickle down his cheeks.

James decided to play a hunch and use his few times of finding himself back in the past as a lever.

"That was one of the other times I ended up back in wartime Grasceby. I was hiding just off the rough path that lead to the clearing where Edward was preparing to commit suicide, but he hesitated. I could see you but you didn't spot me. Did you see the little girl at all?"

"No, there was no little girl, but he seemed to be looking down towards a spot just a few yards from the base of the tree. That did seem odd. He seemed to change his mind but I thought he was going to do it and shouted to stop him. He slipped on hearing me and fell, hanging himself in the process. I, I was…" he started crying and held his face in his hands as Mike moved to come between James and his Granddad. Eric stopped him.

"No, it's all right, I was too far from him and he was too high up the oak tree for me to have done any good. I panicked and ran through the woods doubling back. Walking up the road to the main entrance rather than by the woodland path. I acted as if nothing had happened, I was a coward. When I think of what Edward and the aircrew like him went through on their sorties and there was I, a coward and unable to save his life."

Mike was silent but hanging on every word, as was James who unbeknownst to the other two was recording it all using his smartphone.

"But Granddad, who found this chap, Edward?" Mike asked quietly as he helped Eric to sit back down next to the window table.

"The military police were sent to bring him back to the base and knowing his usual route they went through the woods to the cottage he shared with his son and daughter in law. They'd had a little girl a year earlier and she was Edward's pride and joy, even if he didn't fully get on with his daughter-in-law. Not finding him at the cottage and discovering he had set off for the base through the woods, the MP's retraced their route and found the side path to the clearing. There he was, looking for all the world as if he had committed suicide. They got him down and took him to the airbase then an officer went to see his family at the cottage to give them the sad news. After that, it was posthumously decided he was guilty of negligence and complicit in the death of his fellow crew on the ill-fated Lancaster.

I've lived with it all my life and never thought I would meet the person responsible for not delivering the replacement part. He was a mystery to everyone and was thought to have been a figment of Edward's imagination.

"Yet you knew I existed and could have come forward to confirm his story about a Mike Barracks." said James.

Eric sighed and with a sad look, nodded.

"Eric. For what it is worth, I don't think you could have done anything to save him and you were not to know by shouting you'd make him slip and hang himself accidentally. But you could help him now. He was my grandfather and I would like to clear his name. Will you make a statement about what happened all those years ago and help me clear Edward's name?" James was hopeful and patiently waited as Eric sat and stared out the window. Finally Eric looked back at him.

"It would be the least I could do to right the wrong that was done to Edward Portisham."

25: Reconciliation

A couple of days later, James arrived at the industrial estate and chuckled at the sign above proclaiming 'Arthur and Sons Haulage', knowing now that it had been a slipup all those years ago and should have said 'Arthurson Haulage'. Greg had called saying he had found something that would interest him but had been coy as to what.

Intrigued, James entered the control tower haulage headquarters to be greeted by both Mike and Greg, Sandra remained in her chair behind the desk, somewhat bemused at seeing him visit once again. She still had not wormed out of her bosses why he was a regular visitor while not seeming to be connected with any interest of the firm itself, according to the records she was privy to.

The three walked down to the museum section but before they reached the main entrance they stopped at the door that lead down into the records room. Mike used his key and opened the door leading them down into the cooler depths and switched the lights on. The fluorescent lights were bright and James blinked, wondering what they had found for him as his sight recovered from the brightness. Greg looked quite smug and looked at James.

"So, you could say it was a very fortunate find. I was down here taking another look at the various filing cabinets that hold not just paper records but some of the smaller items that were either found on site or have been donated to us over the years."

"We don't yet have room for everything to go on display so items that don't seem to merit a high importance end up down here. That's where Greg made the discovery," added Mike.

Greg walked over to one of the cabinets and pulled open a drawer two thirds of the way down. It was quite slim and James wondered what on earth could be in there. Greg held up an envelope that had not been sealed and showed James the text. It said:

No records exist for this airman circa 1944/45.

Greg held the envelope up, indicating for James to cup his hands then shuffling the envelope until a patch of fabric fell out into them.

James gasped and stared in disbelief. It bore a name, looking for all the world it had been hastily stitched but saying:

BARRACKS M

It was dirty and some of the cotton from the stitching was coming loose but it was unmistakably the one Edward had handed to James on board the doomed Lancaster.

James was speechless becoming emotional as he looked at it, remembering pinning it to his chest whilst in the upper gunners turret.

"It must have come off when I rolled out of the Lancaster just before it crashed. I never gave it a thought."

"Well, according to the slip of paper inside the envelope, it was found, quite dirty, near to the runway edge a few years back and handed in to the previous owners. We're lucky they kept it. They must have tried to find out more, but drew a blank.

Hence the comment on the envelope about no records for the name. Of course, we now know why," said Greg as Mike put out his hand for the name badge and envelope.

"What I'll do is put this on display with a note that the records of this airman have been lost but based on the fabric it is from about the mid nineteen forties era."

"OK, yet another clue to say I was really there and I didn't hallucinate it all," mused James.

"Well, we're still finding it hard, but neither of us are going to say anything. Let's face it, how on earth could we explain it if science says you can't time travel!"

James just nodded and with that they put the envelope back in the drawer and headed back up to the ground level.

#

James sat at home at his desk in deep thought. Something had been bothering him over a few sleepless nights and Sally had begun to wonder if he was falling ill.

For a while since it had occurred, he had begun to have nightmares about the bombing raid over Germany and it was the odd incident of the German fighter, the Foche Wolf 190 that had not attacked, that kept replaying over and over again in his drifting sleeplessness.

The previous night had been particularly vivid as he recalled how the fighter had come up on the starboard side and flew along side them. James had trained his turret and aimed the guns at the fighter, but something had stopped him firing them. Why hadn't the fighter shot them down? They were easy prey for the pilot and it would have added to his kill rate, but instead the pilot had tried in his own way to indicate the bombs stuck underneath the Lancaster. It was as if he realised that even if he didn't shoot them down, they were probably doomed anyway as they couldn't land with live bombs on board.

But something kept drawing James to the side of the FW 190. There was a serial number on it and he could tantalisingly see it in his dreams, but it just wasn't quite clear enough. On a hunch he began to search the web for German WW II records but most of what he found covered land based operations until he finally found links to the Luftwaffe service records in English and slowly made his way through the official documents. Finding a possible useful form for requesting information, he filled it in as carefully as he could with what details he could remember and clicked on 'send', although he felt there would be little hope of finding out who the pilot was.

#

A couple of months went by. As James lay in bed, he heard the letter box clatter and for the umpteenth time he leapt up and raced downstairs to see what the post contained.

Scruff was a good dog, sitting guarding the fallen envelopes on the floor and James could see that most were the usual mix of bills and unwanted junk mail.

But one with an official stamp from the MOD caught his eye and his heart raced in anticipation. He called up to Sally who quickly donned her dressing gown and came down to join him in the kitchen.

She put the kettle on as James nervously looked at the letter.

"Well, it's not going to open itself now is it?" she said, understanding why he was hesitant.

James kept turning the envelope over and over until finally Sally plucked it from his fingers and sliced it open with her knife, then handed it back to him. She went back to slicing the loaf of bread ready for the toaster and James carefully pulled out the several page letter and began to read.

Sally realised he was very quiet and knew not to say anything, but buttered four rounds of toast, placed two on a small plate and put them down in front of James who was still engrossed in reading the letter. His eyes darted back and forth across, then gradually down each page taking in the information. Normally Sally could read James' face but this time it was a different matter.

He looked up at her, Breaking out into the broadest, happiest smile she had ever seen him display.

"They have reviewed the evidence supplied to them and have reached a conclusion. In their opinion, based on the confession of Mr Eric Arthurson, whom they confirmed was stationed at RAF Grasceby in 1944 as part of the ground service personnel, Flight Sergeant Edward Portisham can be cleared of any wrong doing in respect of the crash of the Lancaster on June 6th 1944 with the loss of the crew and aircraft. The admission that a part was defective and may not have been replaced, as per the original evidence presented by Mr Arthurson at the time of the hearing, along with a review of Flight Sergeant Portisham's own statement and account of the ill fated flight, including the recent discovery of the identity tag of Mike Barracks, provides ample proof that Flight Sergeant Portisham acted with the highest of honourable intentions expected from a member of the RAF. As such his posthumous dishonourable discharge has been revoked and instead he has posthumously been awarded the Distinguished Flying Medal for meritorious service."

James stopped as he began to cry and Sally came around and held him close. There was a small package included and inside was an oval silver medal with the effigy and titles of King George VI, the monarch at the time of the second world war, with a ribbon of violet and white diagonal stripes.

"Sorry, I was a bit overcome. Having actually experienced what those airman went through, to receive this medal would be have been important to them and meant a lot. Real shame that Edward never got to receive this when he was alive.

All because of me…" trailed off James as his mood turned sombre.

"Hey! Don't go there. How the heck did you know what was going to happen? It's not your fault, even if I still struggle with the idea you were actually back there. But you are not to blame so that's an end to it!

Funny how we haven't seen Edward or Jenny for the last couple of months. Perhaps now they are reconciled we won't see either of them again?" Sally wondered and looked around just in case they materialised. James realised she was right, as always and his spirits lifted.

"That might have been the reason Jenny was still here, well at least in one sense. I wonder…"

"What?"

"I wonder if we can get Edward's remains moved and a new inscription added to the family headstone? Do you think the Reverend Cossant could get permission?" James pondered as Sally sat looking across at him, contemplating it.

"It's possible. Mind you it was already allowed once bringing all your family members together again at the churchyard, so they might say enough is enough. But worth a try."

#

The permissions were granted, various dignitaries consulted, Phil and Jo helped to dig up Edward's remains from the original, unremarkable plot. Five weeks later on a sunny Sunday afternoon, a small gathering took place at Graseby Church for a brief service, then a short walk to the Portisham family plot.

Flight Sergeant Edward Portisham was reburied alongside his son, Jack, daughter in law Barbara and granddaughter Jennifer in a moving ceremony conducted by the Reverend Sarah Cossant. Several RAF dignitaries from the local air force bases were present and as the the small coffin holding the bones of Edward was slowly lowered into the vertical hole next to where Jennifer and Barbara Portisham had been buried close to Jack's grave, the officers gave a salute.

A faint low hum could be heard in the distance and one of the officers spoke.

"Ladies and gentlemen, may I have your attention please. Squadron Leader Derek Myers in attendance. In consideration of the surrounding the false accusations against Flight Sergeant Edward Portisham, it is my pleasure to announce that there will shortly be a fly past of the Lancaster from the Battle of Britain Memorial Flight over Grasceby and in particular this church, then over the original RAF Grasceby airfield. I can hear it now so if you can wait a short while it will fly over from the east off to our left."

As he fell quiet the drone became louder and James felt a lump in his throat as it began to bring back memories of his one and only sortie. The deep thrum of the four Merlin engines became louder but with additional engine sounds and as they all looked up, the Lancaster flew over, gracefully, slightly angled for the crew to pay their respects. A Spitfire and a Hurricane flanked the Lancaster and as as they all flew past, the officers and James all saluted. Edward's ghost appeared next to James and saluted too looking at James with a proud expression on his face, mixed with a tear. Apart from James, only Sally and Harriet could see him but they in turn kept quiet knowing this moment was for Edward.

Without any of the living souls knowing, Jack, Barbara and Jennifer appeared by Edward's side, the family reunited and reconciled at last.

26: The dead spot

With Edward now at peace with his family, James and Sally found Wolds View Cottage tranquil and it was clear that there were no more surprises lurking in the shadows. Even when they called out for any of the family members to appear, none did, which surprisingly made James a little sad.

It was late morning and he was sitting in his, originally Edward's, favourite kitchen chair, sipping at his hot coffee as Sally read the local report in the paper covering the reburial and fly past.

"You know, I'm surprised that the local TV news hasn't been in touch," mused James.

"Now listen you, sometimes it's best if you don't get too much publicity, do you really want to talk about how you can see ghosts and over the years have discovered you had a family you never knew you had, even if they are all dead!" Sally offered as she put her mug down.

"Sage advice my love, sage advice indeed." He was going to add more but his phone beeped and he looked at the incoming text ID. "It's Mike at the museum." He opened up the text, read quickly and his eyebrows went up. "Mike says can we pop round to the museum this afternoon. It's important." Sally nodded and so they set about sorting out a light lunch, taking Scruff out for a quick walkies before heading down to the museum for two o'clock.

Greg met them and shook their hands, waving them into the main building and indicating towards Mike's office. Sandra looked up and smiled at them, wondering what was going on. She was sure she would be able to find out. She always did.

Mike stood up and smiled, greeting them both warmly.

"Pleased you could come, I have some news for you. We're going to set up a new display about the Lancaster crash with details of how Edward was exonerated but naturally I am not going to mention how you found some of the information out. We'll put it down to 'sources said…' something like that.

Our plans to build up the museum side of things has taken a good turn in that we have now secured lottery funding to extend and build the VR centre, also additional display space and we will be linking up with the other RAF historic venues. It is pretty exciting; I can tell you.

To be honest we've had such a downturn with the haulage business and it seems tourism is the way forward, so we're joining up with Lord Grasceby's Estate as their tourism plans have done very well for them."

"That's great news Mike, but, well, you could have said that in the text, there's more isn't there?" Sally looked at James wondering about his lack of tact in this instance.

"Don't mind him, Mike, he's getting on a bit now you know and was looking forward to his afternoon nap!" she winked at Mike and Greg, who smiled as James screwed up his face at Sally.

"No offence was taken, I just felt that you'd like a walk to see something we've managed to find. Come with us and we'll show you."

Mike and Greg both headed for the door, James and Sally following them. James wondered for a moment if they were taking the path that would lead back to the entrance near to their cottage, but before they reached the turn off to the clearing of Edward's childhood and sadly, his end, there was a faint second path branching off to the right which they took.

James looked at Sally, puzzled, he was losing his sense of direction in the woods as the trees were pine and quite densely packed. The undergrowth looked like it had been trampled down quite recently. Suddenly the trees thinned out and ahead of them were the open fields of the farmland that James knew lay on the other side of the road from Wolds View Cottage. He noticed a section, not quite semi-circular in appearance, containing quite weak looking wooden fencing off that had seen better days. There was little growing inside it and the ground looked quite rough and lumpy. Mike indicated to Greg to take up the story.

"Because so many aircraft were lost from RAF Grasceby, we'd never thought about any of them crashing nearby until the recent turn of events. So I started to dig in the local news and talk to the nearby farms and it turns out that this is the si ..."

"... site of the crashed Lancaster from my flight." ended James excitedly.

"Yes, old man Harris across the way was twelve when he heard an almighty bang and rushed out with his father. Tthey saw the plume of smoke over here from that farmhouse over in the distance. This is their land. They did try to help but the Lancaster was an inferno and so they figured no one had survived.

Since then, little has grown on that bit of land so in the end they fenced it off and left it as a sort of informal memorial to the Lancaster crew who perished."

Mike took up the story. "So, we've stepped in and bought it off them and plan to erect a memorial to the Lancaster and the crew who died here whilst trying to get home. So near, yet so far. When it is finished we'll add the names of all the crew and include a certain Mike Barracks now we know someone did know he existed at the time, even though we also know it was a false name. He was still there with them and based on your account of what you did, you even downed an enemy plane so in that respect we all owe you a debt too. Although it does feel odd adding 'Barracks' to the list. Greg has discovered something else in the archives that was a revelation." Mike indicated to Greg who waved for them to head back to the industrial estate and the museum. As they began to walk back he told them of his discovery.

"When I came across the name badge for Barracks I remembered that a lot of local folk and even some who are elsewhere in the country, have sent in diaries kept by relatives who had been stationed here during the war. There was a lot to go through but one from a WAAF by the name of Shirley Hammerton caught my eye and is a revelation.

She was based at RAF Grasceby from 1943 until it was decommissioned in 1948. Her diaries are so immaculate and detailed that sometimes you read them thinking you are experiencing what she went through as if it were happening now. Sadly she died in 1987 and on finding her diaries just a few years ago, a relative sent them to us knowing we'd set up the museum.

She has an entry for the night and morning of your mission. Did you know that it was part of operation 'Overlord'?

James shook his head and Greg explained.

"Bomber Command conducted a bombing campaign to deceive the Nazis into thinking that what we now know as the D-Day landings were going to take place further up the coast. For the number of aircraft deployed losses were quite light really, so you were unlucky. Shirley made brief notes of the Lancs and crews going out from RAF Grasceby in case she had to contact family about any crew lost. She mentions that most came back, but she did note that one Lancaster was suddenly short of a crew member before setting off as their upper gunner, Kevin Bonderson, broke his leg that day. Then suddenly Flight Sergeant Mark Chapman stated over the radio before they were due to taxi out that they were OK as a *Mike Barracks* had joined them but was a newbie."

"Ahh, that's what Edward meant when he said 'Bondy' had broke his leg, it was this Kevin Bonderson," realised James.

Greg nodded. "Plus, you did mention someone had broken their leg and that corroborates it. She goes on to write that Chapman was the pilot and as they were heading back the wireless operator, Basil Harris radioed that they suspected some of their bomb load had not dropped. Then they lost contact so assumed the Lancaster had been downed.

It surprised the airbase when the Lancaster did a high level fly past so the tower could see who they were, then on the second, a very low pass, some people reported they thought *two* people had dropped out close to the rear of the Lancaster, although others said they only saw one. So there you are, although the reports are conflicting, the fact that some say there were two aircrew falling out of the plane again confirms what you told us and what Edward had stated in his official report of the crash.

Again it comes down to the fact no one could find you that cast doubt on Edward's story. Shirley clearly mentions a Mike Barracks in her diary entries for the fateful day and later when there was an investigation into the crash. For some reason her testimony was not considered important enough to be included. It all seems to come together."

They headed back to the museum and Greg showed James and Sally the diary in question. It was quite a sobering experience to realise that someone's care and attention to detail not only brought home what it had been like to be based at RAF Grasceby during wartime, but that it also helped confirm once again what James had told everyone. They returned home to find Scruff eagerly awaiting them.

Walkies were in order!

#

A week later Sally thought she heard someone walking on the front footpath and wandered through into the hallway to the door just as there was a light knocking on it.

She opened the door to find a man about James' age with an elderly man sitting in a wheelchair.

"Hello, can I help you?" she asked cautiously.

"Good morning. Mrs Hansone?"

"DS Hansone, yes, again, can I help you with anything?"

"We're sorry to just drop by but my father was adamant that he wanted to see a Mr James Hansone and he was given this address. You see he was in the war and was contacted by the German records office."

Sally stood at the doorway, electrified at what was dawning on her and turning back shouted up the   stairs.

"James, JAMES! There's someone important to see you." She looked back to the two people. "Are you able to get into the cottage?"

"Yes, we can leave the wheelchair out here and Grandfather can use his crutches for the last bit. Do you have a reasonably high chair though, low slung sofas and the like are awful for him to get up from?"

"Err, yes, tell you what come into the kitchen, through that doorway. Would you both like something to drink? Tea, coffee, a cold drink?"

"Tea for me, white and no sugar," the grandson said.

"Could I trouble you for a glass of water, I have some pills to take. Then a coffee would be nice if I may be zo bold," the elderly gentleman said as he carefully got up from the wheelchair and his grandson helped him with his crutches.

James came down the stairs looking a little puzzled and only caught a glimpse of the pair as he reached the bottom step. He walked through into the kitchen looking perplexed at the two strangers that Sally had let into the cottage.

"Sally?"

"Oh James, I think you will be wanting to say hello to this gentleman. Sir's I didn't catch your names but I suspect James will be very interested to talk to you."

The son shook James by the hand followed by the elderly man.

"Sorry, I should have introduced us better. It's my father that is the important one here, but I am Keith Beaumont and this is my father, Heinrich, usually called Henry, actually, but I'll let him explain."

James shook their hands as the penny dropped.

"Heinrich?"

"Ja, I believe you filled in a form fur information of a pilot in the second war. Here are my official Luftwaffe documents and identity card as proof. The details you gave were, how you will say, little? However you did mention the details of my fighter plane, a Foche Wolf 190 and the serial number on zee side that identified me as the pilot. You mentioned a Lancaster that was spared by such a plane?

That was me. My name as you can zee on the card is Heinrich Lorenz Meier. In case you ver wondering, I was shot down over France and captured by the British in November 1944 and transferred to a POW camp here in Lincolnzhire at

Moorby. I was eventually released after the war but given the option to return to the fatherland or remain. I chose the latter. I am a naturalized British person now and have never regretted my decizion to stay. I changed my names to Henry Beaumont and I have a vonderful family, but I owe it all to the mid gunner of that Lancaster."

James felt the hairs on the back of his neck stand on end as he looked into the eyes of this elderly and quite frail man and recognised something about them.

"Why is that? What happened?"

"I was part of a small patrol of our four aircraft trying to catch out any stray RAF or US Army Airforce bombers. Two had already engaged Hurricanes, leaving myself and my colleague, Albrecht Seidel, to look out for any other aircraft. We spotted a couple of Lancasters high above us and so Albrecht chased after one whilst I approached your grandvater's from underneath. However I could see just before I began to shoot that their bomb bay doors were still open and that there were several large bombs lodged close to the centre of the aircraft and I hesitated. I had heard of some of our bombers being spared in similar zircumstances and upon seeing that they also had an engine out and another smoking away, realised that they would probably not survive.

To be fair, I also thought it would save my ammunition as it was getting low, but something made me pull up on their starboard side, far enough back that the front gunner could not turn to get me in his sights. I thought the middle turret was out of action until it turned to aim at me and I thought I had made a terrible mistake. But the gunner didn't fire. I was close enough to see the pilot was himself in trouble and the front turret gunner slumped as I watched, but I tried to indicate that they had bombs still underneath and that I was not going to attack them.

I can still recall the look in the upper gunner's eyes, utter fear in them. In fact, your eyes, remind me of them. Strange indeed. Are you related to the gunner by any chance and that is why you sought me out?"

"Err, yes, my grandfather was on that plane, I'm not sure of his role but it could have been the upper gunner." James lied and Sally gave him a slight look without giving anything away. She handed over the drinks, Keith took them and helped his grandfather to take his pills with the water.

"My grandfather was Edward Portisham and he passed away a long time ago but left information which told us about the German pilot that could have shot him down but didn't, so I wanted to look into it and see if I could find out who the pilot was. I will be honest, I didn't think you'd be alive today."

"Neither did I! Ze fact is, I didn't shoot him down and he didn't shoot me down, it shows that some of us could get on if we wanted to."

"If you don't mind me asking, where do you live?" asked Sally politely.

"I'm in a care home near Newark and my son here lives in Derby. He is a good son and visits at least once a week and more when he can. If you don't mind, this has been a wonderful thing but I am tired. Keith, may we go home now as it is a long journey for an old man."

"Of course father," Keith replied looking at James and Sally. "Thank you for seeing us, especially at such short notice. Here is my card and if you want to keep in touch then please do so."

James took the proffered card then had a thought.

"Heinrich, Edward's Lancaster almost made it back to the airbase near to here and he was able to get out just before it crashed. There is to be a memorial plaque set up at the crash site. When that takes place, if I can get the people doing it to agree, would you like to be present at the unveiling ceremony?"

There was a tear in Heinrich's eye as he stuttered his reply, but he was clearly moved at the thought. James, then Sally, shook hands with the departing pair and once Heinrich was in his wheelchair, they watched from the front door as Keith took Heinrich back out onto the road to where they had parked.

Closing the door and heading back into the kitchen it was Sally who broke the silence.

"That was amazing to witness and wasn't he canny, looking at you and seeing something in your eyes that reminded him of that gunner."

"Yes, I couldn't very well tell him it was me and that somehow I'd time travelled and ended up on the Lancaster that he nearly shot down. I think in his state it would have finished him off!"

"Well, you'd best see what Mike has to say as to when that memorial stone will be ready as I don't think poor Heinrich is here on this world for much longer."

"You may be right my love, you may be right," replied James as he fished out his smartphone and gave Mike a call.

27: Memorial and a surprise

The procession made its way along a newly laid flagstone path that allowed disabled access, much to Heinrich and Keith's delight. At the head was the Reverend Sarah Cossant, Squadron Leader Derek Myers, representatives of surviving family members of the lost crew along with Mike, Greg, Sandra, Harriet, James and Sally.

It had taken a couple of months but once Mike had discovered how frail Heinrich was, he insisted the work be speeded up and indeed it was completed in record time. They gathered around the five foot high granite monolith which now had the names of the aircrew lost on that fateful flight.

In memory of and the bravery of:
Pilot: Flight Sergeant Mark Chapman
Wireless Operator: Basil Harris
Bomb Aimer/Front Gunner: Neville Trumper
Mid-Upper Gunner: Mike Barracks
Navigator: Anthony Anders.
Flight Engineer: Flight Sergeant Edward Portisham
Rear Gunner: Flight Sergeant Jack Jackson
June 5th/6th 1944

Sarah conducted the ceremony then Squadron Leader Derek Myers, James and Mike all laid wreaths at the base of the monument which was inscribed with the words *Lest we forget*.

As Sarah finished a lone RAF sergeant stepped forward and played the Last Post on his bugle. The remaining family members of the crew, many of whom had not known where their grandparents had died, were particularly moved at the ceremony as they paid their respects.

Finishing off, James, the Squadron Leader and Mike Arthurson stood to attention and saluted the memorial.

Without any of them knowing, including James, behind the gathered crowd the six crewmen of the mission appeared and saluted the memorial before fading away, reunited at last.

#

"Okay Sally, where are we going?" James asked as, for once, Sally drove them towards Lincoln then turned off and headed to a small airfield. They parked up and who should be waiting for them but Mike and Greg looking pleased with themselves.

"Good to see you again James, Sally. Right follow me, just have to sign you in and get you to sign a couple of forms."

"What is going on?" asked James.

"Oh, you didn't tell him then Sally?" asked Greg as they filled in various forms. James began to sign them as it slowly dawned on him that they were flight documents.

"No, why spoil the surprise. I can see he's guessed part of it. Mike and Greg both have pilot licenses for light aircraft and are taking us up for an aerial view of mid Lincolnshire, especially over Grasceby."

James smiled as they indicated for him and Sally to follow them out and over to a Cessna. They got in and strapped the safety belts on as Mike and

Greg ran through the pre flight checks, then contacted the airfield for permission to taxi and take off. They had to wait a few minutes as another light aircraft came into land, then they were off.

James couldn't help but think it was completely different from the roar of Merlin engines and there was a slight lurch as they left the ground and began to climb.

Off to one side but changing direction as the plane slowly turned, they could see Lincoln Cathedral, proudly standing overlooking the city. Then Sally pointed off to one side and James realised he could see Boston Stump, St Botolphs church tower, one of the tallest in the country way off in the distance.

James remembered something he'd learned whilst browsing online. "According to the International Bomber Command Memorial information, they used both as navigation points. They also used familiar roads and rivers too." Sally nodded and James couldn't help but think she looked funny with the headset on. Then he thought about how he must look and just chuckled to himself making her look at him wryly.

"Nothing, just a thought I had. This is much smoother than in the Lancaster, eh Mike?"

"Wouldn't know, not allowed to fly it!" came the reply, with a chuckle from Greg.

It didn't take long before they passed close to Wragby, then swung round the periphery of Horncastle as Mike set course for Grasceby.

Sure enough within moments James recognised the roads he had driven on ever since his first diversion all those years ago and a lump came into his throat at the memory. He was brought back to the present when Mike said something that he had to ask him to repeat.

"Down to the right hand side, there's Grasceby, the church, rectory and manor. I'm swinging a little off to one side as we're coming up on the industrial estate and airfield. There's a section of woodland and, there, can you see your cottage?"

James looked down and spotted it as Sally tried to peer over his shoulder and grinned. "Quick before you miss it. Look down towards the memorial site," called out Mike.

They did as they were told and both let out a gasp of astonishment.

The fenced off area of the memorial crash site was filled with poppies, in the shape of a Lancaster with the granite memorial at the nose end …

"How spooky is that?" exclaimed James.

"Not really, Greg and I had the area dug over in fact it was Phil and Joe who offered to do it for free, so once we'd dug out a few feet down and recovered any remaining fragments of the Lancaster, we covered the site with topsoil and deliberately planted the poppies in the hope they would flower all at the same time in that shape. Fitting tribute eh?"

"Yes!" chorused James and Sally. James quickly fished out his smartphone and waited as Mike brought them around for a second closer pass.

Mike came on again. "We have another surprise for you. Sally and I were in touch with various people so look off to your rear or you'll miss it."

James looked back and a tear welled up in his eye.

The Battle of Britain Memorial Flight with the Lancaster, two Spitfires and a Hurricane raced past and James spotted several crew members waving at them. They waved back but by then the flight was well past and James realised he had missed the chance to take a picture and said so.

"They're actually on the way to a display but as it wasn't much of a change to their flight plan they agreed to do the flyby for us. And Greg here has been taking pics and a bit of video too for posterity. We'll send you copies and also put them up online once we get the expanded centre finished."

"Wow, I really owe you so much for all this guys, oh and Sally too! Can we do one more fly past?"

"Just about to turn but then it's back to base." James took a video for himself of the site as they flew by and for a split second thought he saw people down at the site in flight uniforms, standing to attention...

Epilogue

Things afoot in Devon…

Wolds View Cottage felt calm and serene in the weeks after the private flight. Indeed, James couldn't help but miss the mystery of the airman now they had resolved who he was and exonerated him. What a family tree he had!

However, he had fulfilled several local speaking engagements and was now in Devon, having enjoyed the long drive down from Lincolnshire with a couple of stop offs at services. So had Scruff, who seemed to travel well considering the distance. He had a special harness so that he could travel on the back seat, but if James had to break hard or swerve under any circumstance, Scruff would still be safe yet able to watch out the windows.

Something he seemed to relish doing, especially when they'd passed a field with a large herd of cows near to the fencing. He kept up a series of gruffs and whines as they passed by.

Sally had to be away at another training seminar, this time about data protection and the law, so had not been able to take any time off work to accompany them. With no one at home to look after him, Scruff had to be with James. Fortunately, the historical society had been very good and found a B&B that took pets too and would look after them if needed, so things had turned out for the best.

James and probably Scruff, was relieved to finally arrive at the tucked away B&B. It still amazed him that he was now being asked to speak to societies and clubs up and down the country about the original De Grasceby Manor and how he'd helped discover the truth about the first De Grasceby family and their untimely demise. Naturally James tended to leave out the parts concerning the ghostly encounters!

He parked up in the suggested parking slot and got out. With Scruff happily by his side on his leash, James walked up to the green and quite plain old wooden door.

He smiled at the lady who greeted him at a side door marked 'B&B entrance' and said hello.

"Ahh you are?" she asked.

"James, James Hansone. The local historical society booked a couple of nights here as I understand it. Here is the online booking form they sent me with the reference. Oh, and this is Scruff, my Scottish terrier." James picked Scruff up as he had started to whine a little, somewhat unusual for him, but it was a strange new place.

The lady appeared to be in her late twenties, possibly early thirties, James surmised. She smiled at Scruff who started to fall asleep in James arms, whilst becoming quite heavy too. She took the booking form from his outstretched hand and smiled as she looked at the details. "B&B, ahh yes, they don't show that we offer an evening meal and it's a bit late now, but I can rustle up something quick if you like?"

James smiled and shook his head, "Thanks but I stopped off and grabbed something earlier. Scruff's also fed and been good, doing his business at the last services, so hopefully he'll settle down quite quickly. May I ask your name?"

"Oh sorry, a bit rude of me isn't it! It's Jackie. Me and my husband, Terrence, run the place." She held her hand out and they shook.

"Nice to meet you." he said as Scruff half opened his eyes, did a little woof, then went back to sleep again.

"It's alright for some isn't it! He seems pretty good but were you aware that we don't allow pets in the bedrooms?" she said.

James looked at her horrified, thinking there had been a mix up but she saw his pained expression and quickly interjected. "Oh, sorry, pets are allowed but we have a special room for them downstairs with their own special bedding and small space to settle down. That's OK isn't it?"

"Oh, I guess so, he does sleep downstairs in our front room, so he's used to being on his own, I can't see there being a problem." Scruff awoke as if he knew they were talking about him and James put him back on the ground as they headed inside.

Scruff seemed to like his small room as he wandered around the space before getting onto the dog basket. He turned around several times, settling, then turning around a few more times before finally dropping down onto the bedding. His eyes began to droop again, and his ears flopped down, relaxed. He had a bowl of water nearby and James couldn't help but smile, he'd expected Scruff to be the one to be unsettled in a new place, yet he'd just fitted in straight away. James gently stroked his head. "Have a good night Scruff."

Jackie smiled, turned, indicating for him to follow as she led him through a door to the right which revealed an old wooden staircase, quite steep. Before James could comment she chuckled.

"Sorry, it's quite an old building, a converted farmhouse that we think is about three hundred years old or even more. The walls, floors and ceilings are at slight angles and uneven, but people seem to love the quaintness of it all."

"Have you been doing B&B long then?" he asked, noting they went up past the first floor, then the second and guessed he was at the top. Any further and he wondered if he'd be on the roof!

"About five years now, we inherited it from a distant family relation we barely knew, who bequeathed it to us. No one else left in the family, so we decided to move here and renovate it. We seem at last to be hitting our stride with the B&B side of things and of course the good ratings from our customers are helping. Here we are, sorry it's the top room but we're updating the others, adding in Internet Wi-Fi amongst other mod cons. Terry has put a temporary router in your room to give you that if you need it and there is the password on a slip of paper on the side board next to your bed. Is there anything you need? Drinks making facilities are on the table in the corner to the side of the window and toilet facilities are en suite, so I hope everything is OK for your stay.

Here's your set of keys, large one is for the side entrance where you came in, that's the one to use, smaller key is for your room."

James took the keys and smiled at the warmth and hospitality shown so far.

"Many thanks, looks like I have all I need, main thing now is to get some rest, it's been a long drive down from Lincolnshire!"

"What part? I have a cousin up in Tealby, not sure, to be honest, where that is!"

"Oh, that's up near Market Rasen, north of where I am in Grasceby, not too far from Bardney and Horncastle."

Jackie looked lost and shook her head. "I'll look it up on a map someday. Not visited or seen her for years. As you say, it's quite a long trip!" Hope you have a comfortable night. Breakfast is from 7am until 9am, if you could give me an idea of the time you'll be down. I forgot, when you get to the bottom of the stairs there is another door in front of you which takes you into the dining area. That's where I'll be serving breakfast. Full English?"

"Yes please, can we say around eight thirty then?"

"Fine with me. Good night then. Oh, just bear in mind this is an old building and it does creak and groan a bit as the farmhouse settles down in the night."

"Won't bother me, I'm used to that sort of thing. My wife Sally and I renovated an old cottage and live in it so I know what you mean. Good night and see you in the morning."

Jackie nodded then closed the door behind her as she left and James looked around the room trying to decide where to put his bags. The view out of the window was an open expanse of rolling hills and valleys, much to his liking and he prepared for bed even though it was still light, the long drive having taken its toll.

#

It had taken him a while when he and Sally had moved into 'Wolds View' cottage to get used to how the sky could be so dark at night. Even when he and his first wife, Helen, had moved into Horncastle there was a certain reassurance from the glow of the sky due to light pollution from the streetlights. Out in the middle of nowhere there were none, making the bedroom pitch black. He had originally come up with Helen from the city lights of the outskirts of London, a small place called Allbury, so had grown up with a perpetual orange glow filtering through his bedroom curtains. At Wolds View cottage having such dark nights had initially disturbed him. Sally was totally used to the dark, having grown up in Lincolnshire, out in the wilds of the Lincolnshire Wolds, so often berated him when he moaned a little about the darkness. Sally, being Sally and a DSI, continuously informed him that most crime actually occurred where there was more light, not less, as thieves and miscreants were still human and needed light to do their deeds, hence most crimes occurred during the daytime. But it was an ingrained fear of the dark from the primeval consciousness that still swayed public perception, and indeed James.

The B&B was in the middle of nowhere in Devon with not a single streetlight to be seen so naturally his room was also slowly going pitch black. James sighed, turned the side light off and settled down to sleep. After his long journey, he was quickly deep in the land of nod and nothing was going to wake him.

#

He stirred a little, then settled down again. 'Dammed rocking chair, couldn't they sit still for a moment?' He mumbled to himself in his sleep. His mind noted the faint creaking as he drifted off into deep sleep again. The house creaked again and James, dreaming took himself on a wild journey as he ran through walls falling in on him, ceilings lifting off slowly and all manner of strange things swirling around his subconscious. At one point he was flying in a Lancaster but instead of being on the inside, he was riding on top of it! Somewhere deep down he wondered if it was that extra topping of four cheeses on his pizza back at the services that was responsible.

He stirred again, and his eyelids fluttered open a little. There was a faint light permeating the room. His mind was about to dismiss it again when the creaking of a rocking chair caught his attention. He thought for a second then realised that when he'd looked around the room, there was no rocking chair.

He was wide awake now but still snuggled down under the sheets. He slowly poked his head gingerly above them and the room was gently illuminated although he couldn't see the source. He carefully turned over, only to spot his smart phone screen was glowing and he sighed as he climbed out of bed to turn it off.

The charger had been playing up and it had stopped, then started charging again, making the screen come alive.

James tutted at himself for beginning to think there was something strange going on in the room.

He turned to go back to bed and stopped short as he spotted the elderly lady siting in a rocking chair across the room in the corner where the drinks facilities were supposed to be.

She stared intently at, or through, him, he couldn't tell which, before she faded away leaving the room back to normal and the table with the refreshments just about visible again in the dim light.

"Oh hell, can't I get a break from ghosts!" James moaned as he climbed back into bed and pulled the covers over his head. He waited then slowly put his head above the covers again, but it was as he was blind as the room was again pitch black. He reached over and tapped the screen of his phone and it again sprang to life and he quickly glanced over to where the lady had been sitting.

Nothing.

Just the drinks tray and kettle on the small table, no old lady. Relieved, he turned over and finally fell asleep.

He didn't hear the ghostly chuckle of a younger lady as she watched over him that night ...

#

Meanwhile, in his own room, Scruff kept waking up and whimpering as he stood up, turned around and around, then tried to settle down again.

He could sense them, and they needed help ...

Authors Note

Considering that the first ghost mystery was supposed to be a one off book, it still surprises me that this is book four! Once the first sequel was completed it became clear that there was a lot about the fictional village of Grasceby that could be explored. That, along with suggestions and guidance from Lorraine, a genealogist, that there could be more of James past to discover led to more ideas. So, it seemed natural that, as Lincolnshire is known as Bomber County, at some point there had to be a story which explored that aspect of James past.

It didn't take long, as book 3, 'Return to De Grasceby Manor', took shape, before I had an idea of how the ending would lead into book four where James would discover his grandfather and a travesty of justice. Initially I had the idea of involving the black market and that it would be a stolen item that puts the Lancaster with Edward on board at risk. For a long time the story stalled and I couldn't get to grips with it. Then, over Christmas and into New year 2019/2020, suddenly things began to fall into place as the plot developed to end with the story we have today.

Along the way, having known and met Simon Ross of Paper Planes Gallery and from his occasional work at BBC Radio Lincolnshire, I saw the potential for the cover to be done by him and in B/W to give the feel of a wartime adventure. I do hope you visit the Paper Planes Facebook page mentioned near the front of the book as Simon is very talented!

I'd heard of rare acts of kindness on both sides during WW II so it felt natural to try to work that into the story too and in recent years there have been wonderful stories of reconciliation, along with the discovery of sites of crashed aircraft allowing their stories to be told. So a rich tapestry was available to tap into.

The renovation of Wolds View Cottage was inspired by my own parents purchase many years ago and renovation of the cottage they still live in today, that I and my sister grew up in out in the Lincolnshire Wolds. Indeed it is stories told by my father of his own time in the RAF, which occurred after the war, that led to one of the flight crew of the Lancaster having the nickname of 'Ackers' which was Dad's nickname during his RAF years.

Meanwhile, ideas about part of a story based in Devon swirled in my mind and so this forms the basis of the lead in to book five, provisionally titled 'James and the haunted Rectory'. Despite this, along with resolving the mystery in Devon, James will get to discover more about Grasceby Rectory and indeed his past so stay tuned to the Astrospace web site and Facebook pages as book 5 begins to take shape!

And then there is book six to consider …

Newsletter

If you enjoy the exploits of James Hansone as he unravels the many ghostly goings on, in and around the sleepy village of Grasceby Lincolnshire, then why not sign up to the newsletter to keep up to date with upcoming novels.

Those signing up will be the first to receive a *free* mini novel: "Lord Shabernackles of Grasceby Manor" when it is available.

So If you want to know more about the James Hansone Ghost Mysteries or other novels from Astrospace Fiction, such as how to purchase them and where, or when the next book in the series will be released, then simply sign up and you'll be the first to informed. There will also be a possible competitions or a give-away so worth subscribing to see what may be on offer soon. Note your information will not be passed on to third parties.

Just head on over to the following link where you can enter your email to be added to the newsletter list.

Note I will not share your email with anybody and it is only for keeping up to date with Astrospace Fiction books and the James Hansone Ghost Mystery novels.

https://mailchi.mp/1c69765ddf7a/jameshansonegm-signup

Best wishes and see you soon: Paul M

'A Ghostly Diversion'

Discover the first book of the James Hansone Ghost Mysteries.

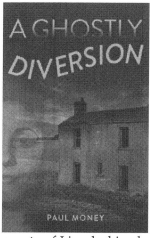

An ongoing set of roadworks.
A dark blue Mercedes.
A diversion.
An abandoned cottage.
A young girls face at a broken window.
A fifty-year-old mystery.

James Hansone faces all the above and much more, all because of a diversion to avoid roadworks one morning. A relative newcomer to the rural county of Lincolnshire, he likes his job, his new home and loves his wife Helen.

He is also a sceptic of all things paranormal.
Until the day of the diversion…

'Wolds View' cottage holds a mystery about a young girl who disappeared fifty years earlier. A missing persons case that's stalled and long forgotten.
As strange sightings begin to occur to him, James Hansone finds himself increasingly drawn into trying to discover:
Who she is;
whether he can find out who or what caused her death
and why he seems to be the only one that can see her…

ISBN 9781907781070 (Paperback edition)
ASIN: B01I83O3HQ (Kindle edition)

'Secrets of Grasceby Manor'

The second of the James Hansone Ghost Mysteries.

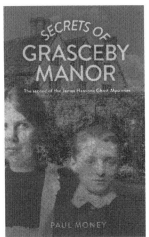

Renovations at Grasceby Manor
A mysterious upper class gentleman in Grasceby Churchyard
A ghostly boy
A servant called Annie
A 150-year-old conspiracy

James Hansone thought he was done with ghosts once he'd discovered the truth about his family.
He was mistaken…

Grasceby Manor stands in several acres of old landscaped gardens and had been the jewel of the village. But now it desperately needed renovation, prompting Lord Grasceby to hire a local firm to renovate the property in readiness of the opening of parts of it to the public.

But as work commences, strange sightings of a boy and a servant girl begin to occur to the workmen and James finds himself increasingly drawn into trying to discover:

The identity of the boy.

The connection to the ghostly servant.

Whether he can find out who or what caused their deaths.

And why a cat seems determined to trip him up!

ISBN 9781907781100 (pb)
ASIN: B071KS6JXR (Kindle edition)

Return to De Grasceby Manor:
and the Search for Helen'
The third of the James Hansone Ghost Mysteries.

*The Ghost of his ex wife
A Mysterious Stag
The discovery of extensive
remains of the original De
Grasceby Manor
Sightings of aristocratic
ghosts by the
archaeological team
The ghost of a little girl
running frantically through
the grounds
A three hundred year old
mystery*

James rushes off to Wales to try to solve what happened to his Ex and why a stag is involved.

He returns back to Lincolnshire only to be drawn into discovering what really befell Charles De Grasceby and his family in the 18th century and a three hundred year old mystery comes to a head.

Available on Amazon UK as Kindle or POD.

The Fragility of Existence
A Sci-Fi/Apocalyptic tale

The extermination of our species was probably inevitable when you look back with hindsight. Every advanced civilisation has almost always wiped out the resident less advanced occupants whenever they came into contact. So it was the same for us, Homo Sapiens. But it wasn't supposed to have happened. We were not to know that though. Perhaps that is a good thing. For the Universe…

Matt and Simone stared out at the devastation and knew it could only mean one thing… Humanity was about to become extinct. Could they escape the fate they had seen befall others in their small village of 'Woldsfield'? They were not going to wait around to find out…

Available on Amazon UK as Kindle or POD.

Keep an eye on the Astrospace publications section of the Astrospace web site for details of all the books.
http://www.astrospace.co.uk/nightscenes/Fiction.html

Non fiction books by the author

Nightscenes: Annual guide to astronomical events for the year.

Published annually with details of the best meteor showers to view, when to see the planets at their best, conjunctions between the moon, stars and planets, special events to look out for plus much more. ISBN/cover changes annually.

A5 format, 74 pages inc covers full colour throughout with approx 100 charts, diagrams and images. Each month has a 4-page fold out spread (print edition only).

Look out for new edition every October.

Available as print or kindle print replica edition.

NightScenes: Guide to Simple Astrophotography.

This book fills a space left by many astrophotography books by concentrating on only the astrophotography anyone can achieve with just a camera, set of lenses and a tripod. No telescope or complicated tracking mount required! Topics covered include capturing: constellations, planets amongst the stars, lunar phases and eclipses, capturing the wonder that is the Northern Lights or Aurora plus lots more that can be achieved with just a basic set up of equipment.

A5 format, 56 pages inc covers in full colour with over 130 images plus tables of data and informative charts.

ISBN 978-907781-03-2 (pb)
ASIN: B07C3S9QL1 Kindle print replica edition

About the Author

 Paul L Money is an astronomy broadcaster, writer, public speaker and publisher. He is also the Reviews Editor for the BBC Sky at Night magazine and for eight years until 2013 he was one of three Astronomers on the Omega Holidays Northern Lights Flights. He is married to Lorraine whose hobby/interest is genealogy/ family history and helped with suggestions involving the historical aspects of 'A Ghostly Diversion' and 'Secrets of Grasceby Manor'.

Paul writes and publishes the popular annual night sky guide to the year's best night sky events, 'Nightscenes' and the 'Nightscenes Guide to Simple Astrophotography'. Both can be obtained nationwide in the UK via all good bookshops and online retailers such as Amazon.co.uk

As an astronomer Paul has been giving talks across the UK for over thirty years and was awarded the Eric Zuker award for services to astronomy in 2002 by the Federation of Astronomical Societies. In October 2012 he was awarded the 'Sir Arthur Clarke Lifetime Achievement Award, 2012' for his 'tireless promotion of astronomy and space to the public'.

'James and the Air of Tragedy' is his fourth novel in the James Hansone Ghost Mysteries series following on to the highly successful 'A Ghostly

Diversion' followed by 'Secrets of Grasceby Manor then 'Return to De Grasceby Manor and the Search for Helen'. A fifth book in the series "James and the haunted Rectory" is in progress.

'Fragility of Existence' is the first Science Fiction novel to be published and several more are planned in the near future.

More info can be found at the Astrospace web site:
Astrospace/ Astrospace publications
http://www.astrospace.co.uk

August 2020

Printed in Great Britain
by Amazon

64349181R00187